A Careless Husband

Two Stories. Only One Truth.

Paolo Sedazzari

A Wild Wolf Publication

Published by Wild Wolf Publishing in 2024
Copyright © 2024 P Sedazzari

All rights reserved. No part of this book may be reproduced, stored in a retrieval system or transmitted in any form or by any means without the prior written permission of the publishers, except by a reviewer who may quote brief passages in a review to be printed by a newspaper, magazine or journal.

First print

Cover Art by Dean Cavanagh

ISBN: 9798321805381
Also available in E-Book edition

www.wildwolfpublishing.com

To Gigi Riva

Prologue

PJ – Video log – Saturday 31st March 2018

"Why do you love me?" she would often ask, making me feel awkward and tongue tied for fear of saying something cringey. She would press me by staring, demanding an answer, and I usually end up saying something like – "I just do." Or "Too many reasons."

But as I sit here now, trying to visualise her, I see it all.

The way her eyes glowed whenever a mischievous thought came into her head. That goofy crossed eyed look she put on when she was messing around. Those luscious lips, her jutting out teeth, her sensuous smell whenever she put on a sweat.

Even the silly irrational stuff like reading the end of a book before deciding if she wants to read it from the beginning. Swearing at inanimate objects when they drop to the floor when she's tidying up. Even her habit of dancing along to really loud cheesy disco music when she's had a few too many.

The sheer striking power of her beauty – the warmth and compassion of her personality which released me from the prison of grief and pain I was in. How I wish I could say all this to her now.

Now that Ligia is gone.

Date: Saturday 8th December 2018
Time: 22:00
Location: Terminal 2, Heathrow Airport

On the tarmac of Heathrow Airport I sat down and wept. I wept for all the people affected.

But most of all I wept for Zico, out of everyone on that long list of people, he had been hurt the most.

Chapter 1
Is This What They Call A Cold Case?

Day 1 of the Investigation

Date: Tuesday 20th March 2018
Time: 12:30
Location: West Byfleet, Surrey

The Sat-Nav sends us deeper and deeper into the green heart of Surrey, a world of neatly clipped hedges, manicured lawns and top end shiny motors. The further we drive, the higher the value of the surrounding real estate.

In the passenger seat next to me is my partner Matt. Both of us were trying to keep our states of high excitement in check. We don't get calls like this every day.

After a lengthy stretch along a sycamore lined avenue without a pedestrian in sight, the mechanical female voice instructs me to hang a right into a winding cul-de-sac. Looking ahead, our final destination becomes clear, it's the house sectioned off by yellow tape and a uniformed police woman in her mid-twenties standing by.

Next to her on the pillar there's a sign that reads – ASGARD in a Runic Nordic Font. Set back, behind a twelve foot hedge is a large two storey house, with white walls and three triangular roofs painted in fire engine red.

From the house next door, the branches of a pink blossom tree arched over to create a canopy entrance to the drive-way, and over the head of the waiting WPC.

I recognise her, it's Gemma Muldrew based at Woking Nick. Her out-going bubbly personality makes her a well liked colleague. I, on the other hand, found her alacrity rather forced and irritating.

I pull up next to her and as I scroll down my window, I am hit by a cold blast of icy wind. Readers will remember the 'beast from the east' that sent Britain into a deep frost in February 2018. Mercifully the beast had moved on, and the temperature was now thawing. Incidentally this cold weather will have a critical bearing on the forensics of this case.

"Good Afternoon WPC Muldrew," I say leaning out and trying to sound cool – "what have you got for me?"

"A dead body in the freezer. A woman."

"Who found the body?"

"The husband."

"And where is the husband?"

"He's sat in the kitchen of his next-door neighbour at number 3. I've requisitioned the kitchen as an incident room."

"We need to arrange for someone from the Trauma Treatment Unit to talk to him."

"Already done Sir. They are on their way."

"Excellent work WPC Muldrew," I said getting out of the car, hoping to get a smile from her. But she remained ashen faced, her normally rosy cheeks drained of colour, apparently shaken. This may well have been her first murder case.

"Have you seen the body?" I continued.

"No. I haven't Sir – I'm…not. I'm a bit squeamish Sir."

I am as well, but I wasn't going to admit that to her.

"Well, we need to check that the victim is definitely dead. That's procedure."

I lift the crime scene tape, about to go under when I hear a loud shout of "Wait!"

My head snaps back to see the familiar bespectacled face and lank messy hair of my long-time partner and car companion Matt.

"You don't want to go into the crime scene until Roy gets here."

Matt, as he is most of the time, was spot on. Roy was our head crime scene forensics guy – and not a fan of mine. On a number of occasions, he had berated me for contaminating "his" crime scene, and once in front of a whole load of people.

But I needed to establish that the body was actually dead. This was in my Regulation Homicide Handbook. The woman might still be alive and requiring immediate life-saving medical attention.

I had myself a dilemma. As I considered it, I paced around on the road looking over at the neighbouring houses – an assortment of twitching curtains and faces at the window.

I did not want to provoke the ire of Roy, at any cost. His public telling off still smarted and I would do most anything to avoid that happening again.

I made my decision. If the victim was still alive and in need of medical attention, there was nothing that the three of us could do. We should wait until a trained medical person arrived. "I need to get an ETA from Roy. If he's not here within fifteen minutes, I am going to have to go in check she's actually dead.

"You call him" – and I handed Matt my phone. "He likes you better. I'm going to see the husband."

The front garden of number 3 had two more pink blossom trees, in early bloom with the first stirrings of spring. They flanked me as I crunched my way up the gravel drive way and pressed the doorbell. The door was opened by a chunky late middle-aged woman in thick round glasses. I introduced myself and asked to be shown to the man in the kitchen.

The age of the people living here became immediately apparent when she opened the door to an expanse of furry shag pile carpet on the floor, and fussy floral papered walls with pictures of wildlife in ornate frames.

As I passed through the hallway I hear the tick-tocking of a clock from the living room. I look right and observe a tall grey haired, gaunt lined face man, standing up watching me through the open door.

I walk towards him, about to introduce myself, but the woman steers me away. "No the kitchen's this way." The tall man stares at me as I walk away.

I passed through the open kitchen door and there he was sat at the table.

His head was arched downwards and gazing down onto a mug of tea going cold. He was aged forty-ish, around 5ft 10, slim build with dark brown shoulder length, studiously messy hair and parted in the middle. A ski-slope nose led down to a large crater of a dimple in the middle of his chin. His chestnut brown eyes were moist and appeared foggy with pain. His mouth hung open slightly and he was breathing hard.

He was the picture of a man who has lost everything.

I went straight into it – "Excuse me Sir. I am Detective Chief Superintendent Ferdinand. Are you sure your wife is dead?"

The man did not even look up.

"Are you sure the body is your wife?"

Still no response. Instead he lifted his head to stare gloomily out the window.

"Can I please have your name?"

Nothing. I look out the window with him and see a cherry red Peugeot 205 pulling up next to ours.

"The name of your wife?"

More nothing.

"Sir I realise this is very traumatic, but I do need your help. Medical help is on the way to treat you for shock."

Silence.

I resorted to pleading – "Can you please tell me what happened?"

He continued to look blankly out the window. He didn't move, his face didn't flicker. He wouldn't even acknowledge my existence. It was as if I was invisible and inaudible, just like an evening at home with the wife.

Presently an ash-blonde woman aged around mid30s dashed into the room. I immediately spotted the chestnut eyes and nose shape as that of the silent man. The pronounced dimple, however, was absent.

"Hullo Madam – and who might you be?"

"I'm Samantha. I'm her sister."

"And who might he be?"

"His name is…Paul – PJ." She equivocated before

saying his name.

"Paul – PJ?"

"No just PJ."

"That's his Christian name?"

"Yes."

"What's the surname?"

"James."

Pause.

"Can I be alone with my brother?"

"Well actually we've requisitioned this kitchen as a make-shift incident room."

Samantha's eyes glared with fierce defiance.

"Oh – ok then." And I left them to it.

I shut the door behind me and approached the woman with the chunky eye-glasses. I said whispering – "I will need to take a statement from you at some point."

The tall man was still standing in the living room as I went out the front door. He had the look of a Nazi War Criminal. I could picture him brandishing a dentist's drill and asking the question 'Is it safe?' over and over.

Outside I sneakily grabbed a peak through the kitchen window that PJ had been staring out of. I saw Samantha's eyes narrow as she was apparently listening to PJ talking. What can those narrowing eyes mean? Was she wincing – or was it suspicion?

Walking back towards the crime scene at number 5 I call over Matt.

"Call the nick – get them to run a check on a PJ James – resident of West Byfleet."

The familiar white Vauxhall Astra of Roy our CS Guy pulled up. As he got out, I walked up to him – "Hullo Roy – you'll be pleased to know we have protected and preserved your crime scene. Nothing has been touched or moved. But you must establish immediately that the victim is definitely dead."

"Yes, yes." He muttered at me impatiently. The man really didn't like me.

"We are going to have to seal off the whole street as a crime scene. Not just the house. And also, the area around the back garden."

I was about to ask Roy a question when I picked up some movement in my peripheral.

I shouted out – "Oi! Where do you think you're going?"

It was PJ and Samantha getting into her cherry red Peugeot. I sprinted towards them to prevent them leaving.

"I'm taking him home. He can't stay here. It's too upsetting." Samantha blurted at me as I approached.

PJ was still wearing his vacant shocked expression.

This man was a vital witness, and a highly likely suspect. There is no way I could let him get away from us without being questioned.

"WPC Muldrew will take you to the station. He'll get treated there for shock and trauma – and he must wait there until I get to take a statement from him. AND NOT BEFORE."

More uniformed coppers had shown up by this time, the place was now crawling with Old Bill. But Roy was not ready to let me into the crime scene – so I went back to see the neighbour.

Time: 14:00
Location: 3 Odin Court, West Byfleet, Surrey

"What do you say to a man who's just found their wife dead in a freezer?" Said the woman as she led me into her living room. "I made him a cup of tea. I couldn't think of anything else to do." I resisted the temptation to suggest that perhaps a glass of champagne would be more appropriate. In my appraisal my impetuous manner and inappropriate comments had been commented on. I even once had to stop my partner Matt from making a formal complaint about me. Instead, I ask – "Did the man say anything to you?"

"Not a dickie bird."

"So how did you know he'd found his wife dead in the freezer?"

She ponders this before saying, "That nice policewoman told me."

"So what have you recently seen or heard coming out of that house?"

"I heard nothing from Number 5 since Friday night."

"And what did you hear Friday night?"

"A row. A massive row."

Here we go – our first lead. "Right. Who Between?"

"I couldn't see. I only heard the voices."

"One male – one female?" Sorry – that was a leading question.

"Yes."

"Do you know PJ James at all?"

"Who's that love?"

"Your neighbour. The man that was in your kitchen."

"Oh him. Only by sight. Never spoken to him. I say hello to her. She seems nice."

"And what might her name be?"

"I don't know."

I recalled the grey haired, lined faced man looking at me from the living room.

"Who was the other man in this house when I came in earlier?"

"Yes – that's Fred my husband."

"Where is he now?"

"I don't know. I think he's gone to the shops."

Isn't that rather dodgy? Your next door neighbour is found dead in the freezer and then you decide you need to go to the shops?

"Why has he gone to the shops?"

"He always goes for a walk to the shops in the afternoon. He's a man of routines is our Fred."

My phone pinged. A text from Matt – "Roy is ready to let you see the crime scene."

"I am going to have to take full statements from you both. I will be coming back this evening. It's very important I speak with Fred as well."

Time: 14:30
Location: 5 Odin Court, West Byfleet, Surrey

Outside the taped house Roy was waiting for me. He handed me some latex gloves and shoe covers. I quickly put them on and he lifted the crime scene tape for me. The front door was opened and Roy led me inside, telling me –
"No sign of forced entry anywhere."
"Any sign of a struggle?"
"We haven't found anything yet."
Once into the hallway, to the left was the sitting room and in front of me was the doorway to the kitchen. I chose the kitchen.

I was in the same space as number 3, but the interior was stylistically the opposite. There was no shag pile carpets, instead we have gleaming floors, white walls, an open plan Scandinavian style kitchen in sparking white and gleaming chrome.

Coming out of the kitchen and into the living room on one side of the wall there was an assortment of pictures. I recognise the long hair and dimpled chin of PJ in all of them, standing next to a parade of different people, with cameras, clapperboards and lights as props. On more than two of the clapperboards were written the words 'Shipton Village'. That rung a bell, it's a popular TV show. The photograph collection gave off an overwhelming whiff of smugness.

I turn left into a dining area with floor to ceilings windows that opened up into a large garden. There were no signs of any children living there, it was all too neat and tidy. But I see a cat flap in the bottom corner of the glass.

In the far corner on the sideboard was an open lap top connected to two square Bose speakers about nine inches high.

In between the speakers were three framed photographs. In one – two smiling brown skinned mixed race boys – one aged around 5 and the other around 8 – cherub faces like Botticelli paintings. The boys must be either adopted, or from another partner.

The second photograph is of a middle aged tanned couple and a young woman in between them. She has long straight raven black hair and a vivacious smile

The third picture is of one of the mixed race boys in the first photograph. Here he is around 15 with flowing black locks, in front of the woman with the raven black hair.

While staring at the photographs, Roy taps me on the shoulder and leads me towards the garage. I braced myself. "Do I have to see the body?"

Roy looked back at me with an expression that said, "I can't believe you're a policeman."

As I stepped into the drafty garage, I immediately felt a drop of temperature. The large freezer was against the back wall with a black and silver Mercedez backed up against it.

Fear gripped me as I looked towards the freezer.

Roy lifted up the freezer door. I couldn't put if off any longer – I took a couple of steps forward and then I saw her.

A complexion once tanned and healthy, was now icy blue with white flecks of ice on her eye-brows and cheeks. From a head injury, blotches of red zig-zagged across her frozen face.

While looking at the body, Roy said into my ear "I cannot establish the kill location yet. I am going to run some Luminol around the garage to see if there are any traces of blood that has been cleared up."

He went on: "When I first lifted up the freezer door I found the body in a zipped up sleeping bag with two thick black dustbin bags over her head. I took photographs. I had to remove the bags. There was lots of blood inside the inner bag."

"Is the head injury the cause of death?" I asked.

"Can't say for certain yet."

12

This was the fifth corpse I had seen in the course of my duties. All were distressing and I don't know how anybody gets used to it. This one I found especially distressing because moments before I had seen her so happy and alive in those photographs on the wall.

I looked away and shut my eyes. The image of her frozen blue and red streaked face projected onto my eyelids.

I couldn't help it, I began to weep.

Yes you didn't misread that. I began to weep.

I felt an embrace. An embrace of empathy and warmth. It was Roy.

"Come on son. Let's find the person who did this."

I often feel an urge to crack a joke at the strangest moments, I think it's to diffuse the intensity of the situation, and I gave way to it this time.

Rubbing my eyes I said, "is this what they call a cold case?"

Thankfully Roy had walked away from me by this time and was out of ear-shot.

I walked out of the house in a daze and was still with moistened eyes when Matt came up to me. "The name of the woman who lived in this house was Ligia James, wife of PJ."

He pronounced the name Ligia as lij-ee-ah.

"How do you spell her name?"

"L-I-G-I-A."

"What country is that?"

"Portuguese… I think."

So we had a name of the victim at last. Though unconfirmed.

As I sat in my car gathering my thoughts, I get a text from WPC Muldrew: "PJ James's brief has arrived at Woking nick. He's ready for questioning."

Chapter 2 – The Harpo Marx Impression

Date: Tuesday 20th March
Time: 16:00
Location: Woking Police Station

PJ came into the interview room still wearing his face of abject misery. Next to him was his brief, a familiar face with whom I had jousted with many times in the past – the formidable Jennifer Janus. She tended to get the lion's share of the juiciest crime cases in this district. I had always known Jenny J as an elegant power dresser, and recently she had taken to applying a smokey eye make up, which gave her something of a middle-aged goth look. From her wide eyed unflinching stare I deduced Jennifer Janus had recently had a round of Bottox.

I look at PJ and I put on my best conciliatory voice:

"Thank you Sir. Please sit down. I realise you are suffering from an unimaginable trauma. But I do need to ask you some questions. I have no intention of keeping you here any longer than is necessary."

PJ took his seat, next to Jennifer Janus on his left.

Gazing at my notes I fired off the first of my prepared questions:

"When did you last see your wife alive?" PJ looked down at the desk.

There was a long silence until – "No comment."

I sucked in air. I wasn't expecting that.

My next question: "Do you know where your wife had been in the days leading up to her death?"

"No comment."

"Do you know anyone who might want your wife dead?"

"No comment."

"Can you tell me about any of her friends?"

"No comment."

"Where does she work?"

"No comment."
"How long have you been married?"
"No comment."
"Will you be prepared to formally identify the body?"
"No comment."

I sat back reeling with incredulity. I looked at Jennifer Janus to his right, her Bottox poker face gave nothing away.

> **PJ – Video log – Saturday 31st March 2018**
>
> In my first encounter with DCS Ferdinand I was in total shock – shut down mode. I couldn't hear or see people properly. It was like I was underwater, and I just wanted to drown. So I wasn't able to communicate, let alone process anything that had just happened.
>
> I was numb. I was not hungry for revenge. I was not burning with the desire to know who did it. All I knew was that I had seen Ligia's lifeless body, and I was never going to see her ever alive again.
>
> But I really wanted to help. I so much wanted to provide the information to help him find who did it.
>
> In that first police interview my impulse was to try and be as helpful as possible. But my lawyer told me to say absolutely nothing to the police. I was told that's standard. She insisted because, she said, that in my confused state I would tell the police something that wasn't quite correct or consistent. The police would then pick up on it and use it to force the case of my guilt.
>
> I looked up at the end of the interview and saw the look on DCS Ferdinand's face, and it did occur to me that by not answering any questions I was helping to cement in his mind that I was the guilty one.
>
> I had lost Kelly, my first wife, through a sudden accident some years before. Back then I went through the most extreme grief, and in the months after Kelly's death, I tried to comfort myself by thinking that now that I had the most horrible thing imaginable happen to me, I would never experience the same sort of pain again. But I was wrong.

> The pain I was going through with Ligia was much, much worse.
>
> When I started to think about what might have happened – and who might have done it, I thought this all must have been to do with her recent use of cocaine, and the sort of company she had been keeping because of it. But I couldn't say that to the police on the record. I didn't want to smear her name.
>
> I had suspected that she had been a drug mule on a recent visit to Brazil to see her relatives. I remember she had gone somewhere directly after the flight, and not come straight home, and my imagination had dreamed up a scenario where she had held back some of the drugs she had brought into the country from the gang.
>
> But I wasn't thinking these things during that first police interview. My immediate reaction was shock, and I became numb and unresponsive to everything and anybody around me.

Time: 18:00
Location: Woking Police Station

After PJ's no comment interview I paced around the incident room, fuming.

So despite all that shock and grief, within six hours of finding his wife dead, PJ had managed to get it together to get himself the best possible legal representation – and come back with a No Comment strategy.

Barely calming down, I arranged for the paperwork to raise warrants on PJ's phone and PC. I was also going to arrange a raid on his place of work to search his work PC.

But Matt came back to report that it turns out PJ has no current place of work.

PJ James's occupation is a TV Director – which explains the shrine to smugness on his living room wall. But he hadn't worked in over two years. Though his most recent gig was the very popular TV show – Shipton Village.

Maybe high profile jobs like that pay so well you don't need to work again for several years. Well, when we got hold of his bank statements, we'll find out.

From the incident room window I was looking down into the police station car park and was watching PJ sitting alone in the passenger seat of Samantha's Peugeot. I couldn't make out his expression, but I could see he was fiddling with the car stereo. Presently Samantha appeared next to me.

"Something you should know," she said "Ligia has a son from a previous marriage. He's about 16 or 17 years of age, and called Zico – or something like that."

That was most likely one of the mixed race boys I had seen in the photographs in the house.

"How do you spell his name?"

"I don't know."

"Z-I-C-O?"

"I don't know. That's all I know."

I stared at her hard. Her bright chestnut eyes sparkled with intelligence, and I was reminded of the look she gave her brother that I spied upon through the kitchen window. I thanked her and she exited.

Once out the door I called out – "Matt we need to find the son called Zico."

I then called WPC Mudrew into the incident room and complimented on her excellent work as first respondent. This time her face lit up with her familiar glowing smile. Her police head-gear had been removed to release her hair in long brown ringlets. I then shared with her my frustration with PJ's Harpo Marx impression and wanted to know if he had said anything to her before Matt and I had arrived.

"Well it just so happens I turned on my body armour-cam as I approached the house."

I sat forward.

"Did PJ talk to you?"

"Yes."

"A lot?"

"A bit."

I was getting to really like this girl.

"Come on – let's play back this tape."

WPC Muldrew pulled out the SD card and put it into my PC. Now none of what I was about to see would be admissible in any trial – but at least I could get some sort of fix of what the hell was going on with our non-speaking victim/suspect.

I leaned forward in my chair and we were away:

The opening was a jerky shot of grey tarmac. The time code display at the bottom of the screen put the time at 13:19. So 15 minutes after receiving the 999 call.

I hear the rustling of clothes as the moving grey tarmac tilts up to reveal the three triangular red roofs of Asgard, the house of PJ. The house gets larger and larger until we push through the unlocked front door.

Off screen we hear WPC Muldrew's voice calling out.

"Hallo? Hallo?"

Off screen we hear a male screeching voice.

"My wife. My wife. My wife she's dead."

The wobbly camera turns into the living room where we see a man with his head in his hands sat forward on a couch. He is wearing the same V-neck jumper and jeans as when I saw him in the kitchen.

"Where is she Sir?" The voice of WPC Muldrew.

"In there. In there!" PJ shouts and points a shaky hand towards the garage door, and then even louder he yells "In the garage. In the freezer."

The garage door slides open. But the camera jerks back in keeping with WPC Muldrew's testimony that she didn't want to see the body.

The next image I see is back on PJ sitting on a couch still covering his head with his hands. WPC Muldrew gets nearer as he scratches his head. She is so close I can see the dandruff flakes flying off.

WPC Muldrew's says nothing as PJ continues.

"She was doing cocaine. She fell in with a bad crowd! It has got to be something to do with that." This was said in a change of tone – not screechy, but slower, calmer. His voice had a touch of the mockney.

"Do you know where the murderer would be now?"

PJ shook his head.

"I know her first husband was back on the scene. Eduardo."

This statement was made while the camera paid special attention to PJ's Adidas Gazelle trainers.

"They'd been meeting up." He continued.

"OK Sir. I am going to have to seal off this crime scene. We need to take you somewhere outside of here." So we had ourselves some leads – a bad crowd who did cocaine and a first husband called Eduardo. But how much did this bodycam footage reveal? There was no way of knowing at this stage. But at least I got to hear the fucker's voice beyond those two words – No Comment.

"Thank you WPC Muldrew. Excellent work," I said after the viewing, and WPC Muldrew beamed again.

 "It's been a tough day. I need a drink. Fancy coming along?" WPC Muldrew offers.

"I'd love to," I say "but I've got a mountain of stuff to get through."

Presently I looked out the window to see WPC Muldrew, now out of uniform, walking out the car park with someone I recognised – the peroxide ambulance chaser journalist for the Surrey Star – Jane Barrow. This set off alarm bells.

I got out my phone and bashed out a text to Muldrew – "Fanx once again for your wonderful work today. Have a well earnt drink on me. Be careful what you say to the vulture lady from the Surrey Star."

She replied ten minutes later with a – "Jane is very nice. She's offered to help us with a call out for information. Rest assured I will not reveal any sensitive stuff on the case."

Was my rest assured? No. Not really.

Time: 20:00

Location: Woking Police Station

Roy came into the incident room holding up a see-through plastic zip up bag containing the laptop I had seen in the house. Just what I was waiting for.

"My team did some forensic on this. We've emailed you the report, but the top line is this – no activity at all since Friday night. A Spotify playlist got activated at 9.35 pm and got switched off at 10.25pm."

"May I see that playlist?"

Roy fired up the lap top and clicked onto the Spotify playlist. The playlist was titled "Ligia's Disco Party" and this is what was on it:

PLAYLIST
Ligia's Disco Party
Created by **Ligia James** · 16 songs, 1 hr 20 min

TITLE	ARTIST
♥ Boyfriend (Repeat)	Confidence Man
♥ Keep on Dancin' - Original Mix	Gary's Gang
♥ Born To Be Alive	Patrick Hernandez
♥ Rollerskating Jam—Disco Rap Mix	Dr. Packer, Casual Connection
♥ Blind—Frankie Knuckles Remix	Hercules & Love Affair
♥ Ask Me	Carol Jiani
♥ Fire Island	Village People
♥ Asi Me Gusta	Chimo Bayo
♥ Toda Menina Baiana	Gilberto Gil
♥ Instant Replay	Dan Hartman
♥ Le Freak - 2016 Remaster	Chic
♥ Open Your Heart	Madonna
♥ Funky Guitar - FPI Funky Mix	Tc 1992

20

An eclectic mix of dance music, not just disco, I observed.

I then did a skim of her email correspondence – much of it was in a language I assumed to be Portuguese. Would Surrey Police go to the expense of hiring me a translator? They bloody better. There was a lot of correspondence to Zico, who must be the son that Samantha mentioned, and an Eduardo. That was the name PJ gave as the ex-husband in WPC Muldrew's body-cam footage. So now we had email addresses for the son and ex-husband.

I asked Roy about her mobile phone.

"It was with her in her jacket in the freezer. The phone was in there for so long it cracked and so we can't get access to the data. But we are going to run some tests on the state of the phone, so we may be able to tell how long she was in the freezer.

"So can we establish a time of death?"

"Impossible to say – the freezer has monkeyed around with that. As you know, normally a body's temperature would give you an indication, but the freezer took her body to minus 4 and kept it there. Unfortunately, there were no flies inside the freezer to lay any eggs."

I forwarded the email addresses of Zico and Eduardo to my partner Matt The Stat so he can contact them, while I flicked through her picture library. I always feel uncomfortable looking through other people's photographs, but I had to do it, especially with the paucity of information I was getting from the husband.

Scrolling through the years, I felt I was getting to know Ligia. The mother, the daughter, the party girl. In most pictures she is dressed down in jeans, trainers and t-shirt, occasionally she's glammed up for a formal occasion. In every picture she is either smiling or pulling a humorous face.

The picture of PJ and Ligia together were becoming less and less frequent. A constant was the young mixed race lad – I watched him grow up in pictures from an 11 year old to a tall athletic young man. But I only saw one of the boys grow up.

I saw a picture of five young women standing outside a village bar in a country that is not the UK, in amongst them is Ligia, her face is now familiar to me, with the same flowing black hair and the same glowing smile.

I found a relatively recent picture of the married couple together by the mantelpiece in the house. In the middle of them is a trophy – a metallic statue about three foot high of a goldy brass coloured woman with wings holding up a globe. Perhaps it's some showbiz award. I looked closer at Ligia's smile, it seemed frozen, doubtful. But that always happens when you stare long enough at the smile in a photograph.

I was in the car making my way back to the crime scene, when I get a phone call from a Matt full of brio telling me that, on Saturday night, the son Zico had filed a missing person report with the Met Police on Eduardo Pinheiro.

"This has got to have something to do with the case," he said, and sent over a photo of Eduardo Pinheiro to my phone. He was black, with a broad forehead and a wide pronounced jawline. Short back and sides, with a slight quiff. I was also sent a full length picture, which showed him wearing a chef hat and to be very long legged and tall – about 6 foot 3. Not someone who would get easily lost in a crowd.

Date: Tuesday 20th March 2018
Time: 21:00
Location: 3 Odin Court, West Byfleet, Surrey

It was imperative to speak with the next door neighbours who had heard rowing on the Friday night. With your older witnesses you need to speak with them quickly while the evidence was still fresh in their mind. Leave it a few days and that vital evidence could get lost forever in their foggy brains.

The name of the chunky woman with the thick glasses was Rose Barraclough. The husband was called Fred – a retired accountant. His voice was a complete contrast to his menacing Nazi war criminal appearance. Instead he spoke in a Yorkshire accent as thick as black pudding.

"She were a ray of sunshine, always cheerful always saying hello – but him – not so much as a dickie."

A Yorkshire man using rhyming slang? Is that suspicious? Maybe – but let's move on.

"So when WPC Muldrew brought him over, did he say anything to either of you?"

Rose and Fred reply to the negative.

"Did either of you see or hear him call his sister?"

Negatives all around.

"Or his solicitor?"

More expressions to the negative.

"So this row you heard from the house on Friday night – male and female voices – could you make out any of the words?"

"You're a loser! I heard her say that a few times," said Rose.

"And what was the male voice saying?"

"Couldn't hear," says Rose.

"What about you Fred?"

"I couldn't hear either."

"Did you hear them row often?"

Rose looked over to her husband.

"Every couple of weeks."

Fred nodded.

"The thing is though," Fred chipped in "We never could see them rowing, so we can't be sure if was them two who live next door doing it."

"But the female voice sounded foreign though." Rose chipped in.

"You talked about the night of the last row. Loud music was being played."

"Yes Love. That stopped suddenly."

AH! That would be the Spotify play list – I thought.

"You didn't think to complain?"

23

"No it wasn't too loud. That's why we could hear the rowing over the top."

"Can you remember any of the songs?"

"No sorry."

"Come on – can you remember a lyric?"

Rose thought for a bit, scratched her head.

"Anything? What sort of music was it?"

"This bloke was singing Prawn."

"Prawn?"

"Yes Prawn. Over and over – and then the music stopped."

"But the rowing went on?"

"No the rowing stopped after the music stopped. It was dead silent after that."

I showed them the picture of Eduardo on my phone – "Ever seen this gentleman around?" That drew a blank.

I was making to leave when Fred chipped in – "We need to mention the cat."

"OK. Tell me about the cat."

"He came into our back garden Friday night."

"Oh yes. Their cat came in and turned on our burglar lights in the back garden," said Rose.

"OK" I said, "why would that be important?"

"It means someone visiting the house next door, because the cat always runs away into our back garden when they get visitors."

"Nice. You are turning out to be top class witnesses. What time was that?"

Rose closed her eyes as she thought.

"Oh yes I remember – just as Graham Norton was about to start."

"Where you watching live TV?"

"What do you mean?"

"I mean were you watching as it was being broadcast, or were you watching it on the Iplayer?"

"What's an iplayer?"

24

Right a quick reference to the Radio Times shows that on a Friday night Graham Norton comes on at 10.30. So that snippet of info gives us a kick-start to our timeline:

At just before 10.30 a visitor arrives to the house (maybe).

Time: 22:00
Location: Woking Police Station

In the reception area I saw a young brown skinned man, aged around 18, being comforted by an out of uniform WPC Muldrew who evidently had been called back from the pub. I instantly recognised the man's emerald eyes, striking cheekbones and flowing locks from the boy in the photograph. Now his flowing locks had transformed into dreadlocks that were bleached white at the tips. But here there was no smiling. He had clearly been crying.

I approach the young man. "Hello I am Detective Chief Superintendent Ferdinand – Will you answer some questions for me?"

He nods.

He confirmed to me that Ligia's name was pronounced lij-ee-ah.

"You live with your father?"

The boy nods again

"And I understand you reported your father missing. When did you do this?"

"Saturday night. He didn't come home Friday night. He's a chef at a restaurant and when his work called at 7pm asking where he was, I got worried and called the police."

Zico's voice was unusual, it was hard to attach it to any specific region or country. There was a little bit of London there and a little bit of somewhere else.

"The name of your father is Eduardo Pinheiro?"

He nods.

"Is he also Portuguese?"

"No Brazilian."

"Do you know where your father keeps his passport?"

"Yes it's still there – in the drawer."

"Does he have any other passports?"

"No. He only has one – Brazilian."

"Where did Eduardo go Friday night?"

"I don't know – he went out on a date – but I don't know who with."

"A date with a lady?"

"I guess so. I think her name was GG."

"Do you have any contact details for this GG lady?"

"No I will have a look."

"What do you think of PJ James?"

Zico scowled and then said, "If you can't say anything good about someone, don't say anything at all."

"Well I totally disagree with that. I wouldn't get very far in my job if everyone stuck to that. So – come on – what do you think of PJ James?"

"No comment."

Aw – not you as well!

In the incident room, on my PC I pulled up the missing person report on Eduardo Pinheiro. On the Friday he went missing he was wearing a green sweater and blue jeans and drove a White Pontiac. I printed out his photograph and forwarded it to WPC Muldrew who had volunteered to lead the door to door.

On my way out of the incident room, Matt pulls me aside. "We have contacted Ligia's parents, and they are coming straight over on the first plane from Portugal to look after Zico. But we need to have the body formally identified now. I just spoke with PJ's sister – he's refused to identify the body. Can we get the son to do it?"

I shook my head vigorously. "No way. No fucking way. We can't let the son do it. Get PJ on the phone – he must do it. PJ has already seen her dead."

PJ – Video log – Saturday 31st March 2018

This was nothing but cruelty. I was at my sister's home. I had just seen my wife dead and I was trying to sleep and blot out the pain. A phone call comes in late into the night. Sam picks up, and the person insists on speaking to me. They were demanding that I go to the morgue and formally identify the body.

I had spent an hour or more being thoroughly examined by the police for any injuries I may have sustained in an attack. I realised then that I would be a prime suspect. They of course found nothing. I haven't been in a fight since my first year of secondary school.

I wanted to co-operate with the police but they were asking too much of me. I could not bear to see Ligia dead again. The police called me again about identifying the body, I just hung up and shut down.

I had already seen the body and called the police. That should be enough for any formal identification.

I just wanted to shut my eyes, go to sleep and never wake up again.

Chapter 3 – The Chablis Trail
Day 2 of the Investigation

Date: Wednesday 21st March 2018
Time: 07:30
Location: Woking Police Station

    I managed to snatch an hour or two of sleep at home, and returning to the nick early doors I discover that the brass had assigned me a team of three investigators. I've worked with these trusty bloodhounds before – I like to call them Huey, Dewey and Lewey. I am not sure if they are too keen on their monikers, their real names are Shakeela, Tom and Vikki.

    Burning the midnight oil, Vikki had been busy putting up the incident room wall charts, including this floor plan of the ground floor of Asgard:

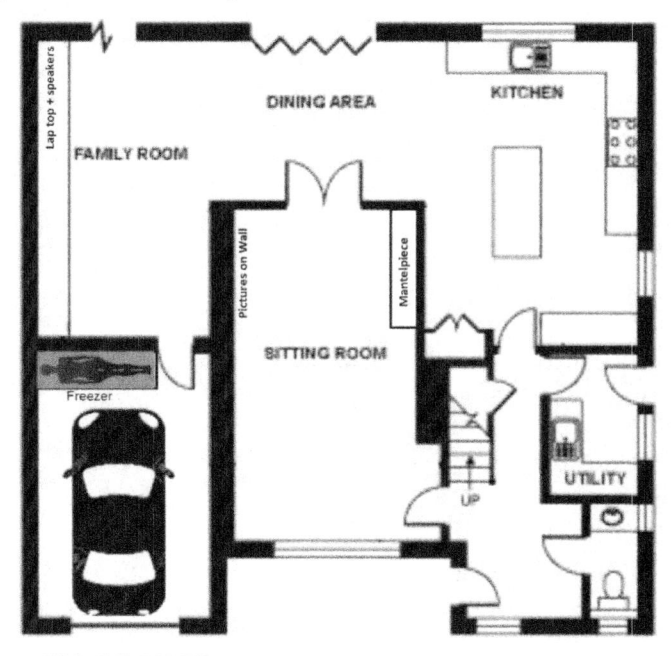

GROUND FLOOR

Also on the wall was a map of the streets of the immediate area, and a chart of the four investigation pillars. I filled it in with the info I had after Day 1 of the investigation:

Evidence	Witnesses	Crime Scene	Victimology
• Body in Freezer • Body put in sleeping bag • Two dustbin bags over head of body • Victim's mobile phone cracked in freezer	• PJ - husband • Fred & Wendy - neighbours • Zico - son • Door to door in progress	• Victim's Lap top • No blood. So cleared up? • Or not killed there • No sign of forced entry	• Son - Zico • Husband - PJ • Ex-Husband - Eduardo (Reported Missing!)

This to be updated as the case progresses.

Looking up at the boards that now surrounded my desk, I felt a rush of nervous exhilaration – the Murder Investigation was up and running.

Settling down to my first coffee of the day, I was angered by the news that Zico had been made to identify Ligia's body. He had apparently done it willingly, saying that he wanted to see his mother one last time and say good-bye, but I am sure he would have found the experience traumatic, and something that would scar him mentally for years to come.

We are supposed to be public defenders and we should have protected Zico from that. Why couldn't PJ identify the body?

Zico was now back at his home in Merton that he lived in with his missing father. His grand parents had arrived at Heathrow from Porto in the early hours and were now taking care of him.

One of my assigned investigators Tom who had managed to get some sleep had been sent to interview Ligia's parents.

While PJ not talking to me was suspicious, and supremely irritating, on consideration of everything, the missing ex-husband Eduardo Pinheiro was top of my suspect list. It was highly likely that his disappearance was linked to Ligia's death. Had he escaped the country? Tom had called in to confirm what Zico had told me – that Eduardo Pinheiro's Brazilian passport was still in the drawer at home. There was no record of him having a second passport.

I forwarded a high-res photo of Eduardo Pinheiro to the team to alert the forces nationwide and put out some WANTED posters. True to their reputation, it appears the Met Police had done next to nothing on receiving Zico's missing person report on Saturday. But this missing person was now linked to a homicide, and now some proper police (that's us, Surrey) were taking over.

I get on the phone to Jennifer Janus, PJ's brief, and left a voicemail: "When is your client ready to come in and give a statement? THIS IS IMPERATIVE! I will be calling again in an hour."

I was hoping that my second interview with PJ would give him the chance to tell me something about the cocaine, the bad crowd and the ex-husband story he mentioned to WPC Muldrew when she first got to the scene.

At a few minutes before 9 am I get an incoming call. "Morning Ferdy – I hear you have a murder case."

The male voice was in an Indian accent, familiar but I couldn't immediately place it. He said the words 'murder case' like it was some jolly adventure.

"It is me Rupal Chakrabharti – Met Police."

"Ah Yes! The blood splatter expert."

Rupal was more than just an expert, he had an evangelical zeal for his job. But his fervour for blood splatter wasn't from any morbid obsession, it was from a passion for forensic detail and the physics of liquids, and any chance he gets to do it he would. He didn't care if it was outside his jurisdiction, or even if he did it unpaid.

"Chakka, do you spend all your time trawling the networks and bulletins for murder cases?"

"No I just check regularly. Come on – tell me about the case."

30

So infectious was his enthusiasm, he made you feel like committing a bloody murder just to give him some splatter to work on.

"At the moment we have no blood splatter. Roy…you know Roy?"

"Course"

"Roy will be running a Luminol test round the crime scene. Rest assured – as soon as a blood splatter turns up, you'll be at the top of my Rolodex."

"I can also get you the services of Brandi The Cadaver Dog."

"Nice. Will let you know."

At fifteen minutes past nine, WPC Muldrew strides into my incident room, holding an A4 piece of paper and in a state of racing palpitation, telling me that the overnight neighbouring door-to-door enquiries had thrown up something juicy.

"OK what is it then?"

"A white transit van parked up round the corner at 6pm Friday night. Right here on Sanderson Way, just one street from the house." WPC Muldrew pointed to the spot on the large wall map:

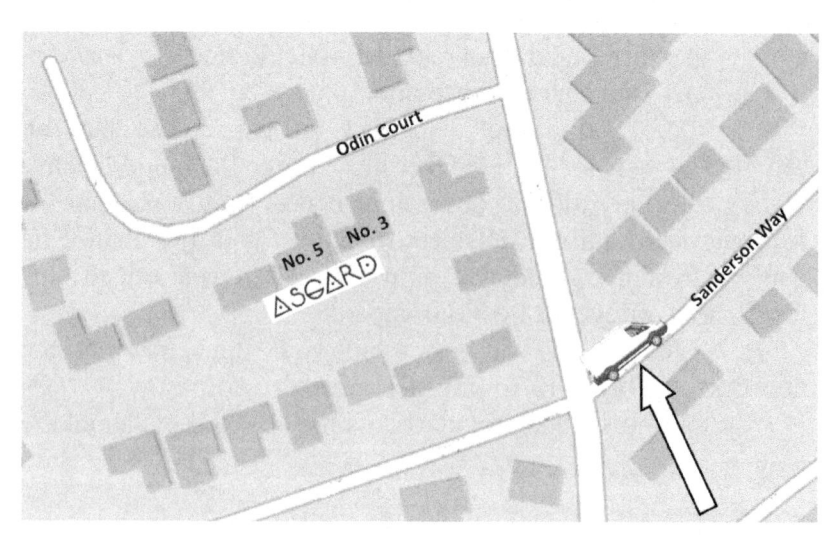

"And what about this van?"

"There were three men inside and….they looked South American."

"In what way did they look South American?"

"The witness said they looked foreign, and he heard one of them speak – and it sounded Spanish."

"Did the witness engage with any of them at all?"

"No but one of the gang came out of the van and urinated against the hedge. The witness crossed his path and he gave him a look as if to say – 'Yeah? What are you going to do about it?' Then as he walked away, he heard them laughing in an aggressive way."

"How do you laugh in an aggressive way?"

"Dunno. Those are the witness's words – not mine. The witness is helping our illustrator put together an identikit. He mentioned that the urinator had a distinctive star tattoo on his left forearm."

"In what way is it a distinctive star?"

"It's an eight point star."

"Eight point star? Is the witness sure it was eight point?"

"Pretty sure. I got the identi-kit illustrator to do a picture." and she handed me the page of A4 with a star with eight evenly spiked points in the middle of a cross:

This was good evidence. You often get four, five, and six point stars – but eight point star tattoos are indeed quite unusual and noteworthy.

Muldrew let a silence hang momentarily as I continued looking at the star, then she said, "It could be a drug gang thing."

"Could well be. I will get onto Interpol. They have a database on drug gangs and their insignia."

Meanwhile Matt had discovered that Ligia worked for an Events Company based near the Strand called Minerva and Shakeela, had been despatched to Ligia's place of work to interview her colleagues.

It unfortunately fell to Shakeela to break the news to Ligia's boss and colleagues that she was now dead. One of the management told Shakeela that on the Friday afternoon Ligia had been told that she and the rest of her department's job has been put a risk – a predictable consequence of a recent corporate take over.

Time: 11:30
Location: Woking Police Station

The Bottox goth lawyer Jennifer Janus had been to reception and dropped by an envelope marked for my attention. I ripped open the envelope to release a wad of photocopied receipts from various business establishments in Oxford, all dated over the weekend. Also included was this laser printed letter on A4 :

> I, P.J. James wish to make an official statement. It has now been over 18 hours since I discovered my wife dead. While I am still in a state of deep shock and anguish, which I do not think I will ever recover from, I am at least able to gather my thoughts to give an accurate and detailed account of my movements leading up to the week-end and up until when the body of Ligia was found by me on Tuesday afternoon.
>
> On Thursday morning, Ligia and I took Willoughby our cat, who had been anaemic, to the vet. That evening we had dinner at home and watched television together.

33

The last time I saw Ligia alive was Friday morning. She got up as usual at 6.30 am – and at 7.30am I gave her a lift to West Byfleet train station to go to her job in Covent Garden.

She did not seem troubled – everything was as normal. I kissed her good-bye as she got out the car and I was never to see her alive again.

At 9am I went for a jog and got back home at 10 am. I made some work related calls and sent out some emails.

At 2pm I set off for Oxford by train. I walked to West Byfleet station. This involved getting a five minute train to Woking, then a 20 minute train to Basingstoke and from there a 50 minute train journey to Oxford.

I got to Oxford at around 4pm and checked in at the Hotel Malmaison.

I am researching a TV series idea on the lives of students at Oxford University. So I walked around the town and visited the pubs and bars popular with the students.

At 8.34pm Friday evening I got a text from Ligia asking me to pick her up from the station. I texted her back to remind her I was in Oxford.

That was the last contact I ever received from her.

Late on Friday night I drew out some money from an ATM near Magdalene Bridge. It is likely CCTV will have picked me up.

I got up at 7.30 am Saturday morning, had breakfast at the hotel and spent the day walking around the town, taking photographs of potential locations and trying to think up ideas for a TV series.

At 3pm I sent a text to Ligia asking how Willoughby was.

She did not reply.

I called her at 7pm and left a message on her voicemail.

I had dinner alone at a restaurant in Oxford, and stayed another night at the Hotel Malmaison.

Sunday was spent walking around the town –

gathering up ideas for the TV Series.

I have a whole raft of receipts from the hotel and various shops and restaurants to verify all of my movements in Oxford over the week-end.

On Monday morning I woke up at 7.30 am, had breakfast, and made my way to Oxford station for the journey home.

I texted Ligia to tell her I was on my way, and asking again for an update on Willoughby. Of course, I got no reply.

I got home at 10 am, alarmed to find Willoughby starving and I fed him immediately.

I assumed Ligia to be at work.

At mid-day I took Willoughby to the vet for a follow up check-up.

When I got home I called Ligia to tell her that Willoughby was responding well to his treatment, but it went straight to voicemail.

I called her place of work, who told me she had not showed up that day. I was now alarmed. Although my concerns were more along the lines of her leaving me, and not that she was dead or in any danger.

I spent the rest of the afternoon and early evening calling her friends. This can all easily be corroborated and verified.

I had a restless night's sleep and when I woke up went on my usual early morning jog.

At 12am I decided to look in the freezer to see if there was anything there I could have for lunch, which is when I made the horrible discovery of Ligia's body.

I immediately called 999 and went into a shocked state of shut down.

As for who could have killed Ligia – I cannot say. Ligia had recently been moving in circles unknown to me for about six months. She had been drinking excessively and taking cocaine. I do not know anything about the person or persons supplying that to her. I know also that she had been in regular contact with her previous husband Eduardo with whom they had a son together. But I do not think for one second that Eduardo would be capable of killing Ligia.

This is all I have to say. Can I please ask you to respect my privacy and leave me alone with my grief?

PJ – Video log – Saturday 31st March 2018

My lawyer said it was much better writing this statement than speaking it in a police interview. This way there was total clarity. That letter was pretty much dictated by me verbatim and was as close as possible to a cast iron alibi. Whenever Ligia was killed, I was far away in Oxford and could not possibly have done it. Furthermore, I had a pile of receipts and an electronic trail proving I was in Oxford the whole period. Including taking money out at an ATM near Madgalene Bridge, Oxford. I believe many or even most ATMs have CCTV.

We hoped this letter would convince the officer in charge of my innocence and so he would then look at other suspects. I hated pointing the finger of suspicion in other directions, but the police needed to focus on the real killer or killers.

Because I hadn't seen Ligia for days I was fearing the worst. It felt strange that she would leave Willoughby our beloved cat alone. Particularly when he had been ill. But I thought it most likely that she had left me.

Time: 11:30
Location: Woking Police Station

After reading PJ's written statement several times I called Jennifer Janus. "Thank you for the written statement, but I still need to speak with your client in person."

"Is that necessary? My client is still suffering from severe shock."

"Yes and your client has still not said one dickie to me. I appreciate he's in shock – but I've got a job to do. Please bring him into the station tomorrow morning at 10am."

"But he said everything he's got to say in that statement."

"Well that's exactly what I need to talk to him about. See you tomorrow at 10am. Bye."

My well of sympathy was rapidly drying out for this PJ and his mask of sorrow. There was a whole raft of questions I needed to ask not covered in his statement. For a start – was everything locked up when PJ came home on Monday morning? Roy reported that a set of keys were in a woman's coat hanging in the hallway. There is no sign of a forced entry, so how did the killer get in? Did the killer double lock when they left? If so, what key did they use? Maybe they exited via the garage. There is a chain inside of the front door, is Ligia in the habit of putting that on?

My next visitor to the incident room was Roy. I offered him a cup of tea, which he declined. He sat down at the big round table and we got down to business.

"Right – cause of death. It wasn't the severe trauma to her head, of which she had two. While they caused one round shaped wound and one smaller wound and a lot of blood loss, the cause of death is asphyxiation."

"How can you be sure it was asphyxiation?"

"We found considerable trauma to the neck and damage to the hyoid bone.

"We also found purple splotches in her eyes, as well as face, neck and lungs – it's called petechial haemorrhages and you get them when you die from strangulation. We also found foam in the victim's airways as she clearly struggled to breath and mucus from the lungs which are also signs of being strangled. We also found an enlarged heart and an altered blood chemistry – all again consistent with a death from asphyxiation."

"So the blow to the head may have been used to knock her unconscious – and then she was subsequently strangled." I offered.

"Quite possibly. There was a lot of mucus and spittle on the inside of the dustbin bag. So it appears that she was strangled with the dustbin bag over the head. Maybe so that the place wouldn't be covered in blood."

"And so the killer wouldn't have to look into her eyes." I suggested.

"Forensics at the morgue reveal that there was large amounts of alcohol and some cocaine in her blood stream. She had been consuming both 12 hours before death."

"Any idea where the sleeping bag she was in had come from?"

"No. Not yet."

"Our big problem is that we can't establish if there is a kill location inside the house. With all the upstairs area, the loft, the garage, the garden, the shed – the forensic search could take weeks – even months."

"Sounds like a job for Brandi the Cadaver Dog."

"So Rupal called you too - eh?"

PJ – Video log – Saturday 31st March 2018

Samantha was telling me I need professional help, but what could they do? Just plug me with anti-depressants?

The police kept calling, offered me a free PTSD counselling service. But I was suspicious of that. They were probably going to use the counselling to try and get incriminating information on me. If I was going to do anything like this at all, I was going to arrange it privately.

I couldn't help it, but in the days directly afterwards, I kept playing and re-playing in my mind my life with Ligia.

We had been together for 8 years and my memory of our first meeting is as clear as yesterday – May 2010 – at a bereavement counselling meeting.

She was talking about the pain of losing her youngest son Leandro in a car accident. She spoke English fluently, she was so eloquent it was hard to believe she was not speaking in her first language. But the way she spoke with her Portuguese accent, she was lyrical, enchanting.

We started seeing each other, and exploring beyond her veil of sadness, I found a joie-de-vivre that shone through and energised me. Slowly but surely my sorrow and grief melted away.

When you lose someone you love – you have an aversion of getting close to someone new for fear of suffering that debilitating loss again. So at first I was reluctant to let Ligia into my life, but when I did – she healed my pain. But now she's brought it back ten-fold by leaving me. I went to sleep hoping never to wake up. I just wanted to be back with Ligia.

I have hundreds of pictures of Ligia, but there is one that I keep seeing when I shut my eyes. In this picture she is smiling knowingly and looking at the lens and raising her finger over her mouth to shush whoever it is who is taking the photograph, most likely me. I have no memory of why she was doing that, but when I see it now as I shut my eyes, I fancy that she's saying to me now – "there's no need to get hysterical, stay calm, stay silent. There's no need to tell the police anything."

Time: 13:30
Location: Woking Police Station

24 hours into the investigation, I still had no solid information on Ligia's movements leading up to her death. So I was very grateful for the next snippet of vital information – the report on Ligia's bank card activity. On the Friday we had these four entries:

Time	£	Payee
12.31	£3.20	Rymans
12.44	£9.99	Waterstones
18.31	£18.20	The Marquis, 51-52 Chandos Place, WC2 4HS
21.24	£12.24	Bestways, Food & Wine, West Byfleet

The last two entries were of particular interest. The Marquis is a pub just off The Strand close to where Ligia worked, while Bestways is an off licence directly by West Byfleet train station.

Looking at the map of West Byfleet, Ligia's home in Odin Way is a mile and a half from the station. So a thirty minute walk. Ligia was at Bestways at 21.24 and the Spotify play list was activated at home at 21.32. So to get home in 8 minutes, Ligia either got a lift, a taxi, or ran very fast.

The train timetable reveals that a fast train to West Byfleet left Waterloo at 20:53 arriving at West Byfleet 21:21. We would request to see CCTV from British Rail, I needed to find out if Ligia had a companion – or was being followed.

And who was she drinking with at The Marquis? £18.20 is the cost of a bottle of wine or a round of two or three drinks. Surely she wasn't drinking that quantity of alcohol alone?

Bestways, Food & Wine, being just a five minute drive away was our first port of call.

Time: 14:30
Location: West Byfleet, Surrey

We spoke to the cheery man who was on the till on Friday night. He recalls Ligia and knows her by sight. He showed us his stock records which reveal that £12.24 bought her a bottle of Chablis – a quality French white wine. The man said she appeared quite jovial, smiling as she usually does. He did not see Ligia get into a car and did not note whether she was with anyone.

The man's cheeriness turned to distress when I told her I was investigating a murder case, and Ligia was the victim.

Stepping outside Bestways I see a Taxi Rank one door away. We go inside and show the people working there our photograph of Ligia. They recognise her as a woman who used their services from time to time, but their records show that she did not take a cab from them that Friday evening. Did she get an Uber?

So we have a burning question. How did Ligia get home in 8 minutes to activate that Spotify play-list ?

Or did someone else activate the Spotify playlist? According to PJ he was far away in Oxford at the time.

Next Matt and I took a train up to the Marquis, the pub off The Strand. We needed to identify that drinking companion.

Time: 15:30
Location: The Marquis pub, Covent Garden

The Marquis is a narrow wedge shaped pub, situated on a crescent road turning off The Strand. It had stain glass windows to give the tourists some of that Olde English charm and posters promoting drink promotions and the weekly pub quiz.

I approached the lady behind the bar holding up my police ID and demanded to speak to everyone who worked at the pub on Friday evening.

The bar lady went to the phone, dialled, and handed me the phone.

"Hullo this is Ted – I worked Friday evening. How can I help?" The voice sounded keen.

I told him I was going to send him a photograph of a woman and I wanted him to tell me if he remembered serving her.

After five minutes I called him back.

"Yes I do. She's a semi regular. I think she works nearby. What's this about?"

"Answer the questions first and I'll tell you. OK. Who was she with?"

"A bloke. He's a semi regular also."

"What did this bloke look like?"

"Normal – about 30ish – not fat, not thin."

I rolled my eyes. Vague descriptions are the bane of my life.

"What was his ethnicity?"

"White."

So not Eduardo then.

"Do you recall where they were in the pub?"

"They were sat at one of the tables near the bar."

"Did you overhear any snatches of conversation?"

"No. I'm not one of those nosey barmen."

"Were they rowing?"

"Not that I noticed, they were just chatting."

"Were they kissing, or touching each other?"

"Not that I saw."

"Did you notice anything unusual about them?"

"No – nothing."

"Any observations. Anything?"

"Well yes…err…"

"Come on tell me…."

"I don't know if I should…"

"Yes you should – you must – what is it?"

"I saw the man hand something to the woman as she went to the toilet. She came back and gave something back to him."

The lady behind the bar showed me their sales records for the evening. £18.20 bought her a bottle of Chablis. A Chablis trail was emerging.

The lady allowed me to look along the sales records of that evening to find that a second bottle of the same Chablis was bought at 19.02 – some half an hour later. This was put on a different card.

We can now take that card number to the bank, who will hopefully give us the name of the card holder and Ligia's Chablis companion.

This was a serious lead. This put us on the verge of identifying the man that was with her the night she was most likely killed. This man who was getting drunk with her – and supplying her with cocaine.

Chapter 4 – Brandi The Cadaver Dog
Day 3 of the Investigation

Date: Thursday 22nd March
Time: 08:30
Location: Woking Police Station

From the newsagent on the way into the nick, I picked up my copy of The Surrey Star, our main local weekly newspaper. This is what ran on the front page:

Surrey Star

March 22 2018 • www.surrey-star.co.uk • Established 1954

HOOKED IN
Janet Ellis talks to us about her debut novel
Full story on page 18

HAND TO GOD
Win tickets to see provocative play
Full story on page 20

Cold Case Murder

Jane Barrow reports

A West Byfleet man returned from a business trip to find his wife, dead in his garage freezer with severe head injuries. The man PJ James - a television director of some renown - is now being treated for shock, and helping the police while they try to determine the exact cause of death .

There was no sign of a forced entry or a struggle, though raised voices was heard from the house on the night of Friday 16th March. With the body being frozen, the investigators are presented with a difficulty in determining the time of death, but are a hopeful that her mobile phone that was found with her in the freezer will provide a clue.

PJ James made the grim discovery on the afternoon of Tuesday 20th March, and the police are appealing for witnesses for anybody seeing something suspicious the days before around Odin Way in West Byfleet.

Ligia James

They are specifically interested in identifying a gang of three men who were seen parked nearby in a white transit van. One of the men had on his forearm a distinctive 8 point star tattoo. (Pictured below)

The victim - Ligia James (aged 39 pictured left) was a woman from Portugal who worked for an Events Company in Covent Garden and has an 18 year old son from a previous marriage. She was known to have connections to South American drug gangs, and a quantity of cocaine was found in her blood stream.

This is the first recorded homicide in the West Byfleet area this year.

Have you seen a man with this tattoo? Contact Surrey CrimeStoppers on 0800 555 111

As the lead investigator in the case I had no need to read the article, nevertheless I gave it a skim. Towards the end of the piece, a phrase jumped out – "A QUANTITY OF COCAINE WAS FOUND IN HER BLOODSTREAM".

45

I grabbed my phone and called WPC Muldrew. She answers the phone with her customary cheeriness, which I cut through -

"Never mind that. What the fuck did you say to the Surrey Star?"

"What?"

"Have you seen today's paper? A front pager written by Jane Barrow, the woman you went for a drink with."

"What's it say?"

"Stuff about some known connection to a South American drug gang, and cocaine in her blood stream."

"I didn't tell her anything like that."

"You must have done."

"I wouldn't tell her anything like that. I promise. I swear."

"Gemma – you've let the case down. You've let us all down."

"Look! The night I went for a drink with her I just told her that I'd found a dead woman in a freezer – and that was it. I called her up the next day to give her the info on the 8 point star tattoo – and that was it."

"Well it can't be …you must have leaked stuff."

"I didn't even know about the cocaine in the blood stream."

I went silent on this – if that was true then someone else leaked.

Then Muldrew spoke again – "You've never liked me – is that what this is?"

"No it's not that."

"Ah! Thought so."

"No I don't not like you. But you must have told her about this drug gang thing."

I went silent and she jumped in – "I swear to you I never, I NEVER, said anything about a South American drug gang – nor anything about cocaine."

"OK I'm sorry. I believe you. Sorry for accusing you. But if you didn't tell her – who did?"

Now I know Roy wouldn't leak anything about cocaine in the victim's blood stream to the press and I didn't want to offend him by asking (and I was too scared). Then it occurred to me that PJ James may have given Jane Barrow the drug gang angle, for the very obvious reason to deflect the finger of suspicion away from him. That would explain the spurious "TV director of some renown" guff. I was about to call Jane Barrow, but then remembered my previous conversations with her, and the whole a-journalist-never-reveals-their-sources bit.

Next – Matt charges into the incident room. He'd been onto the bank and got that all-important name on the zapped card at the pub – Andrew Goddard. That's the same name as someone who works at Minerva – Ligia's Events company.

We had ourselves a named suspect – and so we were off to Covent Garden and to the offices of Minerva.

As I was putting on my jacket, I get a call that I had a visitor in reception. I walk down to see a distraught Zico sat with his two grandparents.

"I've seen the papers. They are making my mother look like a bad person. You must stop this."

As I fumbled for something encouraging to say, I looked at him helplessly, he went on:

"I would see my mother at least once a week, I spoke with her on the phone constantly. If she had anything to do with a drug gang I would have known."

Zico had every reason to be upset. This local newspaper article was the first press story on the case, and it was very likely the nationals would use that article, along with the South American drug gang angle, as a springboard and take their speculations in that direction.

"Zico. I know your mother was a good person. I will find her killer, but I have no control over what the press write."

"But you must tell the press she wasn't with a drug gang."

I felt cornered into making that promise, but of course at this stage I had no evidence either way.

47

After that very uncomfortable encounter I was relieved to get in the car and drive up to Covent Garden. In the car Matt phoned ahead to be told that Andrew, or Andy, Goddard had called in sick. Apparently he was too grief stricken by Ligia's death.

So we turned around back to Woking nick and I got Matt on the case to get Goddard's home address – and a warrant to search his flat. This was on the grounds that he had been with Ligia's on the night of her death, obviously knew she was dead, and yet had not come forward.

My next big appointment was a hastily arranged 1 'o'clock-er with the grieving man himself – PJ James. I was hoping that now PJ would be able to give me something concrete to go on. If he didn't do it, then surely he will have some knowledge or insight on who did. He might be able to tell me something about this Andy Goddard. He may have an idea of where Eduardo Pinheiro would be. He could shed some light on this South American drug gang angle.

Time: 13:00
Location: Woking Police Station

"No comment."

Said PJ – for the 17th time. He sat in the interview room, once again with Jennifer Janus sat next to him. This time his messy hair had lost all shape and his five o'clock stretched beyond the night and into the early afternoon of the next day.

Aside from my previous set of questions, I also asked about the drug gangs and whether he had spoken to the press.

"When you spoke to WPC Muldrew, she said you mentioned that Ligia had got herself involved with some bad people. Can you tell us about that?"

"Have you spoken to any members of the press?"

Same two words each time. I had questions about keys and locking up:

"Was the house locked up when you came back on Monday morning?"

"No comment."

"I see you have a burglar alarm. Was that turned on or off when you came back from Oxford?"

"No comment."

In a final desperate plea for help I tried this: "What you know could be invaluable to finding your wife's killer. Don't you want to help?

"No comment."

I walked out the room in disgust and let Matt deal with the niceties of calling the interview to a close and seeing the witness/suspect out.

I waited for them in the car park. On spotting the three of them, PJ, his sister and Jennifer Janus, I collared the latter – "I have a warrant to search your client's phone," I barked holding up the said bit of paper close to her face. "Hand it over. NOW!"

PJ – Video log – Saturday 31st March 2018

After that second interview I was desperate to answer the questions. But my lawyer told me that I should not under any circumstances, no matter how uncooperative it made me look. She said this strategy would force them to look at other suspects. Otherwise they would just get into the minutia of my alibi and try to unpick it.

In any case there was very little I could offer that was useful. I knew nothing about Ligia's associations for the last six months, I'd overhead her talking on the phone to people – and frequently in Portuguese.

In the last six months, she hadn't been her vivacious self. She seemed troubled. I asked her a few times about it. But she wouldn't tell me. I so wish I'd pushed her now. I wanted to help solve her problems.

I handed over my phone to DCS Ferdinand the second he showed his warrant, I even gave him the password. Searching my phone would reveal that we had a few squabbles – mainly over money worries – but they would find nothing sinister – no threats, no warnings. They will find I did nothing wrong.

As far as I'm concerned he can keep the phone – aside from Samantha my sister and with both my parents gone, I had no one else I would want to contact and no one I would want to contact me.

Some people from the press had somehow got my phone number, maybe the police had leaked it to them. But I never answered any calls and just let them leave a message, to which I would not reply.

Ligia was upset with me because I hadn't worked since Shipton Village. She thought the worse of me for that. I tried to explain to her that this is the nature of the industry I am in. You can be out of work for two or three years and then you have more work offered to you than you can handle.

I was on the verge of something good coming along. I was waiting, hoping, on that, and our marriage would sail out of the choppy waters and back to happier times.

She died before we had the chance to reconcile, to tell her once again how boundlessly I loved her. That's what was compounding my sadness.

Time: 13:00
Location: Woking Police Station

I held it in my hands, this silver palm sized rectangle peeling off at the edges could be the key to opening up the case. I give over the phone to Roy and instructed him to give me any text and phone call info ASAP.

Within fifteen minutes, Roy emailed me this text exchange between husband and wife:

> Can you pick me from West Byfleet Station half nine?
> 23 January 20.51

> OK
> 23 January 20.55

> OK to do a station pick up @7?
> 6 February 17.55

> OK
> 6 February 18.06

> Station pick up @6.30?
> 16 February 18.05

> OK
> 16 February 18.07

> Can I get a station lift? Train comes in at just after 7pm.
> 1 March 18.25

> OK
> 1 March 18.28

> Will be @WB Station @7pm. OK to pick up?
> 8 March 18.15

> OK
> 8 March 18.25

> Can you pick me from the Station @9.25
> 16 March 20.55

> Sorry darling - No I'm in Oxford. Remember? X
> 16 March 21.55

> How's Willoughby? X
> 17 March 15.00

> How is Willoughby? I need to know …..X
> 17 March 18.55

> What's Up? Why won't you pick up? I need to know how Willoughby is. TALK TO ME
> 18 March 14.04

> Good night see you tomorrow. I LOVE YOU. XXX
> 18 March 21.07

What do you make of that? Not much chat. And no kisses or affection except for the final few texts – and all one sided. Certainly not painting a picture of a couple madly in love with each other. But then not at each other's throats either. The text exchange did confirm what was in PJ's written statement.

I looked at his outgoing calls. There was no 999 call on the Tuesday, no call to his sister or call to Jennifer Janus. He must have made those calls on his landline.

The report came with a comment from Roy that PJ had installed a SafeWiper application which allows you to delete texts without leaving any trace. This app was downloaded on the Sunday. You don't download an app like that to not delete any texts. **So what texts did he delete?** I am sure PJ would be very forthcoming if I asked. Not.

As I sat digesting this info, Matt phones in. He's in a street in Colliers Wood outside the address of Andy Goddard. The job was to get Goddard, hawl his ass over to Woking nick to be questioned by me, while a team of four search his flat. But the grieving Goddard was not at home, leaving Matt like Samuel Beckett, waiting for Goddard. But the ever resourceful Matt had found his facebook page and learnt that he was due to DJ at the Fox & Grapes – a pub on Wimbledon Common that evening.

Roy then informed me that he had downloaded all the info off PJ's phone and he was finished with it. So I arranged for a courier to send PJ back his phone, but not before getting the tech team to put a bug in it. It's OK I had a warrant for that also.

I grab a sandwich on the way to my next appointment of the day. I was seeing a man about a dog back at the crime scene. I was looking forward to this.

Time: 14:00
Location: 5 Odin Court, West Byfleet, Surrey

This German Shepherd was a force of nature. Brandi's talent is being able to find where dead decomposing human flesh had been for a period of ten minutes or more. His training meant he could identify that from a specific person having been given their scent.

He began with upstairs at Asgard. The handler put Ligia's t-shirt under the dog's nose and then led him into each room. Brandi thrust his nose into every nook and cranny, sniffing loudly, making the occasional grunt.

On to the spare bedroom, the curious thing there was that the cushions on the bed had been arranged lengthways and placed under the sheets as if to form the impression that someone was sleeping there. Nevertheless Brandi found nothing there.

So down the stairs we go and Brandi heads straight to a spot just below the mantelpiece area, he starts to bark. His tail wags frantically – the dog looks up at his owner and appears to be smiling as the handler slides a chocolate biscuit into his mouth. The dog gobbles it up with appreciation. He barks. He wants more.

The handler then takes this black and tan furry wonder around to the kitchen – nothing. Then to the garage. Brandi once again barks loud at the spot just below the freezer. This is where the body would have been dropped while the killer opened the freezer door. Another biscuit for Brandi.

Next they take him to PJ's Mercedez car parked in the garage – nothing. They put Brandi inside the boot of the car. He sniffed around, but nothing.

The grounds outside – nothing. The back garden – nothing. The shed – nothing.

Though something else came from going out in the garden that may prove significant. **The key to the shed was still in the shed door.**

So on Brandi's advice pinpointing the area below the mantelpiece, Roy tossed some Luminol around the area. While he did this I looked at the Mantelpiece itself, which was adorned with two small trophies from the broadcasting

53

industry – about nine inches high, neither weighty enough to be able to do anybody any injury.

It would be a cliché to say the Luminol lit up like a Christmas tree – and it didn't. They were only faint traces of purple, just a few smears and a splatter *(see illustration)* – but it was enough to make Rupal Chakrabharti almost wet himself. He finally had himself some blood splatter.

I too was pleased. We had established ourselves a kill location.

I had never worked with Brandi the Cadaver Dog before, and it was amazing.

Before the handler took him away, I went over to shake his paw.

We now have reason to believe that Ligia was struck by the mantelpiece – a plastic bag was put over her head, she was struck again and then she was strangled. She was dead there for a period of ten minutes or more. Before putting her in a sleeping bag and moving her to the freezer.

Roy then took me to the fridge and opened it up for me. Inside the door was an open bottle of Chablis.

"It's a 750ml bottle. There's 500ml left inside, so minus 250ml – enough for a large glass of wine."

I said, "So this must be the wine she was drinking when she was killed. She surely would not be swigging straight from the bottle. Any sign of the glass she was drinking from?"

Roy opened up an adjacent wall cabinet – "all the wine glasses are in here. I will do a search on each one."

So the killer most probably put the wine and glass away after killing her, and cleared up the blood.

Roy had more to say: "Something else that seems significant, but of what I don't know yet. There is a long trail of microscopic fibres starting from the spare bedroom all the way across the landing and down the stairs – straight to the front door. The fibres are green wool and blue denim. So not the clothes that Ligia was wearing."

"So, like someone's been dragged upstairs?"

"Exactly. Or been dragged downstairs and out the door."

"That could be very significant. Though it could be just them ejecting a drunken guest from a couple of weeks before, and nothing to do with the murder."

Before leaving, I instructed Roy to take a look in the shed. The fact that the key was still in the lock might lead us to something.

Time: 16:00
Location: Woking Police Station

Back at the nick I got Tom my graphics guy to add the kill location and fibre trail and other details to the floor plan that was up on the incident room wall.

GROUND FLOOR

- Lap top + speakers
- FAMILY ROOM
- DINING AREA
- KITCHEN
- Pictures on Wall
- Blood Splatter
- Mantelpiece
- SITTING ROOM
- UP
- Fibre Trail
- UTILITY

Pillows arranged to look like a body

- DRESSING ROOM
- Fibre Trail
- DOWN
- BEDROOM 1
- BEDROOM 4
- BEDROOM 2

56

Next I got him to put up a chart of my five main suspects:

Andy Goddard	Fred Barraclough	The 8 Star White Van Gang	PJ James	Eduard Pinheiro
• Was with Ligia the night she died • Has not come forward as being with her the night she was killed • Gave her cocaine	• Neighbour - looks suspicious • Went to the shops • Close to the crime scene	• Seen in the vicinity • Urinated in hedge • Laughing "aggressively"	• Found Ligia • Giving no information	• Ex-husband • Disappeared

Eduardo's disappearance cannot be co-incidental to the death of Ligia, which makes him our suspect number 1. But this Andy Goddard was drinking with her the night we think she was killed. He could hold the key to what happened.

Matt comes in, with a strange smart-ass smile playing on his lips.

"Matt – you do realise that smiling like that makes you look like a jerk."

"I've identified that eight point star." He said, still smirking like he didn't care and then paused for effect.

"Come on tell us…" my partner can be really annoying at times.

"It's the logo of Steaua Bucharest."

I looked back at him blankly as he went to his PC to show me the logo on the web.

"They are Romania's leading football team."

I looked at the logo on the football team's website. Yes it was identical.

57

"So we are looking for a South American drug gang who are fans of Romanian football. Well that narrows it down."

After we considered this, I said, "Come on get your coat. You and me have got a night out down the Fox & Grapes."

Time: 20:00
Location: Fox & Grapes, Wimbledon Common

Matt and I eased our way through the packed pub on Wimbledon Common. We picked a spot to sit, on the edge of a table in a raised area so we could observe the DJ at work across the room.

Andy Goddard was in his late twenties/early thirties of medium height and medium build. On the top of his head was a wisp of light brown, razor cut spiked hair and below a weak chin.

Observing from the other side of the bar, I saw a young woman came up to him, he leaned over to chat, not smiling, then I saw him surreptitiously put something in her hand. The woman walked away in the direction of the toilet.

I stared hard at him as he pulled out a piece of vinyl and placed it on the turntable. Could I be watching a killer on the decks?

I then turned my attention to the disco orientated music that Goddard was selecting. I Shazamed the next three tracks:

Le Freak – Chic, Keep on Dancin' – Gary's Gang, Fire Island – Village People

Look familiar? I went out to my car to refer to my case notes.

Yes all the tracks were on Ligia's Disco Party play-list.

When I returned the crowd was getting down to 'Born To Be Alive'. The singer was signing "I was Born, Born, Born, Born, Born to be Alive."

Could this have been the Prawn record that the neighbour Rose was on about? That was the song that was playing loudly just as the music abruptly ended, so possibly the song that was playing when Ligia was attacked.

I Shazamed the next three tracks. Again all from Ligia's Disco playlist.

This was looking ultra-suspicious. I went outside to call the nick to tell them that the warrant to search Andy Goddard's place was going to be actioned that night.

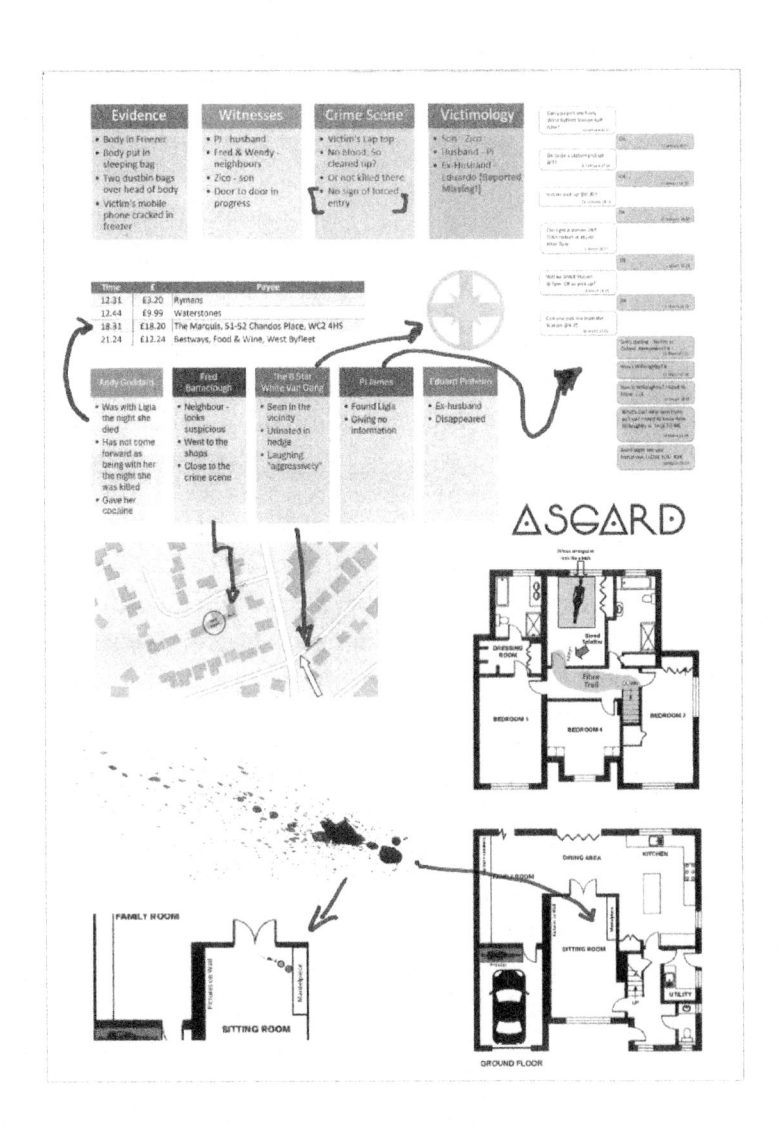

Evidence
- Body in freezer
- Body put in sleeping bag
- Two dustbin bags over head of body
- Victim's mobile phone cracked in freezer

Witnesses
- PJ - husband
- Fred & Wendy - neighbours
- Zico - son
- Door to door in progress

Crime Scene
- Victim's Lap top
- No blood, so cleaned up?
- Or not killed there
- No sign of forced entry

Victimology
- Son - Zico
- Husband - PJ
- Ex-Husband - Edwardo [Reported Missing?]

Time	£	Payee
12.31	£3.20	Rymans
12.44	£9.99	Waterstones
18.31	£18.20	The Marquis, 51-52 Chandos Place, WC2 4HS
21.24	£12.24	Bestways, Food & Wine, West Byfleet

Andy Godballs
- Was with Ligia the night she died
- Has not come forward as being with her the night she was killed
- Gave her cocaine

Fred Barraclough
- Neighbour looks suspicious
- Went to the shops
- Close to the crime scene

The B Star White Van Gang
- Seen in the vicinity
- Utmost in hedge
- Laughing "aggressively"

PJ James
- Found Ligia
- Giving no information

Edward Potheiro
- Ex-husband
- Disappeared

ASGARD

Chapter 5 – Waiting for Goddard

Date: Thursday 22nd March
Time: 23:00
Location: Colliers Wood

"I couldn't have killed her. I loved her."

Goddard said before I officially started the interview. I said, "Mate you've just given me the most common reason for murder. Listen – one of the reasons you are top of the suspect hit parade is that you were with her the night she died. So if you knew Ligia was dead, why didn't you come forward?"

He had that wounded look of smouldering resentment carried by men with heavy chips on their shoulder. Of course being police, it wouldn't do for me to jump to conclusions about people just from visual first impressions.

"I didn't know she died on Friday – in the paper they said her body was found on Tuesday. So I didn't know that I was with her the night she was killed."

Goddard shifted uncomfortably in the imitation leather couch. We sat in the living room of his rented apartment, decked out in scuffed and tired Ikea furniture, personalised by a poster promoting a rave from a by-gone era, and his collection of vinyl records sprawled on the floor. Meanwhile Matt and two uniform on over-time searched the flat.

"OK so we know you were drinking with her at The Marquis in Covent Garden. Tell me about it."

"We'd just been told that afternoon that our jobs were at risk of redundancy, our whole department was affected. Well …the whole department of six people. It wasn't a bolt out of the blue because we had been taken over about two months ago. We were told it was going to be 'business as usual' but we all knew that very soon the cull would start. It was still a shock to be called in at 3pm on Friday afternoon and told that we would most likely be out of a job in a month. So we hit the

61

pub to drown our worries. Two other people from work came with us – but they left after about half an hour."

"What were you talking about?"

"The redundancy pretty much took up everything. We talked about how much of a pay off we could expect to get, how difficult it would be to find anything else that paid anywhere half decent. Then we talked about forming our own events company. She wanted to call it Pegasus."

"So you went back to her place in West Byfleet?" Sorry I shouldn't do leading questions.

"No I did not. I said good-bye to her by the steps of Hungerford Bridge. She was going to walk over to get to Waterloo and I was going to get the tube home. I was telling her to keep her chin up and that she would find another job easily.

"She was really worried because her husband hadn't worked in over two years, and he just spent all day at home playing video games or out playing golf, while pretending to be trying to find work."

"So what time did you say good-bye?"

"It would have been around half eight. I didn't realise it was the last time I was ever going to see her." On those words his lower jaw wobbled as he started to blubber.

"OK – let me tell you why what you are telling me sounds shady. On the night she was killed, when Ligia got back to her home in West Byfleet she put on a Spotify play-list that contained loads of tracks identical to what you played tonight."

Wiping his eyes, he said: "That must be Ligia's Disco Party play-list. I compiled that with her. That's why I was playing tracks off it tonight, as a tribute to her."

Stroll on, I thought. I gave Goddard my I-am-not-convinced look.

"We worked in the same office, our desks are next to each other, so I spent a lot of time with her. We talked about music, sharing tracks."

He handed me his phone. "Look she texted me on the train home."

The text read: "That Pegasus idea has wings!"

"And I can prove I came back here that night. My Mac will show that I looked at a few web pages on Friday night. I shared a few tracks on facebook. Did some chatting. That will all leave a digital trail. Saturday morning I did a Park Run in Wimbledon Common. I met up with a few people and they will all vouch that I didn't seem like someone who has just killed someone."

Goddard now was twitching anxiously when the search moved to the kitchen. He started closing his eyes as if trying to ease some pain.

"So she died Friday night?" He asked.

"It looks that way yes. Listen do you know anything about her ex-husband Eduardo Pinheiro?"

"Ligia mentioned him a lot. It was sad because that car accident and the death of their son broke up their marriage."

"Do you know if she had made any arrangements to see him?"

"Well they conversed frequently because they had their son Zico."

"What about the husband – PJ?"

"Well it's obvious he did it."

"Why do you say that?"

"She must have come home a little bit tipsy playing her disco play-list and annoyed him. He had go at her, she had a go back. They had a row and he killed her."

"Oh really? Thanks for solving the case for me." I cracked sarcastically. I asked – "How did you know she was playing that playlist when she died?"

"You told me…listen. Ligia hated P.J. They had a bitter argument the day before at the vets. He said he didn't want to spend any more money treating their cat. He was going to just let him die.

"He said all this in the vet's reception area and Ligia went mental and they had a massive row right there in front of loads of people."

He went on: "Ligia never said anything good about PJ. I was hoping she was going to leave him."

"So you two had a thing going?"

"No we were just friends. Platonic. But to tell the truth. When I said good-bye to her on Hungerford Bridge, I felt hope. I was hoping she would have a row with PJ. I was hoping she would leave him and I would have to put her up. But I knew she wouldn't move out without the cat."

"So what else did Ligia say about her husband?"

"Ligia was at the end of the road with him. He hadn't worked for two years. All that stuff about Chloe Lund...."

"Wow! Back up. Who the fuck is Chloe Lund?"

He looked at me incredulously. "You know. Chloe Lund?"

He said this as if he was saying 'Dah!' I hate it when people do that.

"No I don't know Chloe Lund. Please enlighten me."

"The star on Shipton Village?" He said still adopting that tone.

"OK come tell me about this. Before I charge you for being annoying."

"PJ got sacked off Shipton Village because he was harassing his lead actress Chloe Lund."

"How do you know this?"

"Ligia told me. Ligia was wondering why PJ hadn't worked for so long and what he was doing all day and so she went snooping on his computer. She found an email from the production company, talking about him 'over-stepping the line' with Chloe Lund. Ligia then contacted Chloe Lund directly. Chloe told her that she refused to play Tippi Hedren to PJ's Alfred Hitchcock.

She said to Ligia that Chloe laid it out to the production company – either he goes or she goes. So they got rid of him."

Matt called me over and showed three see-through plastic sachets of white powder. "We found them under a false bottom in the kitchen drawer." Matt explained.

I dangled one of the sachets in front of Goddard.

"Our boys have found your secret stash of coffee mate."

Goddard became teary eyed – "That's it then. My life is over." He declared with a big sigh of resignation.

"Take it easy son. I may decide not to nick you for this. I am going to blackmail you instead."

As Matt drove us home I filed the report on finding the drugs, but said we were holding back on a prosecution on Andy Goddard, as he had now agreed to work for us as an informant. We found just three grams in his kitchen, and his low rent living arrangement did not say to me 'big time drug dealer.'

If Goddard was guilty of murder, I wanted to nick him for that, and not the cocaine. A drug prosecution would simply result in yet another my-client-has-the-right-to-remain-silent caper, which was the last thing I needed right now.

Aside from being a murder suspect, Goddard was apparently a confidante of Ligia, and that was insight I needed.

Day 4 of the Investigation

Date: Friday 23rd March
Time: 09:00
Location: Happy Pets, Weybridge

I got a call from the front desk to tell me what while there had been no actual sightings of anybody with the distinctive eight star tattoo, three members of the public had called in to inform us that the logo is that of the Steaua Bucharest football team.

At 9am I am out the door, and our first visit for the day was Happy Pets in Weybridge. The establishment was a sanctuary of calm, a large luxury hut encircled by woodlands.

We spoke with the young receptionist – Hannah Wiles – she was mid to late 20s with long dark brown hair. The compassionate warmth in her face was off-set by large biceps and fierce tattoos. She had been working the previous Thursday and confirmed that Ligia and PJ had what she described as a "blazing row" in front of her, corroborating Andy Goddard's story.

"It was over the money spent on Willoughby" she explained.

That name Willoughby was in the text messages between PJ and Ligia, and in his written statement.

"That's the name of their cat. He wanted to cap the spending at £600 and if it went higher than that, have him put to sleep. Ligia kicked back saying it was her money and she would spend whatever it costs to treat Willoughby."

"So when you say row? What do you mean? Were they shouting? Did they threaten to attack each other?"

"Well it wasn't just a row. There was obviously other stuff going on. She clearly hated him with a passion."

"Can you remember any of the words of this row?"

"She called him a 'Good for nothing.' He shouted back at her saying, 'Shut up. Just shut up for once – you whining bitch.' That word 'bitch' really stings. When a man calls his wife a bitch…that's the end of the line for me. That's an abusive bridge too far. That's when I told them to leave the reception."

In PJ's written statement he returned to the vets on Monday, so I asked about this.

"Yes he did – on his own – or just Willoughby. He apologised for the row. I just laughed it off. He seemed normal, calmer. He paid the bill without any fuss. We're not especially expensive, our rates are the same as any other vets, and if you've got insurance…"

"It's Ok, you don't have to justify your rate card to me."

"So I hear Ligia's dead?"

I nodded.

"That's horrible. She was such a sweet woman. And it's him that did it?"

"We don't know yet."

"Well I can quite easily believe that he did."

How significant was this? Doesn't every married couple have a bitter row at the vets?

PJ Video Log – Saturday 31st March 2018

I love that cat. Willoughby has been part of my life since he was a kitten, and was in that house with me all the time when I lived there alone. For a long time, he was my only companion, and sustained me spiritually through that period of isolation.

I was delighted when Ligia took to him so quickly and regarded him as her own pet.

My comments about Willoughby was supposed to be humorous. They got totally misconstrued. Everyone knows that vets are rip off merchants. A furry protection racket. They prey upon people's emotional attachment to their pets and willingness to pay whatever it costs to keep them alive. I too would pay whatever it costs to treat Willougby properly. But I didn't want our love for our pet to be taken advantage of.

Time: 11:00
Location: Weybridge

After the vets I swung by the residency of Samantha James. She lived in a block flats set back from Weybridge High Street.

The door opens and Samantha's face drops on seeing me.

I spoke in my best formal voice: "You have given your address as the temporary residence of PJ James. I just wanted to check that he is indeed staying here – and not being a fugitive." Then in an attempt to put her at her ease, I dropped the formality and added a – "Only doing me job like."

"Well he is here. He's in bed."

"How's PJ bearing up?"

"Not good."

"Can I say hello?"

"No you can't. His solicitor is not here."

"I just want a chat."

"Well he doesn't want a chat."

"Can I see him? I need to check that he has not absconded."

"No. He wants to be left alone."

"I am sorry, but I am going to have to insist. He doesn't need to talk to me. I just need to see him."

She led me through her modern stylishly furnished flat and tapped on the bedroom door. A voice said "come in" and she opened the door. There he was, sat in the darkness on the bed playing a video game.

I put my head in and said, "Hello PJ at some point soon we are going to arrange another interview. I am hoping you can finally say something to me."

He looked at me and then looked at the TV screen and carried on tapping on his game paddle.

"I'll be seeing you later," I said.

He got up and pushed the door shut on me.

While I was on this visit, my trusty bloodhound Tom called upon one Dougal MacPherson at his home in Cobham. Filing through PJ's phone, we identified this man as an associate of PJ, who he had formed a TV production company with. In emails and texts, P.J. kept referring to him as 'Frugal Dougal'.

The bloodhound found him working in his shed, editing a corporate video promoting carpet cleaning services.

Tom reported that Dougal had long hair, a beard and a rather severe look. The bloodhound compared him to Matthew Hopkins the Witch-finder General.

Dougal was reluctant to talk about Chloe Lund and Shipton Village, but he confirmed that PJ had got the boot for "crossing the line" with her.

Dougal claimed no knowledge of the state of PJ's marriage to Ligia and that PJ never talked to him about it. "What do you talk about then?" asked my bloodhound. "About the development projects we are working on." The bloodhound reported back that Dougal expressed surprise when he mentioned the proposed TV series about Oxford students, and said he has had no discussion with PJ about this.

Time: 13:00
Location: 5 Odin Court, West Byfleet

I revisited the crime scene to check in on Roy and his CS team. Just that morning they had made a dramatic discovery. He took me upstairs to the spare bedroom – still in place were the pillows arranged to look like a body under the sheets – and he pointed to the ceiling by the door.

"More blood. A very thin spray."

"Rupal will be delighted."

"He's on his way."

"But Brandi did not sit in here."

"It could be the body was not here long enough dead."

Next we went downstairs and Roy showed me a wine glass that had been put away in the kitchen cupboard. This glass had traces of the Chablis that was found in the fridge and had PJ's prints on it.

Smoking Gun? Sadly not. We were in PJ's house, so it was to be expected to find his prints all over the place.

Roy then took me to the garden and showed me the wooden shed, with the key still in the shed door. Inside the shed and under the bench was a stash of camping gear. One sleeping bag, two camper beds and two tents.

Is this where the killer (or killers) got the sleeping bag that Ligia's dead body was put in? They did it in such a hurry, they left the key in the door. Who would know where the key is and that a sleeping bag was there?

"The sleeping bag in here is identical to the one the body was in. So part of a set of two," said Roy.

Yes this was an indication of something – but proof of nothing.

On leaving the crime scene, next door neighbour Rose dashes over and collars me.

"I am sorry to trouble you. It's about the cat."

"Willoughby."

"Eh?"

"That's the name of their cat."

"Well I don't know what they call him – do I? But he's been left all abandoned. There's no one to feed him."

"Oh my god. He must be starving."

"No he's not. Because we've been feeding him."

"Oh well done."

"Thing is though…we're pensioners. Do you think you can get him to re-impurse us for all the cat food we're buying?"

Yes she really said "re-impurse."

"Yes!" I declared decisively. "Send in your bill and be sure to add a little extra to cover your inconvenience. I'll get PJ to pay you your re-impursement."

Was PJ planning on saving on vet bills by starving his cat to death?

Time: 19:30
Location: Woking Police Station

Back at the nick I call a meeting of the team into the incident room. In attendance were Matt, Shakeela, Tom, Vikki and WPC Gemma Muldrew.

We looked at the floorplan, updated to include the blood spray on the ceiling:

Ground Floor   **First Floor**

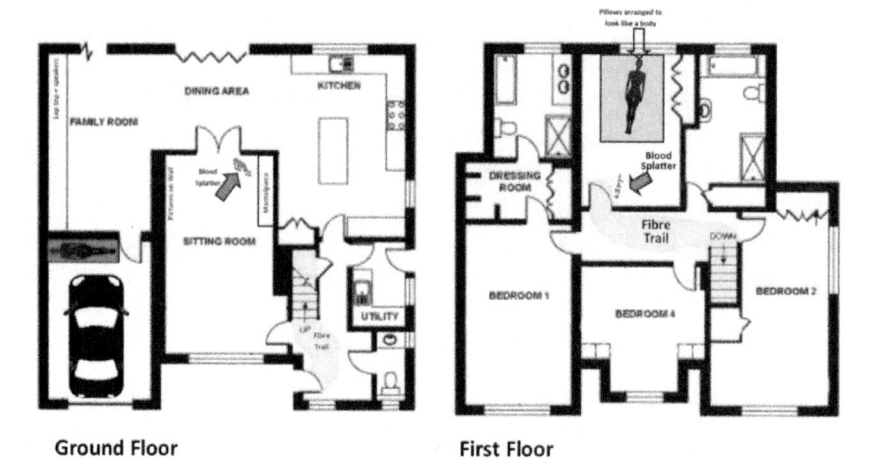

Then we considered our chart of the four pillars of investigation:

Evidence	Witnesses	Crime Scene	Victimology
• Row 9.35 pm • Visitor 10.30 pm • Body in Freezer (must have been put there before 9am Saturday) • Body put in sleeping bag • Two dustbin bags over head • Two severe head injuries • Death by Asphxia	• Andy Goddard • Man at Off Licence • Barman at Pub • Happy Pets Vets • PJ - husband • Fred & Wendy - neighbours • Zico - son • Samantha James - sister-in-law	• Blood splatter in Living room • Blood spray on ceiling • Fibre Trail - Upstairs - Downstairs • Pillows arranged like a body in spare bedroom • Key in Shed • Glass of wine she was drinking from put away • Crime cleared up • No sign of forced entry. • Victim's keys in coat by the door.	• Worked at Minerva - Events Company. • Told job was put at risk • Marriage not in a good place. • Cocaine and alcohol in blood stream • Parents in Portugal • Son Zico • Lost son Leandro • Husband PJ • Ex - Husband (Reported Missing)

Then we ran through the timeline of Ligia's movements – known so far:

71

Time	Activity	Verification
18.31	Ligia is at the Marquis Pub, Covent Garden	bank card + witness
20.34	Ligia sends text to PJ requesting pick up at train station	PJ's phone
20.53	Ligia boards train at Waterloo	Station CCTV
21.21	Ligia alights train at West Byfleet	Station CCTV
21.27	Ligia is at West Byfleet buying wine	bank card + witness
21.35	Ligia is at home playing the Spotify play-list	Laptop forensic
21.36	A row ensues	Witness – next door neighbours

In the 'any questions' bit, it was clear that the overwhelming majority thought that Eduardo Pinheiro's disappearance put him at the top of the suspect charts.

"You find Eduardo – you find the killer," said Shakeela in such a dramatic fashion it was as if she was doing it for the benefit of some imaginary TV camera.

"Yes it seems obvious that Eduardo Pinheiro is the killer," I said. "However, until he is found, it remains our duty to examine every piece of evidence and work every lead."

It was agreed to look deeper into his story. Did Eduardo have any close friends that he confided in? Who was he on a date with on Friday night? We would need to go back and thoroughly interview Zico.

"That white van parked nearby has got to be involved." Offered Gemma. "Why else would it be there on a Friday evening?"

As the meeting wrapped, I took a glance at the office clock – half eight. Time flies when you're on a big case.

Some of the crew were off down the pub, but not me – my body was crying out for an early night.

Time: 21:00
Location: Weybridge

While in the car on the way home my phone rings. Being a law abiding citizen, I pull into a lay-bye to answer it.

It was someone from the nick, the unfamiliar voice was highly agitated – "The gang with the eight star tattoo have been spotted in the Hand & Spear pub."

The Hand & Spear is a large pub on a hill close to Weybridge train station, and as I was already nearby, this meant I was the first law on the scene.

Do I wait for back-up, or do I go straight in? The member of the public who called it in had just given the tip and hung up, so I could not connect with them.

It being a Friday night, the pub was packed, and I made the risky choice of going inside back up free.

Most of the large chain pubs in our area have sold their souls to an anodyne corporate décor, but instead the Hand & Spear's interior was all plush green and reds, tastefully furnished like the front room of some Lord of the Manor. I hear that Robert Louis Stevenson wrote one or two of his books while on an extended stay here.

I did a circuit around the bar, jostling in amongst the revellers, many of whom were unsteady on their feet. I was looking downwards trying to see the men's forearms – but it being March and rather cold outside, many were keeping on their jackets and coats.

I tried to ask one of the staff, but they are all being barraged by customers, desperate to be the next to be served. I considered asking some of the punters – but they all seemed too half cut to get any sense out of them.

So instead I do another lap of the pub again staring at men's fore-arms.

Knackers! This is a waste of time. Talk about needle in a haystack with a wild goose chase thrown in. Maybe when the squad cars pull up – we can lock all the customers in, shut down the bar and get everyone male in the place to expose their forearms. Would that be rather drastic?

I went outside, bracing myself from the cold blast of evening air, as I stood and waited for my colleagues to arrive. Then I looked over at the assorted group of smokers.

I saw three olive skinned men in sports casual wear and I can hear them speaking softly in a language that's not English.

One was older by more than ten years. He wore a hat and resembled an old school, chain-smoking football manager pacing the touchline.

I approach the three men, flashing my ID.

"Excuse me Sirs, would you mind taking off your coats so I can see your fore-arms?"

With confused expressions the three men comply – and bingo there it was. That 8 star tattoo on the fore-arm of the youngest looking one.

"OK – that's what I was looking for. You need to come back with me and answer some questions."

The confused looks gave way to annoyance. You could tell that the one with the actual tattoo wanted to punch me. The one with the craggy features and bushy eye-brows looked ready to defy me.

"Will you all please accompany me to Weybridge Police Station?" Then I had to correct myself realizing there is no police station in Weybridge any more. The nearest was Addlestone.

Time: 22:00
Location: Addlestone Police Station

The three men sat looking daggers at me, arms folded. I couldn't blame them for resenting me, I had spoiled their Friday night out.

In my car, the three men identified themselves as Dan Lupescu the eldest one, Andrei Cristea was the craggy one and Mihei Muresan (MM) was the young man sporting the eight star tattoo.

I was petrified they would immediately clam up and so to counter this, I tried to put them at their ease by stressing that they are not suspects. However if any of them had looked at that week's Surrey Star, they would have known that they are very much in the suspect frame.

Mihei Muresan spoke only rudimentary English. But Dan Lupescu was fluent and offered to be interpreter. "They call me Mister Lupe," he told me.

"OK – there was a woman murdered in West Byfleet last Friday night, and you and your van was spotted in the vicinity on that day. Can you tell me if you saw anything?"

Dan Lupescu leaned forward and said in a rolling Romanian brogue – "we not see anyone get killed. We not see nothing suspicious. We not see anyone run away. We just do our job and we fuck off home. Can we go back to pub please?"

"I need to know what you were doing in the area at that time."

"Our job." Dan Lupescu again.

"And what is your job?"

"We are tilers. We do the tiling."

"Working Friday night?"

"Yes working Friday night. It was an emergency job. This woman hired some other tilers who do a botch job. She call us to fix in a hurry because she has her rellies coming over on Monday."

"Rellies?"

"Yes this woman – she is Australian."

On asking for proof of this, Dan Lupescu pulls out his phone and supplies me with the number of Mrs. Raelene Robertson,

I left the room and called her up and it all checks out. She had hired some cowboys who had done a disastrous bit of flooring work. She had her aunt from Australia visiting on Monday and needed it all fixed by then. She phoned around, and Lupe Flooring and Tilling were the first one available and willing to work late night Friday and all day Saturday.

They had spent Friday night ripping up the tiles of the botch job and then all day Saturday and Sunday was spent laying down the new floor.

On Friday night they had stayed at her house until just after midnight. Raelene Robertson was most complimentary of their hard work and the quality of their workmanship and wouldn't hesitate to recommend them. She had even written them a glowing review on Trust A Trader.

Next I needed to check about the urination on the hedge. I went back into the room.

"Now you." I pointed at Mihei Muresan. "Were seen urinating in a hedge at around 6.00 – why would you do this?"

Mihei turned to Dan who translated my question into Romanian. He answered and Dan translated – "The lady run late. We waiting long time. Nowhere else to go."

I later checked this with Mrs. Raelene Robertson who confirmed she had booked them to start work at 5pm, but she worked in the City and couldn't leave as early as she'd hoped, and so left them waiting outside for an hour with no access to a toilet.

"Can I ask what that tattoo is?"

"Steaua." The man proclaimed proudly.

"Is a football team," said the man in the middle, Andrei Cristea.

"Is that the team you support?"

"No I am from Transylvania. CFR Cluj is my team. But I have no tattoo."

Dan Lupescu then leans forward – "will you come to my office? I want to show you something."

I drove them to his portacabin office in New Haw and inside he turned on his computer to show me the spreadsheet of all the jobs his firm had done over the last three years and what he had booked in the months ahead.

He then showed me the hard copies in his order book. He showed me the photo album of all their recently completed jobs. He then showed the tax return he was preparing, and then his Trust A Trader page and all the glowing quotes along with the recent one from Raelene Robertson.

This certainly didn't leave a lot of time for drug dealing or assassinations.

After showing me all this, Mister Lupe said, "I am very upset. We work very hard. This is the first time I drink with my boys for several months – and our evening is ruined because we are arrested."

I apologised, and tried to look suitably contrite, but I had to explain that it was my duty to fully investigate all lines of enquiry.

"You might catch last orders at The Hand & Spear. I'll give you a lift."

Day 5 of the Investigation

Date: Saturday 24th March
Time: 09:00
Location: Woking Police Station

Saturday was supposed to be a day off for me, but I had too much going on inside my head, so instead I decide to use the day to go over the progress in the case, or lack of.

I sat in my incident room, staring at the wall chart of my five suspects:

| Andy Goddard | Fred Barraclough | The 8 Star White Van Gang | PJ James | Eduard Pin|

I had spoken extensively with three on the list – but nothing at all from the other two – Eduardo Pinheiro and PJ James.

While I was contemplating this WPC Muldrew dashes in.

"I hear you got the eight-star gang. Are they looking good for it?"

"No they don't. I've let them go. To tell the truth, I felt bad about ruining their Friday night."

WPC Muldrew began pressing me until eventually I said, "If you want to pin this on a bunch of foreigners, then you need to find another lot."

"What's that supposed to mean?"

77

"Whatever you want it to mean."

"I am not trying to 'pin this on a bunch of foreigners' as you put it. This is a good lead."

"It is – a beautiful lead – but it came to nothing. That's police work."

Mister Lupe and his boys were certainly off the hook for me but the drug gang theory was still live. I was inclined to think that Andy Goddard was innocent, but he was still in the frame. But at least he was talking to me so I can either prove or disprove his claims.

I badly needed intel on Eduardo Pinheiro and PJ and so I go delving deeper into the email correspondence on Ligia's lap top.

Going back to that Spotify play-list. The digital evidence showed that it was activated at 9.32 pm and ran through to 10.45. But Rose and Fred the neighbours said it stopped abruptly before that. The first three tracks played were skipped 20 seconds or less from the end, indicating that someone was there listening to it, but none of the tracks after that were skipped.

So the volume must have been turned down. Turned down on what Rose described as the "prawn" record. Was the volume turned down by the killer because they had just killed Ligia, and they needed to concentrate to work out their plan?

Looking at Ligia's emails, there was a considerable amount of correspondence with Eduardo Pinheiro – all in Portuguese. I translated some of it with my on-line translator and it all seemed to be about arrangements around their son Zico. But I needed the services of a proper Portuguese translator. Someone who would understand the argot and nuances of what they were saying.

Then going into PJ's bank records I found something extremely dodgy. PJ had arranged for Ligia to pay a £750 monthly direct debit supposedly to contribute to the mortgage of Asgard. But our records showed that PJ owned the property outright – there is no mortgage.

But I found an email from PJ to Ligia saying, "Don't worry – the Mortgage is going through fine. I am paying my half with the savings from Shipton Village." If Ligia had found out she was being conned, that surely would have kicked off a marital row of defcon1 proportions.

There was more correspondence with her husband P.J. The tone of which was all decidedly frosty.

Ligia was clearly concerned about P.J. not working.

"I"VE JUST LOOKED AT OUR BANK STATEMENT."

"WHEN ARE YOU GOING TO START WORKING AGAIN?"

Then I see this email from P.J.

"There is nothing to worry about. If it comes to the worst, we can always sell the house in Rye."

"THE HOUSE IN RYE?" They have a second house in Rye.

I immediately arranged for a fast track warrant and called Matt.

Chapter 6 – The Stench of Death and Petrol
Day 7 of the Investigation

Date: Monday 26th March
Time: 09:00
Location: Woking Police Station

The warrant to search the seaside house in Rye wouldn't come through until Monday morning. In anticipation of it, I had asked Roy my silver-haired fox Crime Scene colleague to get ready to come with me. My trusty side-kick Matt was also in on the trip. Matt had given up his weekend to arrange another interview with PJ, but this time Matt was the sole quiz master. I sat this one out, in case PJ's reticence was because of me. But this turned out to be another No Comment non-event. Like the Go-Gos, his lips are sealed. Next time we will try WPC Muldrew asking the questions in a more relaxed environment outside of a police interview room.

As we sat waiting in the incident room, I had discovered from Matt that PJ had not done anything at all about Ligia's funeral arrangements. So the full responsibility had fallen onto Ligia's parents, with Zico having to be their interpreter. Zico had called in to find out if there was any way we could persuade PJ to offer any help. If nothing else, to provide the contact details of any of Ligia's friends that would want to be at the funeral. Matt had spoken to PJ about this at the interview – but PJ just ignored the question. So Ligia's parents found themselves arranging the funeral without any involvement from the husband.

I was surprised that Ligia's funeral was so soon. Apparently, it was Ligia's parents driving this. As Catholics they like to do their funerals quickly. The coming weekend was Easter and so they brought the funeral forward to this coming Thursday before Good Friday.

I was not keen on this funeral happening so soon, we were still investigating her homicide, and her body was key evidence. While Roy assured me that he had thoroughly studied the body, taking numerous photographs and videos, it's always best to have the real thing to re-examine.

At just after half ten, my warrant for the property in Rye pinged into my in-box. We were off to the coast for the afternoon and it was Matt's turn to drive.

I have to confess I find it rather difficult to talk to Matt and Roy about anything other than work. But with a two and a half hour car journey in front of us, I was going to have to try. But I kicked off talking about the case, the only thing that unified us, and I explained that we were not going to conduct a full CS search of the place yet, we just wanted to have a look round and pick up any evidence that jumps out. If we decided from there that we needed to do a thorough forensic search, Roy could seal the place off and get his team down there.

Time: 14:00
Location: Rye, West Sussex

The cry of seagulls flapping around in circles announced our arrival to the coast. We turn off the main road and ease down a winding lane with detached luxury holiday houses on either side. In between the houses on the right was the lapping dark blue sea of the English Channel, looking icy and uninviting.

We pull up outside a smart one-storey modern cottage, with its back looking out to sea from a cliff side.

So how was I to get access without breaking in? Approaching the cottage, I make for the metal door of the garage, built into the side on the right. I spot the chunky burglar alarm in the top right hand corner. Nevertheless I raise both my arms and slide the garage door open, no alarm bells. As soon as I open up, my senses are hit by a blast of petrol fumes, and revealed before me is a white car. The logo says Pontiac. There was someone in the driving seat. The head jolted back and twisted to the side and though the steamed up glass made it difficult to see, it was clear the person was black.

Green tubing was attached to the exhaust pipe and the other end was slid through a narrow gap in the driving seat window.

The reek of petrol and that vile sickly-sweet smell of decomposing flesh assailed my senses. Matt turned to me and explained the obvious – "He must have left the engine running until it ran out of petrol."

On the back window there was a sheet of A4 paper sellotaped from the inside. These words were scrawled in black felt tip:

gia eu sinto muitissimo

I quickly moved out of the garage. Matt pulled down the garage door and the three of us reconvened thirty feet away, opposite the neighbours.

"OK Roy you need to get your team down here straight away." I ordered.

But Roy was not ready to roll – "No this is not procedure. We are on Sussex Police turf. You must call them immediately and report this to them. They will do the investigation."

"Fuck the Sussex Police. We found the body. We do the investigation."

"No. I will NOT be party to this disregard of procedure."

I looked over to Matt for back up, but he seemed to agree with him.

Roy walked away from us and pulled out his phone – "Hello I need to report a dead body."

The Sussex Old Bill turned up about 30 minutes later. The smarmy lead investigator was more like a car salesman than a copper, and I had to explain to him how we came to be there and why I raised the warrant for the cottage. My words were taken down as an official statement and we were sent on our way.

Day 8 of the Investigation

Date: Tuesday 27th March
Time: 09:00
Location: Woking Police Station

With so much of the case hanging on the death of Eduardo Pinheiro, I couldn't concentrate on anything else. Sitting in the investigation room I put a call into the Sussex police at 9.30 am to get an update. The receptionist assured me I would get a call back.

My phone rang fifteen minutes later, but it wasn't my call back, it was Rupal with his report on the blood splatter in the spare bedroom.

"I can tell you two things – it is certainly splash back – as in from a weapon being pulled back after hitting someone, and second – are you ready for this? – The blood is not of Ligia James."

So someone else was violently attacked in Asgard. Could it be Eduardo? Maybe they had a fight there.

My impatience got the better of me and so I call again the Sussex police lead investigator at 10.30 am. He's tied up, he'll call me back, I am told.

"He'd better," I say in a way that I hoped sounded suitably threatening while maintaining a diplomatic professionalism.

With Ligia's funeral on Thursday I had myself an idea. I called up Andy Goddard.

"Hey Andy how's the job hunting?"

"I haven't been made redundant yet," came the flat reply. "With Ligia gone they have one less on the head count, and so strangely I may keep my job. Although this is not the way I want it."

"Remember our little arrangement?"

"The blackmail. Yes of course."

"OK Andy I want you to phone up PJ, but before you do, I need you to sign a statement saying that you are all OK with us recording the phone call. I want you to ask a series of specific questions."

Time: 12:00
Location: Woking Police Station

Matt and I are sat at our desks, pen and notepad at the ready – with the phone system on loud speaker. Here's the transcript of the phone conversation:

"Hello my name is Andy Goddard I used to work with Ligia."

"How did you get my number?"

"Errr I asked for it – from Minerva."

"Who's Minerva?"

"Minerva – the events company that Ligia worked for. They have your number on their file."

"Well they had no business giving my number out."

"Yes I am sorry to trouble you – but I wanted to ask you about the funeral. Is there a song that you think should be played at the service?"

"I don't know."

"Anything at all? You can have a think and get back to me."

"I don't have anything."

"Or a song that Ligia would like to be played?"

"I don't know."

"Do you want to say anything?"

"No."

"Do you want anybody to say anything on your behalf?"

"No."

"Are there any stories…?"

(Interrupting) "Listen I don't care about the funeral."

"OK – (pause) – Ligia was a wonderful woman"… (Andy was under instruction to leave a gap to get PJ to comment, but PJ said nothing.)

(Pause)

"You probably don't want to think about this right now, but Minerva has a death-in-service arrangement. "

(Silence)

"Who do you think killed her?"

"I've got to go."

And with that he hung up. Nothing especially incriminatory in that call. I found it strange that PJ would not immediately know the name of Ligia's employer, and to say he didn't care about the funeral did not fit with a supposedly grieving husband. PJ's voice throughout just sounded disengaged and bored.

At 11.35 am DCS Christopher Harris, the slimy lead investigator at the Sussex police, finally calls me back. He was cheerily apologetic.

"Sorry you've had to chase me. I wanted to get back to you with something concrete."

"Which is?"

"I think you'll be rather pleased with our findings."

"Come on – which is what?"

"Almost certain suicide. We have the tube – garden hosing – going from the exhaust pipe into the car. There is a high amount of toxins and lead in his body. The letter in Portuguese apologising to his ex-wife which is most likely a suicide note. How's your Portuguese? **Ligia eu sinto muitíssimo** is *"Ligia I am so sorry"*.

"I knew that already. Like most people on the planet I have a phone with access to an internet search engine."

"The clincher, and where it gets interesting to you and your case, is that in his jacket pocket we found his phone, and there we found this text correspondence between him and the ex-wife on the Friday night."

"What does it say?"

"The text correspondence pretty much nails it as a suicide. We will of course have a full inquest."

"Can I see the text correspondence?"

"Of course – it's good news for you. This solves your murder case. Sending it over now."

86

He was talking like I owed him a drink. But I am an old school copper – I like to solve my own cases.

True to his word, minutes later I get an email from DCS Harris. Here is that text correspondence he was talking about:

> Eduardo - come over quickly.
> I must see you NOW!!!
> 16 March 21.57

> I have to see you in person. It's an Emergency.
> 16 March 22.10

> What about him? X
> 16 March 22.33

> PJ's away in Oxford - he's away all week-end
> 16 March 22.34

> I am coming over now.
> 16 March 22.35

> Hurry Up. X
> 16 March 22.35

Later that afternoon I discover that I was not a privileged person to get this text information, the Sussex Police had released that text correspondence to the press.

PJ Video Log – 31st March

I was initially upset to hear the news of Eduardo's suicide. Then my feelings gave way to anger, understandably I hope, because it was now clear that

87

> Eduardo had taken Ligia away from me. From all of us.
>
> I know that he had never stopped hoping to be reconciled with Ligia and to win her back. It seems from the text correspondence that Ligia was giving him some hope of that. Maybe Ligia was planning to leave me and get back with Eduardo, but then changed her mind and that's why he attacked her and finally killed her, maybe accidentally or in a fit of rage.
>
> I couldn't help but feel sorry for poor Zico. Losing his younger brother and now losing both parents all at once in such a terrible way.
>
> Last of all, I felt another emotion coming through. Relief. Relief because now we knew what had happened to Ligia. Relief too that now I was proven to be innocent to the police and DCS Ferdinand in particular.
>
> But I was wrong.

Time: 15:00
Location: Woking Police Station

It was highly plausible that Eduardo Pinheiro would commit suicide. In DCS Harris's report he had revealed that he was being treated by the NHS for depression. and a trace amount of anti-depressant Trazadone (prescribed by his doctor) was found in his blood. The death of his son and the subsequent marriage break up are both attributed to a car crash in which he was the driver and was deemed as responsible. As a consequence he carried a terrible burden of guilt.

In the report, one of the people who worked with Eduardo at the restaurant was quoted as saying, "there was a sadness in his eyes." There was also a declaration from a handwriting expert that on comparing hand writing samples, concluded that it is "highly probable" that Eduardo wrote the Portuguese "I am sorry" note.

But in my job it won't do to jump to easy conclusions. After reading and re-reading this text correspondence I mapped out this possible scenario. A jealous husband returns from Oxford early and finds the two lovers and kills them both.

Both bodies were dumped in the freezer, one was disposed of and the other remaining in the freezer for reasons yet to be determined.

This text correspondence was of obvious high significance to my case, but right away I found something amiss. Ligia's email correspondence on her laptop with Eduardo was always in Portuguese. **So why is the final text exchange to Eduardo on the night that she died in English?**

I was going to demand access to Eduardo Pinheiro's phone and get my own people to do their analysis. I wanted the forensic file put together by Sussex Police CS and I would issue a warrant to get them if necessary.

I also wanted my man Roy, even though he has a low opinion of me, to do his own forensic report and I wanted to do my own search of the rest of that cottage.

In the report I noted that the burglar alarm was turned off at 3.57 am Saturday morning. So Sussex Police set the time of death some time directly after that. So how did Eduardo Pinheiro come to have the code to turn off the burglar alarm? Did Ligia give it to him? Had they been using the cottage as a hide away?

As I was reading the report a second time, my superior Chief Constable Hinton dropped in – "Well done Ferdy, you've cleared up the Ligia James murder in less than one week. Excellent work."

"Thanks sir," I replied, "but I didn't really do that much."

Hinton came back with: "You're being modest – you were the one that found the ex-husband's body."

"Yeah but me and Matt are not entirely convinced that he did it."

Then Matt sitting at a desk across the room chipped in: "Yes Sir. It's perfectly possible to stage a suicide. We need to fully look into it."

"Matt's right Sir. Matt the Stat wrote a really good report last year on staged suicides – you should read it."

Hinton's smile slid off his face. "I am not interested in crackpot conspiracy theories. I am interested in our clear up rate," he rattled off brusquely, "you can scrutinise the death of the ex-husband if you have to, but as far as I'm concerned this case is closed."

I was about to say that I wouldn't be doing my job if I didn't thoroughly look at all the evidence, but he had exited by then.

Day 9 of the Investigation

Date: Wednesday 28th March
Time: 10:00
Location: Woking Police Station

Sussex Police then sent me their forensic report on Eduardo Pinheiro's death, which I spent most of the day examining. The accelerating pedal was NOT kept down by his foot, as it is in most suicides of this type, but by a heavy metal tool box. Presumably taken from the garage he was found in. The report concluded that the death was caused by carbon monoxide poisoning,

One thing that jumped out and slapped me around the face was that Eduardo had sustained two large severe head injuries. To go with that, there was dried blood on his head around the injuries and some blood deposited on the car seat head rest. The two head injuries had been there long enough for blow flies to use it as a nest to hatch their eggs. The flies were photographed and had become fully grown.

The head injuries in the forensic photographs resembled the head injuries sustained by Ligia. I showed the photographs to Roy who confirmed this, but Roy said that he would need to actually see the head injuries for himself before saying that they could have come from the same blunt instrument. He was buzzed by the blow fly evidence (forgive the pun), and declared that he would analyse it to establish a time of death.

Just after lunch, Matt came in suggesting we go along to Ligia's funeral tomorrow, saying, "You never know – sometimes the killer likes to make an appearance."

"Yes" I said to Matt "I am curious to see if a certain someone will be there."

Chapter 7 – Don't Thank Me. Thank the Blow Flies

Day 10 of the Investigation

Date: Thursday 29th March
Time: 10:00
Location: Woking Chapel

Suited and booted in black, Matt and I were sat at the back of the chapel scanning the crowd of about 80 people. The killer may be in amongst them. I assessed the congregation to be family and child hood friends from Portugal, a massive turn out from Ligia's work colleagues and assorted friends based in Britain, and a sole representation from the James family – Samantha the sister – standing alone, and looking decidedly awkward. I was interested to note that the funeral was listed under her maiden name – Ligia Valente.

Andy Goddard took to the podium to do his eulogy. I was reminded that his name was still up on my wall of suspects, so I paid great attention to what he was going to say. Maybe his emotions would get the better of him and he would slip up and reveal himself to be Ligia's murderer. Instead he spoke in an even measured tone – paying tribute to the vivacious personality of Ligia. He lightened things up with couple of amusing anecdotes about his work colleague. He did not make a sudden outburst, shouting and accusing PJ. PJ was not mentioned at all, and there was no hint of bitterness in his eulogy.

Next, Zico stepped up with his grand-mother. Just three days ago he had got the news that his father was also dead. I could not even begin to imagine the torment that he was going through. Ligia's mother spoke in Portuguese as Zico translated: – "It is not right for us to be burying a person so young. It is not right that she has been taken from us."

Inevitably the tears started to flow all round.

The exit music was a gentle melancholic version of the Girl from Iponema.

After the service Andy Goddard came up to me saying, "if you need any more help just whistle. I've arranged the wake for Ligia at a nearby pub. I will be playing all her favourite tracks."

I declined the offer, instead Matt and Me get in our car to follow the cherry red Peugeot 205 of Samantha. I lost her at the traffic lights, but she was heading home so I managed to pick up the trail in Weybridge and parked up outside her flat, just as she was opening her front door.

I followed her up the steps and said over her shoulder. "Hullo Samantha. PJ couldn't make it?" She turned round with a start, about to get the mace out of her bag.

"I guess he has more important things on than his wife's funeral."

"What do you want?" She yelled – close to screaming.

"I want to talk to your brother. I want to hear him say 'No Comment' one more time. It's such a clever strategy – he's so cool – so clever."

"Well he's not staying with me anymore. He's checked into a clinic – a sanatorium."

"Well that's against regulation. He's supposed to tell us about his movements. He's still a suspect."

"I didn't think he was a suspect any longer."

Time: 13:00
Location: Woking Police Station

On the way back I picked up The Surrey Star which had come out that morning. Ligia was still on the front page and they had stuck with last week's South American Drug Gang angle, but this time had placed Eduardo Pinheiro into that drug ring and going along with the Sussex Police's version of events. They run with this headline: "Ligia I am so sorry." Jane Barrow went into a lyrical over-drive with this article, quoting Oscar Wilde: "*Each man kills the thing he loves*" and "*Some strangle with the hands of Lust.*"

They had found a new picture of Ligia with her smiling and raising her finger raised to her mouth as if sharing a secret.

Back at my desk in the Woking nick incident room, I find in my inbox this statement announcement from the Sussex Police – "The full inquest for Eduardo Pinheiro's death will be held Friday of next week, but the Sussex police are satisfied that his death is a suicide. It is highly probable the suicide is due to guilt from causing the death of his ex-wife Ligia James."

I jump up from my desk and made for the pub where the wake was being staged, I needed to speak with Zico.

Time: 14:00
Location: A pub in Woking

When I got to the wake, I saw something I did not expect to see – people energetically dancing. In amongst the gyrating throng I spot Zico, eyes shut, lost in the music.

He was celebrating the life of his mother.

I was going to forewarn him about the press and ask him some questions about Eduardo. But I couldn't do it now. I did not want to bring him down.

Day 11 of the Investigation

Date: Friday 30th March – Good Friday
Time: 10:00
Location: Rye, West Sussex

The Sussex Police had wrapped up their investigation into Eduardo's death and so we were now allowed to go back into the cottage and conduct our own search. Let some proper police take over. I invited Roy and Matt over to join me for our second trip to the seaside that week.

On sliding up the garage door I was massively disappointed to see that the Pontiac car had gone. I needed Roy, Rupal and Brandi the cadaver dog to do their work on it. I immediately got on the phone to the Sussex police.

"We passed the car onto the next of kin." Explained DCS Christopher Harris.

"That is?"

"The son – err…."

"Zico?"

"That's him. He's got everything the car and his clothes. We also gave him the body…so he can arrange a funeral."

The poor boy had another funeral to arrange.

Matt and Roy walked around the garage, while I decide to take a shufty inside the actual cottage. Here's the layout:

DECK

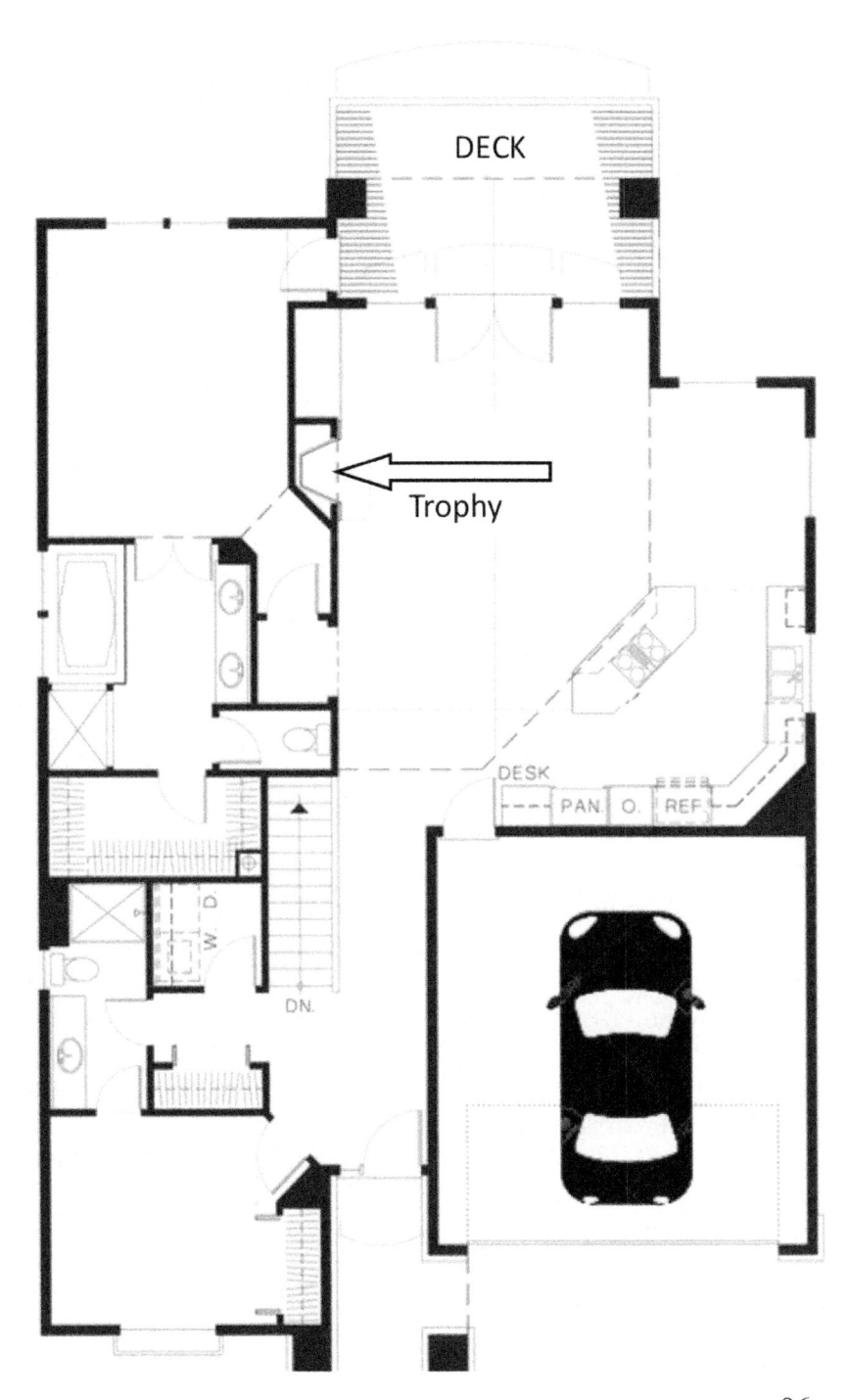

Trophy ←

DESK | PAN. | O. | REF.

DN.

96

Furnished in the Scandi style of Asgard, the living room was sprinkled with a thin layer of sea air dust, as though the place hadn't seen any cleaning action since Christmas. I did a lap of the cottage and returned to the living room. Something grabbed my eye. Above the fire place, is a mantelpiece and on it is a lone trophy. A woman with wings stretching upwards holding a globe. Yes, the last time I saw this trophy was in Ligia's photographs on her laptop and also on PJ's phone. In those photographs this trophy was on the mantelpiece of the West Byfleet home alongside two other smaller trophies. Just near where the Luminol revealed blood stains. Here the trophy appeared gleaming and dust free. Does that mean it had only just been put there? In the last week? I got excited at the potential significance of this because we know that Ligia got hit by a blunt instrument near the mantelpiece at Asgard.

I called out to Roy to come in and bag it.

After the cottage, Matt and me decide to do a bit of door to door. I was to take the houses to the left and Matt the houses to the right. It being Good Friday a good few of the holiday home people were in. After a couple of hours of that, we convened for a spot of late lunch with Roy at the Golden Goose, the inviting looking pub at the end of the lane.

Comparing my notes with Matt we surmised the following – not many people were in on the night of Friday the 16th March and the morning of Saturday the 17th. Those that did, heard and saw nothing. Some of the residents recognised PJ, a few had seen Ligia. None had seen Eduardo. We showed these photos to the pub landlord, who with his bad teeth and scraggly hair carried the aura of a louche old London villain.

He said the same as the neighbours. PJ was often seen about, Ligia once or twice but not for a while. He had never seen Eduardo. "I'm not surprised you didn't get any witnesses that night. The people who live down there are all DFLs."

"DFLs?" Asked Matt.

"Down from London."

I asked the landlord about PJs associates. He said "you need to speak with Chops. He's that man's golfing buddy." He obligingly got on the phone and greeted Chops with a jokey "Chops you need to get down here. The Old Bill want to ask you some questions. Something to do with Operation Yew Tree."

Presently Chops appeared, he lived nearby. He was mid-fifties with dark neat shoulder length hair, wearing a coat with a black velvet collar. His appearance was one of a going to seed debonair gentleman of leisure, balancing his time between the golf club bars and the racing track.

We ordered him a pint of Guinness, sat him down and I said, "First off you can relax. This is nothing to do with Operation Yew Tree."

"Yes I did gather that was the landlord's little joke. Besides those kids won't say anything. I paid them too well. I thought it might be about the landlord and the missing Dalmatians."

"Why do you say that?"

"He looks like the type Cruella DeVil would hire to kidnap some Dalmatians."

"Now that you mention it…"

"Is it about the fellow who topped himself in the garage?"

"It is." I showed him a picture of PJ. "What do you know of this man?"

"PJ James. Blow out merchant."

"How's that?"

"He was supposed to meet me at the club for a hit of golf on Sunday. But he never showed."

Sunday was when he was in Oxford.

"He didn't phone to cancel?"

"No."

"Has he blown you out before?"

"No. He sometimes calls to re-schedule, but never just not turned up."

"Did you call him?"

"I did. He never called me back. The man is obviously a bounder," he said with an ironic smile, but went on: "I am not too miffed. I know he's very busy and all that. What with him doing Shipton Village. Hang on – what's he got to do with that man in the garage?"

"It was his garage."

"My word. How did he get in there?"

"That's what we're trying to find out. So how often do you play golf with him?"

"About twice a month."

Then Roy chipped in. "Can you give us the dates you played golf with him over the last six months?"

Chops seemed pleased we asked this question.

"I do as a matter of fact. I am the last of the Filofax holders."

Out of his coat he pulled out his chunky leather relic of the 1980s, brimming over with paper. He opened it up and flicking through the scribbled racing meeting dates and gambling odds, he provided us with the golfing dates going back to September of the previous year.

Matt wrote them all down.

Chops then started showing concern. He said "Do you know where he is now? Is he OK?"

"He's checked into a sanatorium, being treated for shock and depression. His wife was killed."

"Oh My god. I guess that's why he didn't make my golfing appointment. I hope he's bearing up."

"Well give him a call. He will appreciate some words of support."

"He's a top chap – despite being a one-time blow out merchant. He's going to get me a part on Shipton Village."

It was my turn to be ironic – "Well I am sure he's a man of his word. You got another golfing appointment with him coming up?"

Chops referred to his Filofax.

"16th April."

"When we see him we'll remind him. Last question – why do they call you Chops?"

"My name is Charles Hooper. But also my golf action technique."

After Chops left us, Roy checked the dates of PJ's golfing appointments with the dates the burglar alarm had been turned on and off. All of them matched – burglar alarm off – golf – burglar alarm on. It would therefore appear that only PJ had been using the house at Rye in the last six months. So if PJ had really planned his week-end in Oxford researching his TV series, why did he not cancel or re-schedule his golfing appointment?

Matt then raised the question – if PJ killed Eduardo and staged the suicide, why drive all the way to Rye to do it? Why not leave the car anywhere? In a lay bye for instance?

I suggested if he left it anywhere else, the danger is that the car would have been found immediately and made establishing the exact time of death much easier. You need to stage that kind of suicide in an enclosed space.

The property in Rye was the only other garage he had access to. He couldn't have done it at Asgard, because people would have known immediately where both were killed. Plus in his own garage in Rye he knew he had a heavy toolbox there to use to keep the accelerator down.

Roy said, "I need to take a look at the body myself. I need to see if there are any signs of asphyxia aside from the carbon monoxide poisoning."

To which I said, "It's a shame we weren't able to investigate the crime scene first off, maybe we shouldn't have called the Sussex Police and just done it ourselves as I wanted – eh?"

I wanted Roy to concede that I was right – but I did not get my desired reaction.

"Fuck off. Ferdy."

"Why fuck off Ferdy? Are you saying that because you know I'm right?"

"No I am saying it because you are an annoying…"

Matt intervened. "It's done now, and we had to call the Sussex Police because it's procedure. Look – what we need to consider is that what works in the suicide story note 'Ligia I am so sorry' in Portuguese. The expert said it was his handwriting."

I then suggested, "Maybe he was asked to write it by PJ and he was cut off mid-sentence. Could be. But it's just speculation."

"I have high hopes for the blow flies," Roy said optimistically, "we have the photographs of them all around the car having hatched in his head wounds. If I get the temperature of each day we can get close to pinpointing a time of death."

The three of us all agreed on something – Eduardo's "suicide" in PJ's seaside home in Rye had a very distinct whiff of fish about it – and it wasn't anything to do with the sea air.

PJ Video Log – 31st March

I checked myself into this Sanatorium principally out of consideration for Samantha my sister. It wasn't fair on her to have to put me up and deal with all my gloom. It was clear I was suffering from extreme depression.

Sam took me to a doctor who after a few tests and a thorough examination made no hesitation in recommending I be put under the care of a sanatorium. I was not at all likely to hurt anybody, but I was a danger to myself, so I needed to be put under observation.

At least now an independent professional source can confirm my mental state, though of course I had to pay for it.

I couldn't bring myself to go to Ligia's funeral. It would be just too much wailing and gnashing of teeth. I wanted to be alone in my grief and not share it with strangers, and have a parade of people saying glib things to me like "I'm sorry for your loss."

I didn't want to say good-bye to Ligia and I don't want to have closure. I want her to be in my life forever. If

> that means me being in a constant state of grief – then so be it.

Day 12 of the Investigation

Date: Saturday 31st March
Time: 10:00
Location: Sanatorium, Ripley

It was outrageous that a main suspect in a murder case can get himself checked into a sanatorium without notifying the police, and just as outrageous that some GP thinks he is protecting human rights by not telling me the name of the sanatorium that PJ had been referred to. He seemed to genuinely believe that PJ was suffering from severe depression and should not be subjected to any rigorous police questioning. What a mug.

In the end I had to threaten the GP will all manner of legal reprisals before he finally gave up the name of the establishment. So today Matt and Me were off to the Springwater Health Retreatment in the verdant splendour of Ripley.

The facility was set in its own grounds a couple of miles outside Ripley village and without another dwelling in site. We pull outside the metal gate next to a parked up beaten up Volkswagen Beetle. I get out and peer in between the railings to see a three-storey white walled mansion. From the nearby trees we can hear the soft murmuring call of wild doves and I see a peacock stepping its way across the front lawn. It was the sort of restful bucolic setting a rock star like Keith Moon would check in to do his rehab.

I pushed the gates, they are locked.

I called the number that was on the website and get the ansafone, as I did when I called an hour earlier. Not wanting to go home empty handed I say to Matt, "Let's take a walk," and we proceed to walk around the perimeter of the nine foot brick wall. After a few minutes, I heard a gruff voice from the other side of the wall. "OK Rolling…and…action."

Then I heard another higher nasal voice speaking with these words – "'Why do you love me?' she would often ask. I would feel awkward and become tongue tied for fear of saying something cringey. She would press me by staring, demanding an answer, and I would end up saying something like – 'I just do.' Or 'Too many reasons.' But as I sit here now, trying to visualise her, I see it all."

Then the other hoarse voice – "Hang on sorry – there's a bit of rustling on your radio mic."

I needed to see what was going on so I gestured for Matt to give me a leg up.

With Matt creating a cradle for my feet and labouring under my weight I peered over the wall to see PJ dressed in a charcoal linen suit, sat in a wicker chair while a man with long hair and beard was fiddling with his lapel.

The bearded man then stepped back and got behind a video camera on a tripod. He pressed a button and then declared, "Ok going again…rolling…action!" And off PJ went again: "'Why do you love me?' she would often ask.

I would feel awkward and become tongue tied for fear of saying something cringey. She would press me by staring, demanding an answer, and I would end up saying something like – 'I just do.' Or 'Too many reasons.' But as I sit here now, trying to visualise her, I see it all. "

Matt grunted as he continued to struggle under my weight. To give him respite, I jump down before I started vomiting. Through the wall I can hear:

"How was that?...I would like to do another one. Was the sound of the birds distracting?"

"No. It's a nice bit of atmos."

"But didn't some of it block out what I said?"

"No. Let's go again anyway."

Matt and I walk back and we sat in the car and waited in there for about an hour, listening to TalkSport to pass the time.

Presently the gate opens and out comes the guy with the beard carrying two bags. He was quite beefy and carried a menacing demeanour – he looked not unlike someone who would ride a horse around the Essex countryside looking for witches to burn. Does that ring any bells? Is that how Tom, my investigator, had described PJ's producer friend?

The bearded man put his two bags into the boot of the VW.

I approach saying, "Hey Dougal – how's tricks?"

"Do I know you?" He said with narrowing eyes.

"No. You don't. But we have a mutual friend, though he seems a lot chattier to you than he does to me."

"You talking about PJ?"

I pointed to his two bags in the boot – clearly camera equipment – "so what are you doing?"

"He's asked me to make a documentary about piecing his life together after a tragedy."

"And what are you going to do with it?"

"We don't know yet. He just wanted a record of what he is going through."

On the way home I get a call from Roy with his findings on Eduardo's cadaver. While he identified levels of carbon monoxide poisoning, he did not think it was enough to kill him. It was not ingrained enough into the lungs as if he was breathing it in. "Suggesting he was already dead when the car fumes were all around him," I offered.

Aside from the two heavy head injuries, Roy also found a broken hyoid bone in the neck, which is often found in people killed by strangulation. He also found abrasions on both wrists, and trauma all down the left side of his body, which he thinks took place post mortem. "I am going to spend the bank holiday week-end analysing that blow-fly evidence." He announced.

Day 14 of the Investigation

Date: Monday 2nd April – Easter Monday

Time: 10:00
Location: Walton-on-Thames, Surrey

What sort of person would not go to his own wife's funeral and then get his mate to film a video interview with him to talk about how he feels about his dead wife? Only the worst kind of narcissist that's who. But while this made him look bad, this is not evidence of any murder.

I needed proper tangible evidence so I spent all day of Easter Monday at home, reading and re-reading the reports.

The death of Ligia and Eduardo had made the national papers, and all had the same narrative – ex-husband, who may be connected to South American drug gangs, has a rendezvous with ex-wife hoping for a reconciliation. She rebuffs him, he kills her in a fit of jealousy and then commits suicide from guilt.

On reading, I thought of Zico. His family has been devastated by tragedy – his younger brother dies in an accident and now both his parents are brutally murdered.

I was about to call to tell him that I was going to get to the truth no matter what, but then reconsidered. I shouldn't really be making promises I couldn't keep. My heart went out to him – but I felt powerless.

I had every reason to believe Roy when he told me he was going to spend all of his Easter week-end working on the case. True to his word, in the evening I get this text from him -

"Are you near a PC? I've got some blow fly data you will find interesting."

I replied with a "Please send." Presently I got this -

Report from Roy Hughes, Crime Scene Forensics Manager, Surrey
2nd April 2018

The body of Eduardo was found at 2pm Monday the 26th March.

Forensic photographs were taken of the head wound and other orifices an hour later at 3pm. The photos show that hundreds of blow fly eggs were laid into the head injuries, eyes and ears of the cadaver. Because the life cycle takes two to three weeks to complete, we are given an opportunity to pinpoint a time of death.

The life cycle of the Blowfly

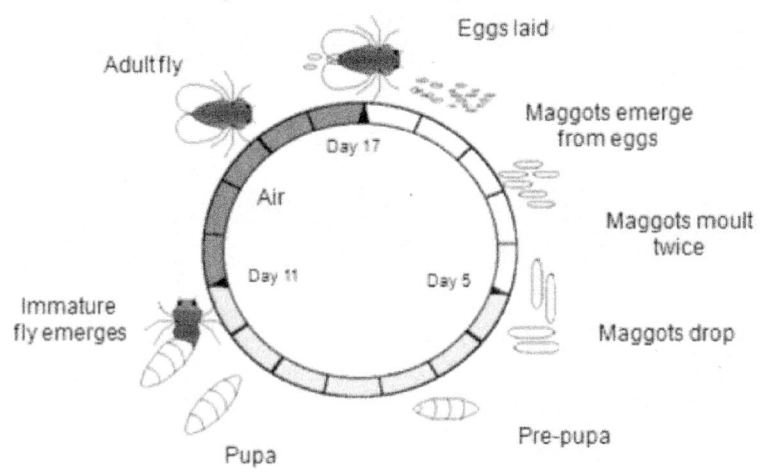

- Adult fly
- Eggs laid
- Maggots emerge from eggs
- Maggots moult twice
- Maggots drop
- Pre-pupa
- Pupa
- Immature fly emerges
- Day 17
- Air
- Day 11
- Day 5

The photos show that the maggots became pupae – and from there the immature flies emerged and turned into fully blown adult flies.

The speed of the cycle is determined by the temperature in the garage.

Here are the temperatures taken from the Met Office for the preceding ten days:

March 2018 Weather in Hastings — Graph

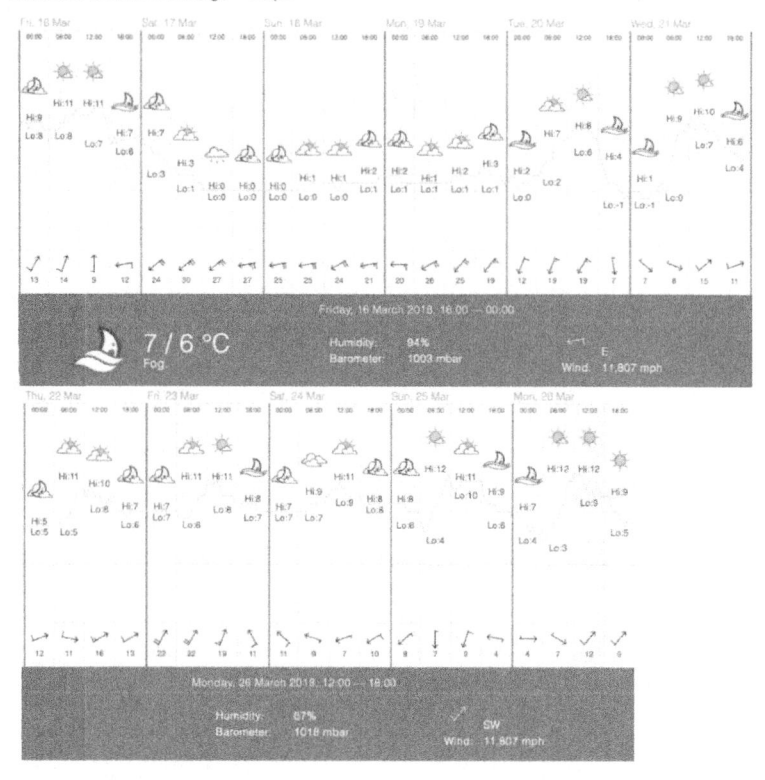

Heat speeds up the process, and so these cool temperatures inside the garage would have slowed it down.

According to my calculations, based on the size of the flies, the temperature in the garage, **the blow fly eggs could not have hatched the eggs in the head injury before 230 hours.**

That's 9 days and 14 hours. Which means not before Saturday morning at 1am.

This is significant because the burglar alarm was turned off at 4am.

It meant that Eduardo was already dead by at least a couple of hours when the burglar alarm was turned off.

I texted Roy back with a "Wow! Excellent Work. Thank you."

107

He came back with "I will get my stats corroborated by an entomology blow fly expert – but it will cost. Don't thank me. Thank the blow flies."

Day 15 of the Investigation

Date: Tuesday 3rd April
Time: 10:00
Location: Walton-on-Thames, Surrey

I came into Woking Nick to find that the incident room was being put away. All our lovely charts and graphics had been placed into archive cardboard boxes like last year's Christmas decorations. With Roy's blow fly findings coming through the night before, it felt premature.

My trusty bloodhounds Shakeela, Tom and Vicki were gone – re-assigned to other cases and Matt and me would go back to our usual base in Kingston-on-Thames.

I called the Springwater Sanatorium wanting to speak with the head psychiatrist that had signed PJ off. But he wouldn't take my call.

Then the post boy came in and plonked an envelope on my desk addressed in a laser printed label:

c/o Lead investigator in the Ligia James case
Woking Police Station
Station Approach
Woking
Surrey GU22 7SY

I opened the letter carefully with an opener. Inside was a single sheet of paper and more laser printed text:

Look into the death of PJ wife #1.
Some people think that was no accident.

Chapter 8 – Deadly Jagged Ridge Holiday
Day 16 of the Investigation

Date: Wednesday 4th April
Time: 10:00
Location: Kingston Police Station

I had buried myself so deeply into the details of this specific murder – the bottles of Chablis, the Spotify play list, the row at the vets, the key left in the shed, the fibre trail, I hadn't even thought about looking into this man's past and previous marriage. How slack is that?

So my first move was to pull out the report on the death of KELLY JAMES nee HILL. Kelly was aged 31 when she died in July 2007. She and PJ, her husband of 1 year, went hiking in the mountains in Cumbria – towards a place called Jagged Ridge, an appropriate name for a place known as an accident hot spot. Despite the scary name, Jagged Ridge continues to be a popular beauty spot for visitors. *(See map below)* Kelly was taking a photo of PJ and she stepped backwards to frame the shot and fell down a cliff. She was killed on hitting the rocks 60 foot below. The coroner returned a verdict of accidental death.

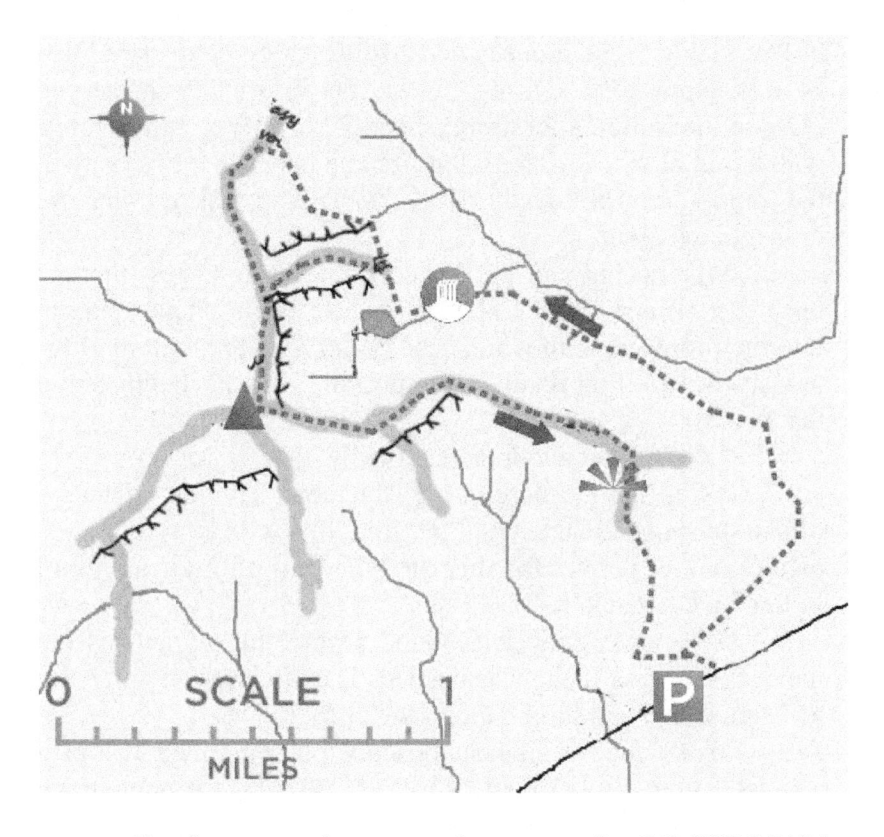

But I saw on the report the name of a PC WILLIAM WINTERBURN, who was first respondent. At the coroner's inquest, he put forward evidence suggesting that it was no accident. Since then Willie Winterburn's career in the police had moved him to the urban setting of Trafford, Greater Manchester. So me and Matt were to take a ride up the M40.

Day 17 of the Investigation

Date: Thursday 5th April
Time: 16:00
Location: A pub in Manchester

Willie Winterburn was now a station sergeant, ruddy faced and developing a burgeoning drinker's nose above a military style brush moustache. At the station he declared that he was happy to talk to us. So we met informally in the pub close to the station after he finished his shift. We sat him down with a pint next to a roaring log fire and handing him a copy of the report on the death of Kelly Hill, I asked what he remembered about it.

Sipping his pint he flicked through the pages, then he put it down, and sipped some more. He sat in silence staring into the fireplace, with white beer froth lining the bottom of his moustache, until he finally pronounced, "I wasn't happy about that verdict."

"Yes? What about it specifically?"

"Well it's all there in my statement. To kick off with – in the husband's statement he said his wife was taking a picture on her phone. **But her smashed up phone was found in her jacket pocket.**

"Then her body was found several inches away from the cliff side – as if she was pushed. The woman had no grazes and scratches from falling along the cliff.

"Also the woman supposedly photographed the man against a grey background of rocks. Why take a photograph with the view behind you, why not take a picture with the view in the background?"

"Right. Anything else that isn't in the report?"

"Obviously I couldn't say this officially. But the man – he just seemed shifty. I got a bad feeling off of him. I heard within months he got himself a massive insurance pay out."

Policemen often go with their nose, we all do it. We try and explain our suspicions as rationally as possible, but so often it's based on nothing more than gut feelings.

"Ah! Just remembered something else about him. The husband – what's his name?"

"PJ."

"That's it. I mean what a poncey name. This PJ pretended not to know that they were on an accident hot spot, but her best friend, the wife's best friend told me, that it was the husband's idea to go hiking in that particularly dangerous spot, because they had gone on a holiday there a few years before. But in his statement the husband categorically said it was the wife's idea. It was as if he was trying to deny it was his idea, because then it would make it look like he set it up."

"Right. Why would the wife's best friend go on holiday with PJ James then?"

"The best friend of the dead woman was also the sister of the husband. She arrived at the scene not long after I got there."

"Right that would be Samantha."

"So why are you asking me about this?"

"Well the husband has just got himself another dead wife."

His eyes widened as he tightened his fist and swung his pint. "I knew he was a wrong 'un."

Time: 18:00
Location: Woking Police Station

A drizzly darkening grey sky and smeared yellow lamplights set the scene for our motorway drive home. Matt and I went over what he had just heard from Willie Winterburn. Do you believe in co-incidences? Your wife dies suddenly and then your second wife also dies suddenly ten years later. When you are taking a photograph and you lose your balance and are about to fall off a cliff, would you have the time and inclination to put your camera away in your pocket?

As we pass the Watford services I get a call from Woking nick to tell me that Zico was waiting for me there.

An hour and a half later, he was still waiting for me, looking distraught. His shiny green eyes underlined by oily dark rings.

"So Zico – what do you want to say to me?"

"Have your people done their examination of my father's body?"

112

"Yes they have."

"Have they found anything different from the Sussex Police?"

"I can't tell you Zico, it's an on-going investigation."

Zico gave a loud huff of annoyance – "The police have also given me my father's car and clothes, you can have them if you want, for your tests."

"Thanks that will be most useful. We will get this sorted as soon as possible."

"Whatever you need."

"Have you got his phone?"

"No the police still have that."

"Well that is majorly annoying. I need his phone because I want to make contact with that woman he was meeting Friday night."

"I'll get onto that DCS Harris for you."

"No I'll do it. I did put in a request days ago."

"You know when we first met, I said if you can't say anything nice about someone, say nothing at all?"

"Yes I do."

"Well I've changed my mind."

This was a Mozartian symphony to my ears. "Well if you want to talk about PJ, I'd like to put it on the record. Let's go to an interview room."

We went into interview room 2, the same one as my first stonewall interview with PJ, I arranged for hot refreshments and to break open our best biscuits and turned on the recorder.

"I have with me Zico Pinheiro – the son of Ligia. First off – were you named after the Brazilian footballer?"

"Yes of course."

"A fine player. OK Zico – what do you want to say?"

"I said this to you before. But I need to stress – I know my mother very well. I spoke with her at least three times a week and she never, ever showed any signs of doing drugs or being involved in any drug gangs. She was always telling me to stay away from drugs."

I thought about the cocaine found in her blood stream, which I naturally did not bring up.

"OK but respectfully Zico you are his son, she may have worked hard at hiding that sort of stuff from you."

"Yes OK but I would have seen signs – give aways. There was never any sign of her being involved in anything like that. I also want to talk about my father – Eduardo."

"I want to say the same thing. I lived with him – and he was never, ever involved in anything like that either. He worked hard, kept fit and went out occasionally. He was never involved in any drug gangs.

"I don't know where the press are getting this from. Do you?"

"I can only speculate," I said.

"Do you think PJ is feeding them these lies?"

"I can't say Zico. It's possible. So what do you want to say about PJ?"

"I never had much to do with him. He never really spoke to me. But this is about what my mother said to me."

"And what did Ligia say about him?"

"Nothing good."

"Never ever said nice things about him?"

"Well maybe in the early days – but nothing I remember."

"She must have liked him at one point, I mean she did marry him."

"They were united in grief. They met at a group for people suffering from bereavement – that was the only thing that brought them together."

"Did they row?" Fuck another leading question. Sorry.

"Yes. I think so. I mean I wasn't there."

"So you don't really have much evidence then really do you?"

"I do – because my mother told me things."

"Like what?"

"She was going to leave him."

"And why was she going to leave him?"

114

"She thought he was a loser."

"Loser? She used those exact words?" Remember that word loser? That's what the neighbours Fred and Rose heard the night of Ligia's death.

"Yes."

"And why did she think PJ was a loser?"

"He lost his job at the TV show – he hadn't worked in years. And it was all over that Chloe Lund – he was obsessed with her. Ligia found out about it when she looked at his emails."

"Then she called Chloe Lund, and she told my mother what a creep he was."

I needed to speak with Chloe Lund.

"Thank you Zico – I appreciate you coming forward."

I turned off the recorder, and I continued "I think we both agree that PJ is the type of self-centered narcissist who might do something bad – but you've given me nothing to incriminate him."

"No wait – turn it back on. I've got something else I want to say."

I flicked the switch back on.

"OK shoot."

"Listen this is why I'm here. I can't stand the press stories. My father was a good man. He didn't have a temper. After the car accident he was always careful. Always. He did not commit suicide and my father did not kill my mother – it's obvious who did it. It's him. IT'S HIM!"

"But why are you so certain it's him?"

"There is something weird about PJ. I was at the wedding. OK Eduardo didn't want to go, and I didn't want to either. But the wedding…it was all mother's friends – all her family – friends from Portugal, friends she'd made in England, friends from work. I saw the invite list – he had no one. Virtually no one. Don't you think that's weird?"

"Yes I agree. But not having any friends doesn't make you a killer."

115

> **PJ's video log – Thursday 5th April**
> So DCS Ferdy started hassling you *(referring to Dougal off camera)* after you left the sanatorium. He might think it's weird that I am doing these video interviews. Like – how can I really be grieving if I am doing this? Well I am actually finding these video sessions very helpful, very therapeutic. It gives me a chance to voice my thoughts without someone being judgemental on the other end. So we are going to carry on doing them. I need to talk about what I am going through. They sent DCS Ferdy's partner with the big glasses and greasy hair to interview me alone. Then about a week later they sent that nice WPC to talk to me here at the Sanatorium. They clearly thought that a different approach and a different person might loosen my tongue. But my lawyer's strict instructions remains to tell them nothing.
>
> But I had questions I wanted to ask them. Like why do you need to interview me when Eduardo has committed suicide? Shouldn't you be looking into that? And if you have – what have you found? Haven't you closed the case now?

Day 18 of the Investigation

Date: Friday 6th April
Time: 09:00
Location: Kingston Police Station

While I shared Zico's views about PJ, and didn't like the thought of Eduardo Pinheiro being Ligia's killer, what hard evidence did we have against PJ? So far – next to nothing.

Finding out about the suspicious death of wife number 1 of course ramped up my misgivings about my mute suspect. But his chess game of silence made things more than a little challenging, preventing me from pulling him up on any inconsistencies in his story.

So we continued digging. Matt had been given the task of doing an exhaustive trawl of the emails on PJ's PC and the text messages on his phone, to shed some light on his private life. He had found that PJ did have some friends, and at one point had quite a lively social life when he was working on Shipton Village.

His friends were, in the main, fellow entertainment industry professionals. But after May 2016 things changed dramatically – he sent many emails and text messages and got barely any replies. So what happened in May 2016? That was when he got the boot from Shipton Village. His social media profile was almost non-existent. He opened a facebook account ten years ago but de-activated it in 2011. He had an Instagram account that he used a bit around 2015, mainly to post some on-the-set photographs, but that had been dormant since May 2016.

I then gave Matt the gig of going to see a chap by the name of Jake Fogerty – a 45 year old resident of Fleet, Hampshire. We had him listed as best man at PJ's first wedding with Kelly.

Jake Fogerty told Matt that he and PJ had met at University studying Media Studies. They had drifted apart as friends, but not fallen out. He revealed a number of things that unsettled him about PJ. First off, calling his cat Willougbhy after Willoughby & Ward the insurance company who paid out close to a million pounds in insurance to PJ after Kelly's death. Jake described this as "distasteful and inappropriate."

He also told Matt that they both attended a university re-union. At first PJ claimed reluctance about going as he had 'nothing to say to them' – and dismissed all of his old Uni associates as losers. Then when he got there he talked about nothing else except for his gig on Shipton Village. Jake described his "supercilious attitude of superiority and talking down to everybody" as repellent. Jake mentioned one wretched soul who was a self-financed indie film-maker, full of naïve enthusiasm, and PJ just totally berated him in front of everyone, saying, "You're not making real films – you're just

117

playing at it." Jake hadn't spoken to him since the re-union.

Andy Goddard called to tell me that PJ had called Minerva about his death in service payment. "Doesn't this make him look really bad?" He said breathlessly – "He was too grief stricken to go to the funeral, but not to cash in on her death."

Towards mid-day I get a call from Rupal – "Thank you for giving me access to the body of Eduardo Pinheiro. It is most enlightening. I can tell you most definitively – that splash blood in the spare bedroom is his." A picture was forming, I fell silent as I tried to see it.

"Hullo Ferdy?"

"Hullo Rupal. Still here."

"This makes a very interesting case even more interesting, does it not?"

The picture came into focus – Eduardo is struck in the spare bedroom and his heavy weight is dragged from upstairs to the front door – leaving that fibre trail of green wool and blue denim. The pillows in the spare bedroom were arranged to look like someone sleeping. Was it to trick Eduardo into thinking that Ligia was ill in bed?

Time: 12:00
Location: Malmaison Hotel, Oxford

Who was the anonymous person who sent me the note asking me to look into the death of Kelly Hill? What was their motivation? Did they know anything that could open up this investigation? I gave the envelope containing the anonymous note to Roy for DNA analysis and he knocked me back saying 'no dice' the envelope was self-sealing and so was the stamp, so the sender would have left no DNA.

But there was hope – "they may have left some revealing fingerprints," offered Roy, so I left the note with him. Meanwhile if we wanted to pin this murder on PJ, I needed to punch some holes in his alibi. He claimed to have been in Oxford all that week-end. So that's where I was off to today. If it checks out that PJ really was in Oxford the whole time, then maybe the hotel staff had overheard PJ speaking on the phone to a contract killer.

The Malmaison that PJ checked into was an upmarket boutique hotel, ironically, a converted prison. It's amazing how a lick of paint, a nice bit of lighting, a few pot plants, some elegant couches and removing the suicide net can transform a penitentiary into a place of luxury. The man who ran the reservation desk was an immaculately groomed Spanish guy – "I don't know if I can help you. I will need to check with head office – this may be a breach of our GDPR policy." He said giving a courteous but annoying smile.

"You don't need to do that. I am not trying to sell anybody anything. GDPR doesn't come into it. I am trying to solve a murder."

I went straight into it – "I am investigating the movement of one of your guests."

And I showed him the mug shot of PJ which was taken on the day he found his wife dead. The man's face lit up with recognition.

"Ah Yes! The Shipton Village guy."

"What do you remember about him?"

"Yes we had a bit of a chat – I remember he was concerned about his cat and he was trying to call his wife to get an update. "

"How do you know about Shipton Village?"

"He told me. He also told me he was in Oxford to do research on a TV series."

Being chatty is just the sort of thing a man trying to establish an alibi would do.

"He's not in trouble is he? He seems like a really nice guy." Asked the hotel man.

He eventually gave me a take away print out of their phone records and bookings for the week-end in question. The hotel operated a key-card system, so he was also able to give me a print out of the times the front door to PJ's room was opened and closed.

119

On the journey home I get a call from Matt.

"Roy has done his testing on the trophy we found in Rye."

"Yes and?"

"Nothing, no DNA, no blood, not even any fingerprints."

Damn! My big hopes of cracking the case remained tantalizingly out of my grasp. I guess it would have been too easy otherwise.

"However…"

Matt did another of his annoying pauses.

"However – what?"

"It's been soaked in bleach. There's no trace of anything else. Just bleach."

So the trophy has been wiped.

"Who soaks their big time TV award in bleach?"

"Exactly!" I was delighted to hear Matt was on the same page.

PJ's video log – Thursday 5th April

The drugs that the sanatorium were giving me were stabilizing my mood, numbing the edges off my most extreme paroxysms. Sometimes I would just sit into space not really feeling anything. But I was now able to read, watch television, play video games. I was functioning, but I was barely living. And I have started dreaming again. Not always about Ligia. About random stuff. Stuff that made no sense, had no logic. But I had ONE recurring nightmare. The nightmare of being taken away, arrested for something I didn't do. I hadn't heard from the police since the visit from Ferdy's side kick. He had run through the usual questions, but still I was under strict instruction not to answer.

Maybe they are finally backing off now. God I hope so.

But if they have concluded that Eduardo had killed Ligia. They should have the decency to inform me. I have a right to know the identity of my wife's killer.

Day 21 of the investigation

Date: Monday 9th April
Time: 10:00
Location: Berners Street Hotel, London

When the name Chloe Lund first cropped up in this investigation a few weeks before, Shakeela, Tom and Vicki all volunteered to do the interview with this apparently well-known actress. Now that I no longer had them at my disposal, it fell to me and Matt to do the interview. We finally got her to agree to one, but as you'd expect we had to go through her agent who got us to sign an NDA that we would not disclose anything in the interview to anybody else. I readily agreed to this although I am breaking it now by telling you this.

We met in a hotel suite at the Berners Street Hotel, under the watchful eye of her up-tight agent sat in a corner.

Chloe Lund had tied back her hair, wore no make up and was dressed down in jogging bottoms. Despite making no effort brushing up for our meeting, it was as if her charisma was something she could not turn off and had no control over. She had a heart shaped face with high cheekbones, a jutting over bite and sparkling blue eyes.

"The man is a creep! " She exploded on me mentioning the name PJ. She spoke fluent English with the faintest trace of a Swedish accent

I have to admit – this is exactly what I wanted to hear. However the second part was not – "I don't want to talk about him."

"Well I would appreciate any information you can provide."

"I don't want to press any charges I just want to leave the whole thing behind me."

"OK – that's understood – I just want some insight into this man. In what way is he a creep?"

"The way he would look at me, obsessing over me. The way he would leer while we filmed the sex scenes. He insisted on meeting one-to-one which he never did with any of the other actors."

"You said to his wife Ligia, that you were not prepared to play Tippi Hedren to his Alfred Hitchcock. I think I know what you mean. But can you explain exactly?"

"I don't want to talk about that."

"You talked about him crossing a line."

"I will NOT talk about THAT!" She snarled at me. The agent leapt up from her chair. It was time to bail.

"OK. One last thing. He obviously has a 'thing' for you. He may be prepared to tell you things that he is not prepared to tell other people. Are you prepared to take a wire, call him up and try and get him to talk about the murder of his wife?"

Her face twisted up and she spats these words at me: "I will NOT take a wire. I will not get involved in your dirty work." The agent was now standing between us calling the meeting to a close.

I was indignant – "Listen Ms. Lund this is not dirty work. This man will not say anything to us at all. He will not help us in any way. You say he is a creep. But by him not saying anything at all – by that I mean nothing – is helping that creep get away with murder. Did you know that he has two wives that died under suspicious circumstances? That's right two dead wives. Ligia the woman you spoke with is now dead. Think about that – and his strategy of silence is helping him get away with it.

"By allowing him to keep silent you are potentially helping a man get away with murdering his wife – twice. I am not sure how your Instagram followers will feel about that if they find out."

"I am not on Instagram," she said with a tart smile.

I still needed her on my side, I dropped the attitude and parted by saying, "OK I am sorry. I respect your decision and I really appreciate you finding time in your busy schedule to speak with me. If you ever change your mind or think of something you'd like to share, please get in touch."

She was still sneering when I left the room.

Day 22 of the investigation

Date: Tuesday 10th April
Time: 23:00
Location: Walton on Thames, Surrey

I jolted awake in the middle of the night from another nightmare. Once again I saw Ligia dead in a freezer, her blue face streaked with congealed blood. On opening my eyes, I remembered Roy's photograph when he first opened the freezer door. Ligia was in a zipped up sleeping bag and her head was covered by two black dustbin liners.

It was 3am. I couldn't call Roy at this time. So I got up and referred to my case file to confirm this. Yes – a zipped up sleeping bag and two dustbin bin liners over her head. Those were the very first photographs he took. All the other gruesome ones were after unzipping the sleeping bag and removing the bin liners.

So how did PJ know it was Ligia in the freezer?

With PJ not saying anything there was no way I could pull him up on the inconsistencies of his story. But what we did have was WPC Muldrew's body-cam video, where he tells her that his wife is dead with complete certainty. But how could he know this without unzipping the sleeping bag and removing the bin liners?

If your wife is missing and you find a dead body in your freezer, would you not want to make sure it was her? Would you not cling onto hope?

I tried to get back to sleep and eventually nodded off, waking up 8am, so I came in to work that morning a little later than I would have liked. Matt was there to greet me with some news: "We've got an ID of the person who sent the anonymous note about the first marriage."

Chapter 9 – Brandi Goes To Merton
Day 23 of the Investigation

Date: Wednesday 11th April
Time: 14:00
Location: Egham

Roy had contacted Matt to tell him that a very firm thumb print was found on the stamp of the envelope of the anonymous letter. Matt had put the print through the system and luckily found a match.

The print belonged to a Josh Viljoen aged 41. Josh had been serving in the army, stationed at Aldershot, and got involved in a pub affray, which is why he was on the database. That was 20 years ago, other than that, his record was clean and he now lived a seemingly respectable life as a fitness trainer in Egham.

So why was this person, apparently unconnected to PJ, wanting me to look at the death of his first wife? Let's go find out.

Josh Viljoen was a sandy haired, lean and muscular man, around six foot two. He looked like the type who would spend the week-end doing a couple of Triathlons and then go for a pint or two with the lads.

"I am not in trouble am I?" he asked nervously as we sat down to questioning him in his living room.

I wanted this guy on my side so I went out of my way to give my reply some added warmth.

"Absolutely not. Far from it. I really appreciate you coming forward with this suggestion. And I respect you wanting to be anonymous. However even though I was aware of PJ's first wife," this of course was a lie, "I want to hear from you directly why you thought the death of the first wife should be investigated."

Fixing me with a grave look, he explained "I

saw the Surrey Star and the business with PJ and his dead wife and it just made me think about what happened when his first wife…" He faltered and then said "I haven't got any evidence myself – that's why I sent the letter anonymous. I am just going over what I've overheard – and what my wife told me."

"Right – who is your wife?"

"Her name is Chun-ja."

"I got out my notepad – can you spell that for me?"

"C-H-U-N dash J-A."

"Chinese origin?" I ask.

"North Korean actually."

"Ah! Interesting – how she get out?"

"Her parents managed to defect in the 60s. She's never been to North Korea herself – only the South."

I nodded with interest. "So what did your wife tell you?"

"She's a close friend of Samantha – who is this man's sister. The day after Kelly's death Samantha came round to Chun-ja all in tears. She was convinced that PJ had pushed her. But didn't want to say anything to the police."

"Were you in on this conversation?"

"No I was in the next room, but I could hear Samantha wailing through the wall."

"What did Chun-ja say to this?"

"She was trying to calm her down – saying 'are you sure?' That it could just be an accident." I didn't hear everything that was said, but Chun-ja told me that Samantha felt guilty because she had introduced Kelly to PJ."

"But did Samantha give any specific reason why he thought her brother had done it?"

"She said that she and her brother had gone hiking with her parents at the same spot when they were kids about ten years before, and he talked about it being a good place to do a murder."

Josh made us a cup of tea as we waited for Chun-ja to come home from work. We waited over an hour, but it was worth it.

We were on our third cup when Chun-ja walked in. She was a slender woman in elegant black office clothes – her left eye-brow arched with curiosity on seeing a plain-clothes police officer in her living room standing up to shake her hand.

Instead of accepting my shake she turned to her husband.

"Josh – what is going on?" Her accent was Estuary English, no hint of the oriental. She then got angry when I told her about Josh sending me the anonymous note. I did my best placatory voice: "Listen nobody here is in any trouble. Quite the opposite."

"Because I am North Korean I know the importance of keeping a secret. How loose lips can cost you your life."

"But you've never been to North Korea?"

"I learnt about secrecy from my parents. And I am breaching Samantha's trust by talking about this."

"Well that's not the way to look at it. This is about getting to the truth and justice."

I eventually sat down with Chun-ja who confirmed Josh's story, explaining how Samantha had insisted on seeing her the day after Kelly's death. Samantha felt she had no one else she could talk to. "I was saying to her – 'look he may be innocent after all' –but I know she wasn't convinced. But I think in the end she was relieved that PJ wasn't prosecuted. She couldn't bear the family disgrace and eventually she just stopped thinking about it."

She went on: "Sam told me that PJ and Kelly were having money problems. They had just signed up to a big mortgage, and in order to get it they had to agree to paying a large amount into an insurance policy. Sam told me that before Kelly died, PJ had said to Sam – 'I have a solution – Kelly will be gone soon.'"

I asked – "Has Samantha said anything to you about the death of Ligia?"

"She called me a few days ago, just after she'd helped him get checked into a sanatorium. She'd seen that PJ had hired a friend to make a documentary about him and what he

127

was going through after the death of his second wife. She thought it ……well she didn't think it was right. She didn't think it's the sort of thing a person mourning their wife would do." "What else did Samantha say to you?"

"She's pissed off that the bills for the sanatorium are being sent to her."

"Really? Has she paid them?"

"No – she's paid the deposit. She is trying to get the money off PJ."

"Has she said anything about the sort of person PJ is?"

"She said she could believe that PJ was capable of murder because he showed his sadistic side to her when they were kids. He did a lot of spiteful things – inflicting pain on her and enjoying it. OK every older brother is cruel to their sister. But she said this was…on another level."

"Spiteful things like that?"

"She showed me this triangular burn mark on her stomach where he put an iron against her."

As you know I am a squeamish copper, I squirmed just thinking about the stinging pain of a steaming hot iron onto flesh.

"Anything else? Any more examples of this sadism?"

"I don't know. You will have to ask Sam."

This was revelatory. So Samantha had suspicions about her brother over the death of her friend. Is that why she had that strange narrowing of eyes expression when PJ was talking to her in the kitchen? Was that a look of suspicion? A look of distrust?

If Samantha, the supposedly stalwart sister of PJ and his go-to person in a crisis, is doubting her brother's innocence, then this could be the chink in his defence. She could be the key in bringing his fortress of silence down.

PJ's audio testament – Wednesday 11th April

A woman came to see me the other day at the sanatorium. She introduced herself as WPC Gemma Muldrew and told me that she was the first police on the

> scene after I called 999. She was out of uniform this time, which would have concealed her long brown hair that flowed down in ringlets. She was lean and athletic with a cheery disposition which remained when I told her that I hoped that she would forgive me, but I had no recollection of meeting her as I was somewhat distracted at the time. The police clearly thought a more informal approach would get me to open up and talk, and while Ms. Muldrew is way more pleasant and likeable than DCS Ferdy and his crusty side-kick, I stuck to my No Comments.
>
> But there was another reason for doing this. I wasn't thinking of myself. She was asking lots of questions about Ligia and her cocaine use and connection to drug gangs. I did not want to provide any information on that because I did not want Ligia's memory to be smeared by such things. Ligia had clearly died because of her involvement with Eduardo and possibly the drug gangs, but there was no need to rake through the details of that murky side of her life. That would only serve to hurt so many people close to Ligia, not just me, but her parents and Zico.

Day 24 of the Investigation

Date: Thursday 12th April
Time: 10:00
Location: Kingston Police Station

Matt was on the phone. "I've found something of gargantuan proportions." (Matt has his own curious lexicon.)

"I've been scrutinizing the data supplied by the Malmasion Hotel and PJ's booking at the hotel came in at 21.56 hours – it was a phone transaction. I repeat – **he did it over the phone.** When the person at the desk took the card payment, they had to tick the box whether the client was there or not, and the person ticked he was not. That's why he took the three numbers at the back of the card, which you don't do when the card holder is there. Their phone records also show that the hotel took an incoming call from PJ's mobile at 9.55 – and his own phone backs that up."

"But in his written statement he claimed to have booked in at the Malmaison at 4pm" "Right. But there is no record of that – and there are no records of him calling the hotel earlier. That 21.55 call is the one and only call he made to the Malmaison."

"He could have made the booking on-line?" I suggested.

"No it was a phone booking. I checked with the bank and the card transaction went through at the same time at 9.55."

"You're right that is gargantuan," I agreed.

"There's more – the Malmaison have electric card-keys and he first entered his room at 12.57am – Saturday morning. The records shows that he did not pick up his keys until 12.55 am. That was when the front desk created the card-key for him."

Matt put in another one of his dramatic pauses, as I digested this info. Then he pronounced – "This makes him being at West Byfleet at 21.35 to kill Ligia completely possible." Yes indeed – we had ripped open a massive chunk in PJ's alibi.

I sat back taking this all in.

Then I realized I still needed an explanation on the Eduardo Pinheiro story, which reminded me – those fuckers at Sussex Police had still not given over Eduardo's phone. Damn the expense! I got on the phone and arranged for a courier to bring the phone over right away.

Time: 16:00
Location: Kingston Police Station

The sun had sunk low, bathing the office with a soft orange glow by the time Eduardo's phone arrived. Before handing it over to forensics I scrolled through it and picked up the most recent phone and text messages. I found a

130

correspondence in Portuguese to someone listed as GG – and one text contained the phrase 'Noite de sexta-feira' which I looked up to discover is Friday night in Portuguese.

This GG then called and texted Eduardo a number of times after the presumed day of his death – Friday the 16th March. I called GG's number.

"Hullo? Hullo? Do you speak English?"

"A little." The voice was distant and hesitant.

"Do you know an Eduardo Pinheiro?"

"Eduardo Si. Yes?"

She said something in Portuguese. It was a question but I couldn't understand.

"I believe you were with him on the night of Friday the 16th."

"I no understand. Sorry."

"I will get an interpreter to call you…"

"I am in Brazil. Good bye."

And she hung up.

I then found the text correspondence between Eduardo and Ligia. Everything had been in Portuguese until the final exchange beginning with the 21.57 text from Ligia – "Come over quickly. I must see you NOW!" **Looking at my timeline – this was 1 minute after PJ had called the Malmaison to book the room.**

What if that text was not from Ligia, but from someone using her phone and trying to lure Eduardo to the house?

I noted that Eduardo had dialed out to Ligia straight after that text with a phone call that lasted 112 seconds.

"What about him?" Came a text from Eduardo at 22.33 – 34 minutes after Ligia's first text in English and after a visitor had arrived at Asgard at 22.30. What if that text had been sent from someone other than Eduardo – and was sent after Eduardo had been killed and was used to lay down an alibi that someone was elsewhere – somewhere like Oxford?

What if that fibre trail in Asgard was someone dragging Eduardo from upstairs to the front door?

131

The fibre was blue cotton and green wool. What was Eduardo wearing that day he disappeared?

Day 25 of the Investigation

Date: Friday 13th April
Time: 09:00
Location: Merton

Today I had booked Brandi the Cadaver Dog to work his magic on Eduardo's White Pontiac. So we were off to the urban village of Merton – Wimbledon's plainer, less elegant sister on the south side of the railway track.

This is where Eduardo lived with Zico, and the Pontiac was now parked inside a small lock up garage in a back street behind a parade of shops.

This garage was part of Eduardo's rented property, which raised the question – why drive all the way to Rye to kill yourself by car fumes when you have your own garage in Merton to do it? OK – maybe he didn't want his son Zico to find his body.

Zico was there to meet us and, hand over in a bag, the clothes Eduardo had been wearing on the day of his death. "There's something I need to show you," he said with an earnest expression as he opened the Pontiac car door on the driving side – "This car, with Eduardo's body still in it, was taken from the garage and put into a truck and taken to the Sussex Police place. Then they called me up to say they had finished with it and could I come and pick it up. I drove it from there to here. I didn't change the seat position. Look at it."

"What about it?"

"It's in a normal position for someone of normal height. Dad was six foot three. If he was the last person to drive it before he died, the seat would have been pulled back."

"You didn't move the seat?"

"No. I just told you I haven't," he snapped irritably.

"Sorry. I am police I need to check these things. I mean you may be moving the seat to..."

"To what?"

"OK thanks Zico. This is good evidence."

"It proves my Dad didn't kill himself."

"It doesn't prove that, but indicates in that direction. Listen Zico you can't be around while we investigate the car..."

"Why?"

"Because you are involved in the case. I'll let you know when we're done."

With Zico leaving I started to feel anger rising up over us not taking control of the investigation when I found the body. I let loose on Roy – "See? This is what happens when you let Sussex Police handle our case."

"Why are you having a go at me?"

"Because you called them in."

"Because that's what we're supposed to."

"And look at what happened. We get to look at the evidence second hand after those sloppy cunts from Sussex County." Shamefully I found myself raising my voice.

Matt dashed over to me. "Ferdy please calm down, the residents are staring."

I turned my anger down to a simmer. It is of course very bad form for the public to hear a police man shouting and using the c_word. I apologised to Roy, whose opinion of me had now gone down even further, if that was possible.

"We will be able to check if Zico's telling the truth from the photographs Sussex Police took," offered Matt.

"If they bothered to take any." I muttered. "Come on let's get the dog out."

Brandi's handler put one of Eduardo's old trainers under the dog's nose to sniff, and then the canine super-hero was let loose on the Pontiac. He ran around for a bit, and then jumped into the driving seat and started barking. That was of course correct, that's where I found Eduardo's cadaver. The body had been there for a week, so plenty of dead cells would have been secreted there. Then we opened the boot, and Brandi leapt inside and sat in it – and once again did his 'I've found some dead cells – give me some chocolate' bark.

As Roy began examining the boot, another member of his team took our own photographs of the blood marks on the driving seat.

Next I was given a six foot three, 88 kilos bendy mannequin corresponding to Eduardo's height and weight. It looked just like a crash test dummy, only this was painted purple. I was nominated as the one to do the lifting exercise as I was around the same height and weight as PJ, and so presumably his approximate strength.

The exercise was to pull the bendy mannequin out of the boot – which took considerable effort. I had to lift the legs up first, rest them on the edge of the boot, and then use all my strength to lift the head part also onto the edge and then let the whole thing drop.

Roy's report found abrasions on the whole of the left side of Eduardo's body. Was that consistent with it being dropped like this post mortem?

I then dragged the mannequin from there to the car door on the driving side, opening the door, and lifting the mannequin, again with considerable effort into the driving seat. I did this by pulling the body through from the passenger seat, and then lifting the legs into the driving seat. The legs were scrunched up a little. When we pulled the mannequin out, it took three of us.

I wanted some form of demonstration of what Zico was claiming about the positioning of the car seat for a tall person. Luckily we had someone on the team who is six foot two. So we got him to sit in the driving seat. (Remember Eduardo was six foot three.) Our test tall person found the driving seat a little uncomfortable for someone of that height and he would have pulled it back to drive. We of course didn't do this. We needed to keep the car as close as possible to how it was found. I then got in and found it OK. So it's possible that the killer adjusted the car seat for themselves to drive it, and may not have thought to adjust the car seat back after putting the dead body into the driving seat, and would not have been aware of the scrunched up legs.

Then Matt suggested I should lift the mannequin from the floor directly behind the car and into the boot, just as someone who would have killed Eduardo did. This was the hardest job of all. Straining I had to arrange the body lengthways – put the legs up first to take that half of the weight and then lift the heavier half up and then slide the body in. I was huffing and puffing and drenched in sweat. As I sat on the floor recovering someone said to me – "Sorry to lay this onto you Sir. But we really should do this all again, but this time put it on video."

So off we went again for the benefit of the video camera.

After lifting the body in, lifting the body out, dragging it to the front of the car, putting it into the passenger seat, we also re-enacted sellotaping the note to the window. Then we did the following demonstration:

1. attached garden hose tubing to the exhaust pipe
2. placed the other end of the tubing inside the window on the driving side, pulled up tight
3. turn on the ignition
4. place the heavy toolbox down onto the accelerator pedal
5. As the car starts filling with fumes, exiting via the passenger seat.

These five steps were caught on video as a demonstration of how a killer might make the killing of Eduardo look like a suicide.

I was driving home recovering from an especially tiring day, when I got a call. My initial reaction was to ignore it but when I saw it was from Roy I knew it was important.

"Hey Roy – what's happening? Sorry again about my outburst today."

"Don't worry about it. You're an emotional copper I've got used to it. Listen – my team have checked and double checked it. The fibres on the clothes that Eduardo was wearing – the blue jeans and green jumper – they are a perfect match to the fibre trail down the stairs and to the front door of the house in West Byfleet."

"Perfect match?"

"Dead right. I have the fibres of his clothes on one microscope next to the fibres found in the house on another microscope – and they are one and the same. I can send the pictures."

"Please do. Eduardo was a tall heavy guy, PJ could not have lifted him for a sustained period of time, so he would have to have dragged him from upstairs to the front door to put him in the boot of that Pontiac. That seals it, I am now firmly in the Eduardo-didn't-commit-suicide camp."

"So am I." Agreed Roy and my heart sung with joy.

Time: 12:00
Location: Kingston Police Station

In order to prove that PJ could have done this, I needed to demonstrate a credible timeline and a sequence of events.

We had established these facts about Ligia's and PJ's movements, all backed up and supported by digital evidence or witnesses. Matt's Gargantuan Oxford revelation *(see page 126)* had added two highly interesting entries into our timeline:

Time	Activity	Verification
20.34	Ligia sends text to PJ requesting pick up at train station	PJ's phone
20.53	Ligia boards train at Waterloo	Station CCTV
21.21	Ligia alights train at West Byfleet	Station CCTV
21.27	Ligia is at West Byfleet buying wine	bank card + witness
21.35	Ligia is at home playing the Spotify play-list	Laptop forensic
21.36	A row ensues	Witness – next door neighbours
21.47	Spotify play-list down in volume	Witness
21.55	PJ replies to Ligia's text - "Sorry darling am in Oxford."	PJ's phone
21.56	PJ calls the hotel in Oxford to make a booking	hotel records + PJ's phone records
21.57	A text is sent from Ligia's phone to Eduardo "Come over quickly."	Eduardo's phone
21.59	Eduardo calls Ligia's phone and has 112 second conversation.	Eduardo's phone
22.30	A visitor arrives at Asgard. Willoughby the cat moves next door and Graham Norton was about to start.	Witness
22.33	Text from Eduardo's phone - "what about him?"	Eduardo's phone
0.57	PJ gets into his room at Oxford.	hotel records
1.09	PJ draws out £150 in cash at an ATM in Oxford.	bank records
3.57	The burglar alarm is turned off at Rye.	digital records
9.21	PJ has breakfast at the hotel in Oxford.	hotel records

Look at the entry on 21.56 – PJ calls the hotel in Oxford, just one minute after replying to Ligia's text that he is in Oxford.

Now look at the entry on 0.57 – PJ enters his room in Oxford nearly two and a half hours after the visitor arrives at Asgard.

This blow by blow timeline now demonstrates that it is perfectly possible that PJ could have killed Ligia and Eduardo.

Why did the Spotify play-list go down in volume at 21.47? Was it because Ligia had just been killed and PJ needed to concentrate to work out his plan? Then he hatched the idea of setting up an Oxford alibi and luring Eduardo to the house, where he could fake his suicide. OK it's only a theory – a plausible theory maybe – but cold hard proof was absent.

The burglar alarm was turned off in Rye @3.57 am. If PJ did it, he would have dumped Eduardo there, set up the

137

suicide scene, but had to be in Oxford for 9am in order to get breakfast at the hotel. How did he get from Rye to Oxford without a car? Was there a second car at Rye? But our investigation of PJ's affairs revealed he had just the one car – the Mercedez which was in the garage in Asgard all along. Maybe he stole a car? Are there any reports of any cars stolen in the area of Rye? Maybe he had a motorbike.

Matt and I had some digging to do. We were going to have to contact all the local taxi firms. Did they get any fares after 4am to take someone to a train station or even straight to Oxford? Did PJ get an Uber? Or did he buy a train ticket to get back to Oxford?

The ever committed Matt volunteered to contact Rye Train station and look at their CCTV between the hours of 4am and 7am on that Saturday.

Date: Friday 12th April
Time: 16:00
Location: Rye Train Station

Matt called from Rye Station to tell me the station had 9 CCTV cameras, meaning that to watch all of them over that 3 hour window would take 27 hours.

"I've got a long couple of days ahead of me. I am going to lose another week-end to this case," he said with a sigh of stoic resignation.

"No – I am coming over. Let's share it." This meant 13 and a half hours each of CCTV viewing – at least we would both get to see some of Sunday.

As you expect between 4am and 5am on that Saturday there was virtually no footfall at the station, but things picked up slowly until the final hour when things got fairly lively. Trawling through CCTV is one of the most boring aspects of police detective work. But if we could spot PJ in any of this footage this would, as Matt would put it, have a "Gargantuan" impact on our investigation.

We were holed up in the small room at the station right

up until just past 11pm. After hours upon hours of viewing that turned our eyes square, we realized PJ would be smart enough to conceal himself with a hat, scarf or glasses. But even so we had seen nobody that could even remotely be PJ.

We left the room rubbing our eyes as our spirits sunk.

But getting in the car Matt offered some optimism. "Assuming PJ is intelligent, he would know that Rye station would have lots of CCTV – so he would go to a smaller station with less or even no CCTV – even if it was further away."

Yes! So looking at the map we see that the second nearest train station to the cottage is Winchelsea. We take a drive over there to see that it's a desolate sleepy station with just a couple of CCTV cameras and a ticket hut that was shut and a ticket machine outside.

"Maybe somebody bought a ticket here after 4am on that Saturday morning. I will get onto British Rail."

Day 28 of the Investigation

Date: Monday 16th April
Time: 10:00
Location: Kingston Police Station

My theories were useless without any substance. What I badly needed was solid hard evidence that PJ travelled between Rye and Oxford in the hours between 4 am and 9.30 am on the morning of the Saturday 17th of March. Some digital evidence, CCTV or an eye witness. If I didn't find this, I would just have to accept the conclusion of the Sussex Police and pack it in. So we were trying to prove that PJ drove Eduardo's White Pontiac with his body in the boot from the Malmaison Hotel in Oxford to his cottage in Rye. A journey that looked like this:

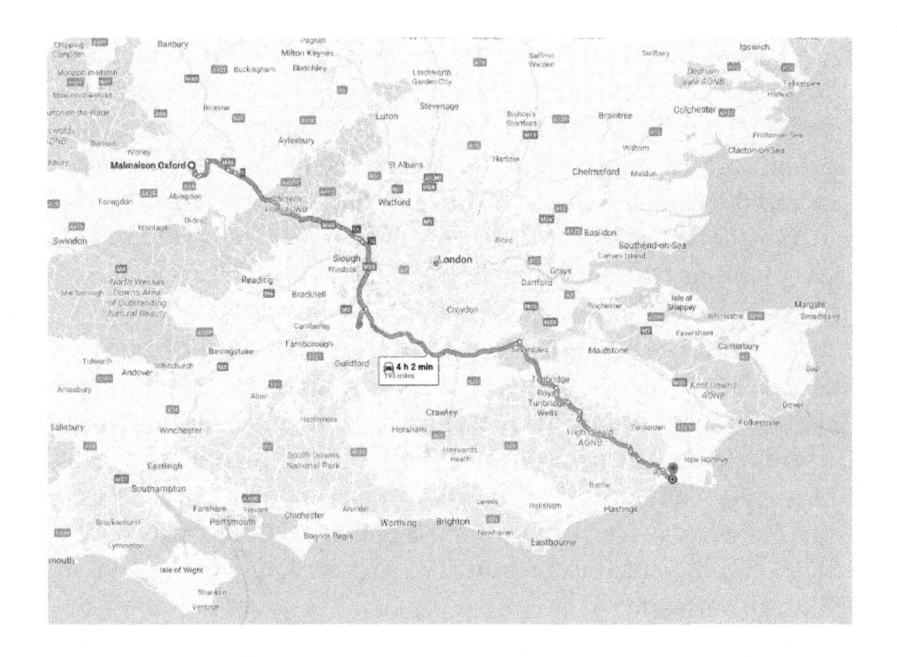

Leaving the Pontiac there, and with no other means of transport, we needed to show that PJ travelled from a nearby Station like Winchelsea to Oxford station. A train journey that looked like this:

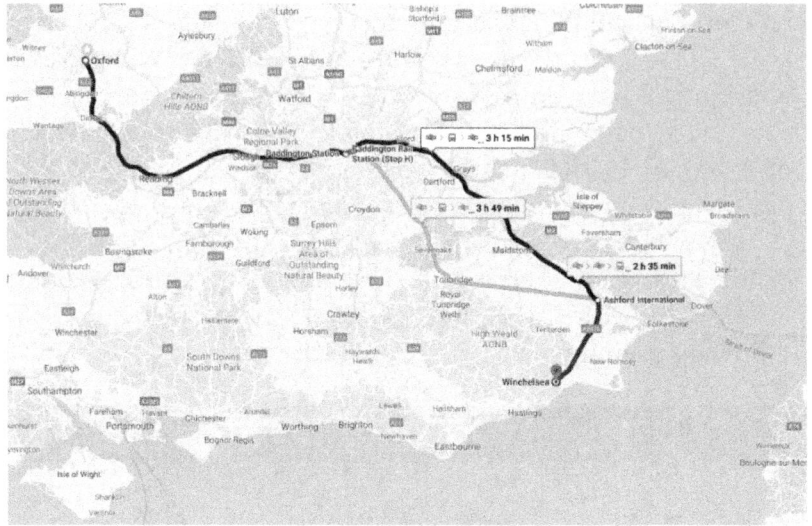

So the walk from the cottage in Rye to Winchelsea train station was around three miles. That's one hour of walking. Assuming PJ arrived at the house in Rye at 4am to turn off the burglar alarm and him needing 15-20 minutes to set up the suicide scene, this meant that he would have arrived at Winchelsea station at 5.20 am. That gives him plenty of time to get the first train at Winchelsea Station at 5.39 am, that pulls into Ashford International at 6.06.

But would he buy a ticket? Would he not just bunk the fare? That's risky – if he got caught by a ticket collector or on the barrier at Ashford he would have to give his name and address to the British Transport Police, and provide proof of it.

It would be safer to buy a ticket, bought by cash so as not to leave an electronic trail. But the ticket hut was shut at this time, so maybe he bought a ticket with his card at the machine. Maybe.

British Rail came back with the data on ticket machine sales at Winchelsea Station for that morning. I was so hoping the name PJ James was to appear on the print out.

No such luck. Instead the first two tickets of the day at the station were bought at 5.31 am by a Mrs. P. Grover – then no more sales until 6.30 am. Damn!

Still – it was worth tracking down Mrs. Grover as she might have noticed some of the other passengers.

The bank gave me the details of a Petra Grover resident of a Sussex hamlet quaintly named Cock Marling. Should I pay her a visit or give her a call? What do you think?

Well I say – get in the car and do it face-to-face. I called ahead first to arrange the meeting. Petra Grover worked in Ashford and I was due to meet her at her home the following evening.

Day 29 of the Investigation

Date: Tuesday 17th April
Time: 10:00
Location: Cock Marling, Sussex

Petra Grover was a plump attractive dark skinned woman with luscious lips in her late 30s.

"Am I in trouble?" She asked with a nervous smile as we sat down in her living room. "I don't believe so Madam. Right!" I said rubbing my hands and getting down to business – "we have reason to believe you were at Winchelsea station at 5.39am on the morning of Saturday the 17th March. Last month."

She thought a bit.

"Yes. I was on my way to Gatwick Airport. I was due to meet a friend who had been living abroad. I can prove all that."

"No need. Did you see anything or anybody unusual at the station at the time?"

"No. Can't think of anything Sorry."

"Were there any other passengers around that time? What do you remember of them?"

"Uh gawd! Sorry I don't remember I was still half asleep."

I slumped back in her settee deflated.

"Sorry," she said again which only annoyed me further. I thought of other witnesses. "The records show you bought two tickets. Who was traveling with you?"

"Ah! Yes I remember – a man came up to me as I was buying my ticket at the machine. He said his card wasn't working and if he gave me the cash, could I buy it for him? The machine only took cards you see."

I nearly leapt out of my chair on hearing this.

"You bought his ticket?"

"At first I thought it was a scam. But he seemed so nice – and with him giving me the cash, I couldn't see how he could scam me. So I agreed. He gave me the cash and a little bit extra. He…"

I saw those luscious lips forming to give me a description. This time I actually did leap up from my chair.

"STOP! STOP! Do not describe him to me. Do not tell

142

me anything else about him." I felt like kissing her, but instead I called the interview to a close.

On the way back in the car I was in high elation, this woman may well have given us the break-through I was looking for. So why did I suddenly terminate the interview?

Very simple. This witness was dynamite and needed to be handled with ultra-care. I did not want her tainted in any way, and give PJ's counsel the ammunition to counter her testimony by saying we had planted an image of who the man should look like.

PJ has a distinctive dimple in the middle of his chin. While this dimple is excellent for identification purposes, it is also susceptible to be used as a tool for witness contamination.

I had learned this from painful experience. In a previous case I had shown the witness a photograph of the suspect, and given a description of the person I hoped it was, and the witness went along with it and said yes – that's who it is – and at the identity parade the person picked out my suspect. At the trial the defence counsel claimed I had coaxed and groomed the witness into identifying his client. It wasn't true – but we nearly lost the case because of that.

Eye-witnesses are not as solid as people think, they rely on their own shaky memory, they are open to suggestion, and they like to tell people what they want to hear. So a good lawyer, which PJ certainly has, is quite capable of destroying the credibility of the evidence.

I was going to arrange for a formal identity parade, and if this Petra woman positively identifies PJ out of the line up without any pre-conception of what the suspect looks like, then we are well on the way to proving our case and sealing PJ.'s fate. I wanted Petra Grover to identify PJ in a parade with other police and his lawyer around. This identification had to be water-tight. Meanwhile we will check the CCTV at Ashford Station, this time able to pinpoint the exact train he would have been on.

If we can establish beyond reasonable doubt that PJ was at Winchelsea Station at 5.40 am – we would be on our way to putting this on PJ. Why else would he be there? Three miles and one hour walk away from his home in Rye and Eduardo's place of death, one and forty minutes after the burglar alarm had been turned off. In our formal interview he never said a word, but in his prepared statement he clearly claims to be in Oxford the whole week-end.

Of course getting someone else to buy his ticket would mean no digital trail of him being there. If he had bunked the fare, while it was unlikely for ticket inspectors to be on the train that early morning, he would have needed to have jumped the barrier at Ashford station. There would be staff at a massive station like Ashford to apprehend him, and even if he would have got away with that, it would have been picked up on CCTV. Once at Ashford he could pay cash to get his train back to Oxford.

It was all starting to fit.

Chapter 10 – The Woman at Winchelsea Station

Day 30 of the Investigation

Date: Wednesday 18th April
Time: 09:00
Location: Kingston Police Station

"I am organizing an identity parade and your client's attendance is highly desirable." I was on the phone to PJ's brief Jennifer Janus.

Her reply was predictable – "He can't. He's in a highly fragile mental state."

"Well he doesn't need to say or do anything. Just stand in a line."

"He's in no fit state to do anything."

I thought of his video interview with Dougal and scowled.

"Well I am arranging for a car to pick him up tomorrow at 10am. No expense spared. If he doesn't comply, we will arrest him and that won't do his mental health any good."

In the meantime we had looked at the CCTV of the passengers on the train from Winchelsea passing through the barrier at Ashford International station at 6.06am. Of the 20 or so passengers we saw a man that could be PJ – but unfortunately could not be positively IDed, because he was wearing a woolly hat and looked down at the floor the whole time. This is a tip for all you would-be criminals and fugitives – all the CCTV cameras in train stations are high up, so if you want to avoid detection just keep looking down and they'll never pick out your face. PJ obviously knew this.

So we established someone who could be PJ at Ashford Station, let's hope we can establish he was definitely at Winchelsea station.

Day 31 of the Investigation

Date: Thursday 19th April
Time: 10:00
Location: Woking Police Station

It was vital that neither of the two VIPs of this identity parade, PJ and Petra Grover, saw each other until the actual parade. So we kept Petra away from the car park so she could not see PJ arrive with his brief.

Petra of course will be behind the glass unseen by PJ. The other men in the parade were hastily assembled. Due to police cut backs, some of them were OB, and some were guys we pulled off the street and given a couple of quid for their trouble. They all had to resemble the suspect in some way, but none had a pronounced dimple on their chin.

It was also important I did not speak with either PJ or Petra, so I was tucked away from the action, up in the booth with all the TV monitors. I sat there watching the screen, wringing my hands as Petra walked up and down the gangway. On the screen I could see Matt looking as jittery as I was, sat in the corner of the gallery with Petra. Then I looked at the monitor showing the ID parade – six men lined up with PJ second from the left with a blank expression – holding up a large card with a number.

In the gallery and with the glass between them, Petra walked two lengths of the parade looking at each of the six faces in turn, saying nothing.

Then she pronounced – "Number 5 – definitely Number 5. I remember the dimpled chin." While I jumped for joy out of sight in the video room, Matt standing next to the woman needed to contain his elation.

"Are you sure?" he asked.

"Yes," she said with slow hesitation.

"Actually just to be 100 percent. Can he say something?"

146

"Like what?"

"Like what he said to me on the day."

"What did he say?"

She quoted, "Excuse me Madam – my card isn't working and the machine won't take cash. If I gave you the cash would you buy my ticket? I can give you a bit extra for your trouble."

In the video booth I got out of my chair and laid out my instructions on the mic. All six of the men were to step forward and say the words in turn. Meanwhile I wanted a camera to be trained on PJ. I wanted to see his reaction on seeing his own words in print before having to read it out. He would then of course know that this ID parade was about Winchelsea station.

We got the wording printed up on six bits of paper and each of the parade men were given them.

I stared at the video screen as PJ was handed his bit of paper. I wanted to study him as he got given what we think were his own words. Did I imagine it, or did he gulp? His face appeared to flush on reading the words.

Number 1 stepped forward and said the words in a Welsh accent. Then Number 2 in a nasal London accent, Number 3 sounded just gormless but could be from anywhere, Number 4 was cheery and a little bit posh. Number 5, PJ – mumbled his words. Number 6 did his bit in an Eastern European accent. Possibly Romanian.

Petra in the booth said, "When he said them at the station he was more upbeat and lively – but yes it's definitely Number 5."

Matt ran into the TV monitor room quite literally foaming at the mouth. "We've got ourselves a case," he pronounced triumphantly.

Establishing that PJ was at Winchelsea station at 5.35am on Saturday 17th March had convinced us both that PJ was our man. But did we have enough to convict?

It was a risk now to let him go back to the Sanatorium, because he could quite easily make his escape.

147

"I think we still need something more," I said. "If we don't tell him that he has been positively identified and if we act all disappointed, he'll go back to the Sanatorium not realizing we are closing in on him."

So Matt and I went out to the car park standing near the car PJ came in on, so that PJ and his brief would pass us. I made eye contact with my suspect but did my best to look defeated and despondent.

As usual he said nothing. Jennifer Janus was about to ask me something but then decided against it. I watched them get into her car, still wearing my façade of dejection.

Back in the police station reception Petra, the star of the show, was hanging around talking to WPC Muldrew.

"Did I do good?"

"You told the truth so you did marvellous."

"Is he in trouble?"

"He is now."

"So how is he doing his scam? I couldn't see how he could. I checked. No money came out of my account."

"This isn't a fraud investigation. It's murder."

"Murder?"

"Yes Murder of the worst kind – his wife, her ex-husband and his first wife. So I will be seeing you again at the trial – hopefully."

"Uh! How exciting."

I thanked her once again and made my exit. I had a lot of thinking to do.

The blow fly evidence and the fibre trail was all good stuff pointing that Eduardo was killed at the house in West Byfleet, but until this ID I had no real evidence that PJ had been doing any of it.

What evidence would make a nice icing on my murder charge cake? I was thinking of Samantha – PJ's sister.

PJ's video log – Friday the 20th April

I had thought the police investigation on me was over, and then I get a call from my lawyer about this identity parade. Doing that identity parade was one of the most Kafka-esque and nerve-racking experiences of my life. I stood there in a line under nasty glaring strip lights, holding up a number 5, with five other men who looked nothing like me. I was trying my utmost to not let my fear show, because that would make me look like the guilty suspect.

I could not see the person who was supposed to be doing the identifying. They were on the other side of the one way glass. I had no idea what the parade was about, where I was supposed to be. Why was the ID parade even necessary when it's obvious that Eduardo did it?

Then they gave me a bit of paper to read. Something about bank card's not working and could someone buy them a ticket. This gave my unease some respite, because I had never uttered those words to anyone ever in my life. This ID parade must be about someone else.

After it was over and I was allowed to return to the sanatorium, I was encouraged when we passed DC Ferdy and his greasy-haired partner in the car park. They looked completely deflated and disappointed. Maybe I was now finally off the hook.

Day 32 of the Investigation

Date: Friday 20th April
Time: 09:00
Location: Woking Police Station

We had to approach Samantha delicately. We needed someone warm and likeable. So that ruled me out, and Matt was not quite empathetic enough. WPC Gemma Muldrew was the perfect woman for the job. I remember when a PC had a traumatic experience involving an especially gory train accident, while we were all making bad taste jokes, Gemma was there by his side to offer support and a listening ear. She exudes natural humanity and compassion. A very rare quality for a copper. So I called her in for a briefing.

"I don't like this" she said dropping her smile after I had sat her down and explained what I wanted her to do. "Why me?"

"You are a very likeable person. You have a winning personality that puts people at their ease. You stand the best chance of getting Samantha to ...."

"Do the dirty on her own brother?"

"Help us get to the truth of what happened."

Gemma countered- "I was first respondent. He seemed genuinely upset about his wife. I think he's innocent – and he mentioned the drug gangs and the ex-husband. They seem more likely perps than him."

I patiently explained that we had built up a mountain of evidence that he had staged Eduardo's suicide and that his first wife had also died under suspicious circumstances.

"We looked at his phone landline records and between him dialling 999 and you arriving – fifteen minutes – he called a lawyer. Surrey's top criminal lawyer. Where did he get that number from? Then he called his sister. Rose and Fred the neighbours heard him shouting and screaming when the police arrived, but they never heard a noise from him when he supposedly opened the freezer door.

"Then we have the death of his first wife. That was very mysterious. I mean what are the chances of someone having their wife brutally killed twice?"

"Couldn't he just be extremely unlucky?" Offered Gemma, obviously with a soft spot for PJ. "Or extremely lucky." I resisted the temptation to say.

"The reason we are asking you to do this is because Samantha, his own sister, has expressed her suspicions that he killed his first wife. She also revealed to a close friend, that PJ subjected her to mental and physical cruelty. He burned her stomach with an iron, and she still has the scar. That's not brother and sisters having a go at each other. That's sadism. That fits in perfectly with a profile with someone who would murder his wife – twice – and not feel guilty about it.

"Listen – you know PJ put up this wall of silence, he's

done it to you – he's done it to everyone. He's not said as much two words to any of us. Well the only words he's ever said to the police are No Comment. So we really need to get underneath this wall of silence.

"Just speak to Samantha woman-to-woman and try and get her to open up and see what she says. That's all you have to do, and if at the end of it, she seems uncertain about her brother, ask her if she'll put on a wire."

"OK I wasn't being insubordinate. I was just asking. I'll do it."

Time: 13:00
Location: Weybridge

We wanted an informal, relaxed atmosphere for WPC Muldrew's chat with Samantha. So Gemma got out of uniform and arranged to meet her at the modern bohemian Café Verditer off Weybridge High Street. Matt and me were not able to sit in on the conversation, so Gemma would record it with a hidden mic inside her bra, and we would listen in the car, a quarter of a mile away.

Here's the interview transcript:

Background noise: soft chattering, clattering of crockery, low volume radio playing BBC6. Our recording starts with Gemma in mid-sentence:

"…that's why I wanted to talk to you. Victims of crime are appointed a support officer but that's only ever for the direct victims. We neglect the victims that are outside of that – people like yourself. You've had to put up with a lot…"

"Yes stuff like being followed by the police on the way home from Ligia's funeral."

"Yes DCS Ferdinand can be rather abrasive."

"He was completely out of order. He made me jump. I nearly sprayed him with my Mace." "It would have served him right if you had."

"Would I have got arrested?"

"Not at all. A lot of my colleagues would have been queuing up to buy you a drink."

They both laugh. Good to hear, the ice was breaking – at my expense.

"I understand that you've had to take a lot of time off work to look after your brother. What do you do for work by the way?"

"I'm a medical journalist. I write for the British Medical Journal."

"That's very impressive. Not working today?"

"Well actually I am supposed to be researching an article on pharmaceuticals. But I can do all that tomorrow."

"Did you miss much work because of what happened?"

"I had to take a whole week unpaid leave, but I am back now. Hope to make some of it back by doing some over time, and a bit of free-lancing. I desperately need that next pay-check. What hasn't helped is the sanatorium demanding that their invoice is paid."

"Can't your brother pay that?"

"He's supposed to. Paul says he will, but he says he can't deal with it right now."

"So you call him Paul not PJ."

"Well that's the name he had growing up, the name he was born with. He changed the name to PJ by deed poll after he left Uni."

"Why did he do that?"

"He said Paul James was a bit bland, forgettable. He thought PJ – as in Paul John – made more of an impact."

The chat goes on to boyfriends, and what shows they are watching on Netflix, until Samantha declared this – "I fancy a proper drink, what do you say to a glass of vino down the Hand & Spear?"

"What a splendid idea."

In the car I rubbed my hands, the alcohol would surely lubricate those truth glands. In Vino Veritas.

With a background noise of the roaring wind and the

rustling inside of Gemma's underwear, the discussion as the two women walked to the pub was close to impossible to hear and transcribe. Gemma seemed to be aware of this and so kept the conversation on the subject of Samantha's work and holiday destinations.

Once inside the pub their voices were now much more audible, though the background chatter was louder and more frantic than the café. Gemma thoughtfully found a quiet place for them to sit. On the first round of drinks Gemma answered general questions from Samantha about life as a policewoman. With the second round of drinks sipped, Gemma brought the conversation back to the case:

"That DCS Ferdinand – we call him Charley Cairoli."

"Who's Charley Cairoli?"

"A clown that was famous in the 70s."

"Oh." She laughs.

"He was totally out of order following you after the funeral. But you were put in a really bad position. PJ was still considered a suspect – and so he was supposed to tell us about checking into the sanatorium. By PJ not speaking to us, not communicating with us at all, it puts pressure on the people around him, like you. How were we to know that he checked into a sanatorium?"

"Is Paul still a suspect now?"

"Officially yes. It looks likely that Eduardo Pinheiro killed Ligia. But there are still quite a few things that make PJ still look like a suspect."

"Things like that?"

"I can't really say. But…you know…there's stuff like that whole thing about Chloe Lund."

"What Chloe Lund thing?"

"You don't know?"

"What? Tell me! She's PJ's friend."

"I am sorry to tell you Samantha, but Chloe Lund and PJ are very far from being friends."

"What?"

"That's why he stopped working on the show. That's

153

why he hasn't worked since then. Because Chloe Lund's complaints ruined his reputation in the industry.

"Had you noticed how his social life changed after he lost his job at Shipton Village?"

"Yes I had. I thought that's just what people in showbiz are like – fickle. What else makes him suspicious?"

"We've had a look at his finances. He was getting Ligia to make monthly contributions to the mortgage on Asgard – when he had actually paid off the house outright. We've seen his bank account, he has loads in there. Which raises the question – why are you paying to check him into the sanatorium?"

"He'll pay me back."

"Will he though? I mean he seems to be a bit dodgy with money. The other thing – big thing – that really troubles us about PJ is over the death of his first wife. Someone got in touch about his first wife Kelly."

"Oh Yes? What did they say?"

"That she died suspiciously."

"And who said that?"

"I can't tell you. Sorry. Kelly was a good friend of yours wasn't she?"

"Yes – we were best friends. We met at University."

"What do you think?"

"I don't know, I really don't…I remember him saying just after he got married – the first time – that he was having money problems. They had just got a big mortgage and in order to get it, he had to sign up to a massive insurance policy, in case either of them lost their job, or couldn't work anymore. I remember him saying to me a few weeks before Kelly died – 'I have a solution'."

"Well that's doesn't necessarily mean…"

"No of course it doesn't. Then I remember when mother died. Father died first and passed everything onto her, and when she died everything was to come to us. The two children. In the end because mother needed care and treatment in her final years, we only got fifteen thousand each, and I was

Ok about it, but he was so pissed off, cursing and blaming everything and everybody including me. He asked me to pay him my half." "What a cheek."

"So I did."

"What?"

"Yes I gave him my half of the inheritance."

"That's terrible. Why on earth did you do that?"

"Because he kept going on about it. Because that's what he does – takes advantage of me."

"We were also told that your brother was very cruel to you."

"Who told you that?"

"I can't tell you. But they told us he abused you psychically. He burned you with an iron – on your stomach."

"I still have that scar. Look. You've been speaking to Jung-Ra? Haven't you?"

"I can't tell you. I am sorry."

"I only ever told two people about that – Kelly and Jung Ra."

"I see it all the time in my job – and it breaks my heart. Women who suffer in silence. They don't speak up. It's not just a husband and his wife, or boyfriend and girlfriend – it's also a brother taking advantage of her younger sister. Who takes her for granted, he expects her to do everything for him, who abuses her. Maybe the physical abuse has stopped but the psychological bullying carries on. Even stuff like expecting you to pay for his sanatorium bills. He says he'll pay you back, but why can't he pay the bills now? He can still function, he can still arrange to do those video interviews, so why can't he sign a cheque? Isn't that an example of his on-going abusive behaviour to you?   "You see that behaviour fits a profile a pattern of someone who would go on to kill their wife. So that's why he's still a suspect…(long pause)…Do you think he could have done it?"

"I don't know. God I hope not."

"So do I. For your sake… (pause)…would you be prepared to take a wire?"

"What?"

"Put on a wire and ask him some questions, you seem to be the only person he trusts and he may tell you things…"

"And you want me to betray that trust?"

Gemma floundered for a bit before saying…"Well Yes."

"So all this being nice to me, that stirring speech about women not speaking up, was all just an act to build up to ask me this?"

"No – not at all."

Gemma was doing so well until we got here.

"Well I'm not going to do that." She stood up. "It's just getting to the truth….."

A slam is heard and for a full minute only background chatter can be heard, then Gemma speaks into the mic:

"Samantha James has left the building."

I called Gemma on her mobile – "Gemma you did great."

"Thanks – but I didn't quite pull it off."

"But you had her wavering. It was all very revealing. That stuff about his mother's inheritance. I could really hear her doubting her own brother."

"I didn't become a copper to do stuff like this."

"But this is vital work. Exemplary work. I'd like, no I insist, on buying you a drink. Me and Matt are down the Flintgate. Come join us."

"No I'm plotted here. Come to me at the Hand & Spear. I don't think Samantha is coming back."

"OK – we're on our way. So you think PJ is guilty now eh?"

Time: 23:00
Location: Kingston Police Station

While we had failed to get Samantha to take the wire, my sense of triumph was all about how Gemma Muldrew had got her to open up to such an extent that she revealed some truths about PJ James – the physical and mental abuse, and taking her inheritance. None of this would be admissible in any trial, but it helped convince in my own mind that my target was a wrong 'un and capable of murder.

In hindsight it was me who messed up. I rushed it, I should have got Gemma to meet Samantha earlier and proposed the wire after a series of meetings. But once I got the idea, I had to do it straight away, because after the ID parade, PJ would have got wind that we were closing in and could have absconded.

Money is the great divider. If you have a favourite band that vow never to reform citing irreconcilable differences, the chances are their disagreements are pecuniary. So I had myself a cunning plan to drive a wedge between Samantha and her brother PJ. Playing the cash card was the way forward. So after the pub, Matt and me went back to the nick and worked late into the night to forge an invoice from the Springwater Sanatorium.

This fake invoice was to Samantha James by name and to give it an extra bit of drama we added some red ink – Final Demand! Please ensure payment is made within 7 days to avoid legal action.

We put the fake invoice in an envelope, put a stamp on it and got it delivered it to her door, ready for her to find the following morning.

Day 33 of the Investigation

Date: Saturday 21st April
Time: 10:00
Location: Walton on Thames

You will recall that we had put a tap on PJ's mobile phone. At just after 10 am we were listening in on this call.
"Hullo it's me."
"Huh?"

"Listen I've had another bill from the sanatorium. Can you pay it?"

"I am…I…"

"Look I know you're depressed and all that. But you shouldn't expect me to pay your psychiatric bills. It's not fair."

"Ok. Ok. If you pay it for now – and I will reimburse you."

"When?"

"When I'm better."

"But when will that be Paul?"

"I don't know."

"Well I need to know. The invoice is a final demand."

"Listen Sam I can't deal with this right now."

The sound of hanging up. I wanted to jump in and advise Samantha to not pay it and get PJ kicked out onto the street. Half an hour later, I was at home playing video games with my son when my mobile lit up. It was a call from WPC Gemma Muldrew. I decide to keep it formal.

"DCS Ferdinand speaking."

"Hello I've just had a phone call from Samantha. She's going to do a wire."

Day 34 of the Investigation

Date: Sunday 22nd April
Time: 10:00
Location: Sanatorium, Ripley, Surrey

We sat outside in an unmarked car ready to listen in. Matt with a Thermos flask of Miso Soup and me with a packet of Monster Munch. Gemma had put the wire inside Samantha's brassier at her flat, and Samantha drove over to the sanatorium for a Sunday morning visit. Here's a transcript of their conversation:

Background noise: Twittering birds, occasional peacocks squeaking and human wails.

"Hullo Sam."

Background noise: A rustling sound, whispered inaudible voices.

"Hello Paul. How are you feeling?"

"In a haze. Still. The doctor gave me something new to take."

"What some pills?"

"Yes some more pills."

"How many pills are you on now?"

"Three."

"Do you know what they are?"

"No – they've all got long chemical names. I'd need a degree in pharmaceuticals to remember them."

"It's not a good idea to take pills when you don't know what they are – or what they do."

"I feel alright on them. I'm not monged out or anything. I guess they're something like Prozac. They just numb the pain."   Background noise takes over.

"I trust them here. Look. About the bill. I'll have a word with the people here, and I'll get it paid. Get the invoice switched in my name if that helps."

"OK thank you. The last bill had nasty red lettering."

"Uh! I hate that nasty red lettering. Gives me the creeps. Yes I'll get that sorted for you. I appreciate all you've done."

"Look Paul. You can tell me. You can tell me everything. I am your sister. I will stand by you forever. Whatever… (pause)…did you have anything to do with the death of Ligia?"

Silence. The faint sound of sighing.

"I am sorry I have to ask. You know if you did do it. I would help you. If you needed me to do anything to help, to hide any evidence, I would do it."

"I understand. I understand. The police have poisoned you against me. Made you doubt me. Let me put your mind at rest. I had absolutely nothing to do with it. I am just a guy –

not a perfect guy – if you put the spotlight on anybody's life you will find something not right.

"It's just – you know – what with Kelly dying as well. It looks bad. Yes I know it looks bad. I've had two wives die horribly. But look at the facts. That's all you have to do, is look at the facts. And then look at me – I'm not capable of killing anyone. You know that better than anybody."

"Of course I know you didn't do it. It's just that I didn't want to be, like one of those people, who were so close to their relative that they were blind to them doing something really bad, because they were …you know.."

"So close to them."

"Right."

"I am not angry. I don't hate you for asking, I hate the people who put those ideas into your head that I may have done it. You know I didn't do it."

"I know. I'm sorry for asking."

"That's alright. You see? You see how mellow I am."

That was it dear reader. No tell-all confession. Nothing incriminating. Not even anything dodgy. It was as if he knew Samantha had a wire on her. But my disappointment was not total. Proper murderers aren't in the habit of making tell-all confessions, not even at the prompting of a close relative. They tend to keep that intel close to their chest. I shrugged it off, it was officially my day off, so I drove home to catch some Sunday afternoon football on the telly. I still had a case against PJ, and would go through it all back at the nick on Monday.

Day 35 of the Investigation

Date: Monday 23rd April
Time: 10:00
Location: Kingston Police Station

I had a series of meetings booked for today. The first was with my partner Matt and the only topic on the agenda was – 'have we got enough to nick him?'

While the suspect himself told us nothing, the blow flies, Willoughby the Cat and Brandi the Dog were able to tell us a lot. I put up a flipchart and we ran through the evidence we had against PJ.

After looking at it all, Matt said, "Our coup de grâce is we can put PJ at Winchelsea Station at 4.30 am Saturday morning, when his statement says he is in Oxford." But in order to prove that PJ did it, we also have to prove that Eduardo did not commit suicide. So I flipped the page and ran over the reasons why we believed Eduardo did not take his own life. Here they are:

1. How did Eduardo know the burglar alarm code? Only PJ was a regular at Rye.
2. According to Brandi – Eduardo's dead DNA will be found in the boot of his car.
3. The final text correspondence between Ligia and Eduardo was in English when previously everything had been in Portuguese. This final text correspondence is bogus. Sent by someone else?
4. Eduardo was clearly attacked in West Byfleet as his splash back blood is on the ceiling of the spare room. Eduardo's head injury would have given him concussion. How then could he have driven from West Byfleet to Rye?
5. The blow fly evidence shows that he was dead at 1am or before – but the burglar alarm was turned off at 4am.
6. The driving seat was pulled forward as if a shorter person was driving the car. Eduardo is 6 foot 3 with very long legs and PJ is 5 foot 11.
7. The Toolbox used to keep the accelerator down. Most suicides of this type use their foot.
8. The trophy appears to be recently moved from the mantelpiece in West Byfleet to Rye.
9. The fibre trail evidence that Eduardo was dragged from upstairs to the front door.

Matt then suggested that PJ put the body in the Sussex police's jurisdiction as part of the strategy – because they were a conspiring police force and he knew they would declare the death a suicide. "Like the death of God's banker Calvi and the City of London Police force." I quickly shut down this line of thinking. The normally sane and sober Matt is sometimes given to jumping down crazy conspiracy rabbit holes. We had zero proof of this and I did not want to present anything like this to Chief Constable Hinton. It was bad enough that we were contradicting the finding of another police force.

Then we considered the evidence of the questionable death of his first wife, and the sadistic treatment of his sister.

We stood back and looked at our board, taking it all in. After a long silence. Matt said, "He definitely did it."

"You think? It's not me getting tunnel vision?"

"No. PJ did it."

"Right! Let's call Hinty and get the briefs in."

So now we needed to convince the top brass – namely Chief Constable Hinton and our law firm Chapman Hendy.

Date: Monday 23rd April
Time: 14:00
Location: Offices of Chapman Hendy, Kingston on Thames

For this meeting we walked across the market square to the plush riverside meeting room of our law firm Chapman Hendy. I was to be presenting to my boss Chief Constable Hinton and Clive Hendy, a barrister of some distinction. His slicked back ebony hair and penchant for waistcoats gave him the appearance of a snooker playing vampire, but this was undermined somewhat by a rotund frame.

I put together a Powerpoint presentation which you can view here. The password is *Ferdy* –

http://vimeo.com/user4249006/ferdy

I ran through my presentation and came to the 'Any Questions' bit. Reading the body language of my audience, I could see that Hinton with his arms folded had misgivings, but Clive Hendy, the courtroom showman, was relishing the chance to present this complex case to a jury.

Hinton began: "OK – let me tell you what's bothering me about this."

"Sussex Police?" I pre-empted.

"Exactly. We had a collar. We had a narrative that was presented by the Sussex Police by their own coroner, their team of experts, and we are contradicting that. We should never do something like this lightly."

"But we are not," chipped in Hendy – "Ferdy has lined up a top team of pathologists and experts to demonstrate that this Eduardo fellow could not have committed suicide." Hendy was clearly my ally on this one.

"Absolutely – everything we are saying is backed up either by digital, forensic or witnesses," I said.

"But there's no smoking gun." Complained Hinton.

"Come on Michael," jumped in Hendy, clearly on first name terms with my Chief Constable – "when is there ever an actual smoking gun? It's never that easy. The woman at Winchelsea is as good as. The missing trophy from the mantelpiece is very convincing. The blow fly evidence is impressive. There's a gaping hole in his alibi at the hotel. There is no smoking gun, but there's plenty of evidential smoke." Hendy – my man.

"OK. Let's do it," announced Hinton.

On calling the meeting to a close I pointed to the picture of PJ and said, "This man is guilty of three homicides. I would stake my entire reputation on this – which in fact is exactly what I am doing."

Day 36 of the Investigation

Date: Tuesday 24th April
Time: 10:00
Location: Sanatorium, Ripley, Surrey

We didn't need to over-do it. We were arresting just the one man, who we believed to be unarmed – so just one car load of coppers was called for – no van or a tooled up special unit. And I scheduled the arrest for just after breakfast so we wouldn't need to feed him at the nick until lunchtime. When you work for the Surrey Police you have to cut the costs wherever you can.

So I had a fry up with Matt at the last remaining greasy spoon caff to be found in Ripley village, immensely looking forward to what to me is the second best part of the job – the arrest.

The best part of the job is, of course, in the courtroom when they finally get sent down. I am hoping you will be reading about that later on.

As you have most likely gathered, PJ's 'No Comment' strategy really boiled my piss, so I was going to use it against him in one last interview, giving him one chance to say at least one thing to me before I formally charge him.

We called up Jennifer Janus to tell her that she needed to be at the sanatorium for 10am and she was parked outside when we got there. She came out of her car on seeing me.

"What's going on?"

"We are going to do another one of those fascinating interviews."

"With four police in uniform? You are going to arrest him aren't you?"

"Come with me."

I gestured for the four uniform to join me and, waving my police ID at the front gate, strode into the garden to find PJ wearing another linen suit, this time pastel blue in colour, and sat in a wicker chair. A picture of leisure and relaxation I was about to destroy.

"Hey. Long time. No speak."

PJ looked at me, then looked at Jennifer Janus, then at Matt followed by the four police. He opened his mouth and I thought he was finally going to say something to me – but then he didn't.

I pulled up a wicker chair and run through the usual caution. I wasn't going to arrest him just yet.

I opened with this: "To lose one wife is unfortunate, but to lose two is just careless."

PJ looked at his lawyer, as if to say can't you stop this? Jennifer Janus jumped in. "Have you got anything appropriate to ask my client? If not. I will call this interview to a close."

"Why didn't you show up to your wife's funeral? Golf tournament on TV?"

PJ glared back at me.

"What's the pay out this time? I guess second time around you lose the no claims bonus. Well the good news is that even though she was facing redundancy, she was still working for the company when she died. So you qualified for her death-in-service payment eh? Well you'd know all about that as you called her company to claim it didn't you? How's that going to look to a jury?"

"That's it. I am closing the interview." Interjected Jennifer Janus.

"Wait. I am going to give your client one chance to avoid getting charged. He has to answer just one question – one question only. OK ready?"

"One question?" Repeated Janus with uncertainty. She wasn't sure how to play this, but I was certain she wanted me to charge her client and go to trial. She would love the opportunity to do her thing in the arena of a courtroom of a high profile murder case.

"Where were you at 5.30 am on the morning of Saturday 17th March?"

"No Comment."

"I have a witness who positively identified you at Winchelsea station at that time. What were you doing there?"

"No Comment."

"Paul John James – I am arresting you for the murder of Ligia Valente and Eduardo Pinheiro. You do not have to say anything." (Notice my use of Ligia's maiden name.)

PJ looked at me with pure hatred in his eyes. A grand feeling as I pronounced, "Take him away."

On this command two uniform appeared on either side of him, one slapped on some cuffs and they marched him out.

I looked over to Jennifer Janus. Her face as usual was impassive, neutral – but I think behind the unmoving mask she was pleased. This was all a game for her, an extremely high paying one.

She said to me calmly – "That abusive interview was totally out of order. I'll make sure that goes on the record."

> **PJ's audio testament – Saturday 28th April**
>
> That pathetic Oscar Wilde joke. He is just feeding off my misery. Yes – I had lost two wives. Both had died suddenly. It was just horrible bad fortune, and to make this the basis for charging me is just plain malicious.
>
> So the nightmare had come true and here I am in remand awaiting bail. Dougal has thankfully leant me this handy palm-sized audio recorder. Now that I've been formally charged, it's now more important than ever that I record my thoughts and tell the world my side of the story.
>
> That DCS Ferdinand is either too scared to take on a drug gang, or maybe he's on their payroll, and so has to pin this on someone else. Whatever the reason he obviously ignored that line of enquiry and just picked on me – the easy target. Would he have arrested me, if I'd answered his questions? Probably. I think he just had it in for me.
>
> The real killer of Ligia is either walking free, or most probably has been found dead. I still think Eduardo is the most likely person – but I don't know for certain. What I do know for certain is that I am totally innocent and I was in Oxford that whole week-end and I can prove it. That woman at Winchelsea station is clearly mistaken or was groomed by the police. Or she saw me around Rye on another occasion.
>
> We are heading for a colossal miscarriage of justice and it has to be stopped.

> He thinks he's won. But he is very wrong. This is not over.

Chapter 11 – Interval – A review of other 'Did He Or Didn't He' cases.

In 1954 the novelist Ernest Hemingway wrote: "A trial like this, with its elements of doubt, is the greatest human story of all... This is the real thing. This trial has everything the public clamours for." This quote was about the famous Sam Sheppard case, but he could have been writing about our PJ James/Ligia Valente/Eduardo Pinheiro affair.

Having read this book so far, I hope you have got the impression that I am a hardworking and conscientious investigator, putting in the hours and regularly burning the midnight oil. However my colleague's Matt's commitment to his job is such that he spends much of his spare time reading up on past cases and compiling reports – I think it's something to do with him not having a wife or girlfriend. So while we were preparing for our court show-down, Matt has taken a look at previous cases similar to ours – a dead wife and a husband in the investigative spotlight. He's compiled this overview of 7 of the most notorious 'Did He or Didn't He' cases?

Sam Sheppard
Bay Village, Ohio 1954

Case Summary: Marilyn Sheppard was clubbed to death in her bedroom in the early hours of the 4th July. Dr. Sam Sheppard claimed to be asleep on the couch downstairs when he heard a noise. He ran up and was attacked by a form with bushy hair and knocked out. When he regained consciousness he saw the form again downstairs, and a struggle ensued. He further claims to have been put into some kind of wrestling choke hold and once again was rendered unconscious. The dog was not heard to bark during any of the attack.

The Investigation: Sam said that the family dog was passive and not likely to bark at intruders. The police were skeptical of Sam's story, more so after he initially denied an extra-marital affair with a hospital colleague which he later had to admit. He was eventually arrested and charged for his wife's murder.

The Court case: In a high a profile trial, Dr. Sam Sheppard was found guilty of second degree murder in December 1954 and sentenced to life in prison.

After a lengthy appeal process the case eventually got to the US Supreme Court and Sam Sheppard was finally exonerated and released.

If he didn't do it who did?: Richard Eberling was a handiman and window washer at the Sheppard household. He later served prison sentences for burglary and admitted to having cut himself in the house a few days before, as if to explain why his blood would be found at the crime scene. He also was found to have two of Marilyn's rings in his possession after a burglary of Sam Sheppard's brothers house. These were the two rings the killer tried to take off during the attack.

Comment: Dr. Sam Sheppard was almost certainly victim of a tragic miscarriage of justice. The initial investigation was botched, focusing on his private life and overlooking the forensic blood evidence, which later revealed the blood of an unknown person at the crime scene (not Sam or Marilyn Sheppard's) confirming the story of an intruder. Richard Eberling is most likely to be the real killer. He died in prison serving time for other crimes

Bibliography: The Wrong Man by James Neff

Video: The Dr. Sam Sheppard Trials Documentary https://youtu.be/MrWoJy0SZqQ

Jeffrey MacDonald
Fort Bragg, North Carolina 1970

Case Summary: According to Dr. Jeffrey MacDonald, he was awakened by the screams of his two daughters and found four intruders in his house, including one woman in a floppy white hat who kept saying, "Acid is groovy. Kill the Pigs," over and over. In his testimony he was attacked with a club and ice pick and rendered unconscious. Military Police found him injured next to his wife and he woke up to discover his wife and daughters slaughtered. On the headboard of their bed, the word "pig" had been scrawled.

The Investigation: The Military police were disbelieving of Jeffrey's story, thinking that he had concocted it from reading about the recent Manson Family murders. They believed there was not enough damage to the crime scene to support his claim of a struggle with three other men, and the murder weapons were found to be domestic utensils from the home. So they charged him with murder.

The Court case: Jeffrey was acquitted at the first army hearing trial. The defence claimed that the military police investigators had not done a thorough job on the crime scene, and they had not followed up the lead of Helena Stoeckley, who was believed to be the woman with floppy hat.

However Jefffrey MacDonald's behaviour after acquittal alienated many, including his step father in-law who had been a supporter of his. Jeffrey told him in 1970 that he had tracked down the murderers and killed them. MacDonald later admitted this was a lie, but said it to give his step father in-law some form of closure. An appearance on a TV talk show failed to ingratiate him with the US public.

A citizen's complaint was filed by one of the initial investigators and a second trial began in July 1979. This time he was found guilty and given a life sentence.

If he didn't do it who did?: Looking into Helena Stoeckley will take you to her then- boyfriend Greg Mitchell an ex-army vet who was part of a counter culture community in the Fort Bragg area. Stoeckely claimed that MacDonald was targeted because he denied Mitchell access to methadone and was very unsympathetic in his treatment of him.

She has apparently confessed to being at the house

when the murders have taken place, and accused Mitchell of the murders. It is claimed that Mitchell confessed to the murders before dying.

Comment: This appears to be another miscarriage of justice. A cursory reading of the facts of the case may make Jeffrey MacDonald appear guilty, but closer scrutiny shows that he was in fact telling the truth. The BBC documentary and Eroll Morris'a book as good as prove that Greg Mitchell was the killer. However Jeffrey MacDonald is still in prison and will most likely die there.

Bibliography: A Wilderness of Error by Errol Morris

Video : False Witness (BBC Documentary) https://youtu.be/fxCByoakms8

O.J. Simpson
Los Angeles, 1994

Case Summary: At just after midnight on the 13th June Nicole Brown Simpson and her friend Ron Goldman were found butchered outside Nicole's house, with blood on the paws of Nicole's dog who was alive. It was assessed that both had died two hours previously between 10 pm and 11pm. The first respondent saw a single bloody glove on the grass, along with bloody shoe prints leaving the crime scene and drops of blood apparently from the attacker's left hand.

The Investigation: This went straight to the estranged husband OJ Simpson who caught a flight to Chicago shortly after the time of the murder. It would appear prima facie that this was the tragic end to a sequence of domestic violence, and when surveying the premises of OJ, Detective Mark Fuhrman found another bloody glove, matching the one found at the crime scene, it was decided to arrest OJ Simpson. After a bizarre low speed car chase with OJ threatening to commit suicide, that was broadcast live on television, he was formally charged.

The Court case: OJ hired the best possible defence team, and after a very long televised trial, he was acquitted.

The problem with the prosecution's case was that Detective Fuhrman was revealed to be a racist cop, and accused of planting the evidence. He took the 5th amendment on the stand which made things look even worse. Nevertheless it was a highly controversial decision, which was contradicted by the civil suit taken out in 1997 by the parents of Ron Goldman. This time OJ Simpson was required to take the stand and he was found guilty of wrongful death. The families of Nicole and Ron were awarded $33.5 in damages.

If he didn't do it who did?: In 1980 the BBC produced a documentary plausibly claiming that OJ's son Jason Lnnar Simpson may have done it, and that OJ's subsequent behaviour was to cover for him. The prominent pathologist Dr. Cyril Wecht concluded that the attack must have been conducted by at least two assailants, which works with this theory. Other than that – there are no other plausible theories.

Bibliography: Without a Doubt by Marcia Clark, Triumph of Justice : Closing the Book on the OJ Simpson Saga by Daniel Petrocelli

Video : BBC – OJ Simpson the Untold Story https://youtu.be/QG5CPhGoT3M

Michael Peterson
Durham, North Carolina 2001

Case Summary: On the night of 9th December Michael Peterson called 911 seemingly distraught after finding his wife Kathleen at the bottom of the stairs, heavily bleeding. She was still breathing but subsequently died of blood loss and had sustained a broken neck cartilage.

The Investigation: With no sign of an intruder, there were only two possible causes of Kathleen's death – an accident or Michael Peterson. Scrutiny of Michael's private life revealed him to be the user of male prostitutes. While Michael claimed that Kathleen knew about this and accepted it, the investigators were doubtful and considered it to be a motive for murder, speculating that she may have found out that night from looking at his PC and a row erupted.

It also emerged that Michael Peterson was involved in another case in 1985 involving a woman dying after a supposed fall down the stairs. Michael was the last known person to see the woman alive. While the coroner at the time concluded the death to be an accident, for the trial her body was exhumed and the medical examiner suggested that the death could be a homicide.

The Court case: While renowned blood splatter expert Henry Lee opined on the witness box that the blood stains were consistent with an accident. In October 2003 Michael Peterson was found guilty of murder and sentenced to life in prison. He immediately made arrangements for an appeal, the case for which was strengthened by the emergence that one of the analysts that testified against him, Duane Deaver, was exposed as having fabricated evidence in a large number of other cases.

A second trial was scheduled for May 2017, but Peterson opted to take an "Alford" plea of manslaughter. This means he can take the reduced sentence and officially plea "guilty" while still proclaiming his innocence. Having served his 8 years, Michael Peterson is now a free man but with a murder conviction on his record.

If he didn't do it who did?: There is no evidence of an intruder. Was it an accident? It has been suggested that an Owl could have got into the house and caused the scratches and trauma to Kathleen's head. It sounds outrageous at first, but becomes plausible after serious consideration, especially when microscopic owl feathers were entangled in Kathleen's hair

Comment: Michael Peterson allowed a film crew to cover his life over a 16 year period leading up to the trial and beyond. While Kathleen's sister disowned him and proclaimed him guilty, it is touching to see how all his children stood by him and believed him all the way. There is just too much reasonable doubt to stamp him guilty. Perhaps if the owl theory had been presented at the trial, the

conviction might not have happened.
Video: The Staircase (Netflix) series

Donnie Brantley
Cleveland, Tennessee 2009

Case Summary: The hairdresser of Marsha Brantley had not heard from her friend and client for a while and thought something was amiss. The hairdresser contacted the husband, Donnie, who told her that Marsha had left him, and he did not know where she had gone to. The police eventually investigated and found that she had taken none of her personal belongings, while Donnie refused to answer any questions on the record.

His wife Marsha Brantley has never been found. She never made any contact with any friends and relatives and is now presumed to be dead.

The Investigation: While Donnie gave conflicting stories to different people, he always took the fifth amendment when questioned by police. Without a body and any official statement from the main suspect, the police faced an uphill task.

The Court case: In May 2014 the case was dismissed because of lack of evidence. He was charged again in December 2016 – and the case was once again thrown out for the same reason. On neither occasion did Donnie Brantley testify and he has never given an official account of his wife's "disappearance."

If he didn't do it who did?: Did she really leave without taking any personal belongings or making contact with anyone at all? It strains credibility.

Comment: This is an especially frustrating case as it is apparent that by isolating his wife and taking the 5th amendment, Donnie Brantley was able to get away with the murder of his wife.

Video: Missing Marsha – CBS 48 hours

Shrien Dewani
Lingelethu West, South Africa 2010

Case Summary : While on honeymoon in South Africa, Shrien and Anni Dewani were in a taxi going through a poor township outside Cape Town, a location where tourists rarely go to. The taxi driver was forced out at gunpoint and the two armed men took over.

Shrien was robbed of his valuables but escaped from the car. The next day the body of Anni was found in the back of the taxi. She had been shot, and a number of valuable items such as watches and jewellery were missing.

The Investigation: A palm print on the taxi took the police to Xolile Mngeni. He confessed immediately and implicated other men, and the trail eventually led to the taxi driver Zola Tongo, who was also acting as a tour guide for the Dewanis. The initial story was that Anni was killed in a struggle for her handbag. After being arrested, Tongo then claimed that Shrien had offered him money to have his wife killed and make it look like a robbery. The guilty men were then all offered reduced sentences in exchange for testimony against Shrien Dewani.

Meanwhile investigators scratching beneath the surface of the life of the newlyweds found that all was not well. Anni Dewani had sent messages to her family that she already wanted a divorce, and it came to light that Shrien had been paying money for S&M rent boys.

Shrien was allowed to go back to England where he got treated for post-trauma stress and depression and was put into a clinic under the Mental Health Act.

The Court case:

There was a lengthy battle between Shrien Dewani's legal team and the South African authorities who wanted to extradite him to South Africa to face trial.

However when he finally was put into a courtroom in 2014, the judge threw out the case on the basis that the accusing witnesses were contradictory and inconsistent.

Additionally there was evidence that text messages and phone calls implicating Shrien were falsified.

If he didn't do it who did? : There is no question about the people who actually killed Anni Dewani. The only question mark is whether it was a contract killing and not a robbery. The angle of the entry and exit bullet wounds pointed to Anni being killed as a result of a struggle, and not an execution.

Comment: A lot was made in the British media when hotel CCTV emerged showing Shrien Dewani meeting up with Zola Tonga two days after his wife's death and passing him a package.

While this looked bad for Dewani, Zola Tonga was not known to be implicated in the murder at the time, and the meeting can be explained as Shrien simply paying the balance to Zola on what was owed for his work as a tour guide, and not paying him for the murder. Shrien's silence on this further compounded media and public opinion against him. The South Africa tourist board preferred the narrative of a killer for hire, as opposed to a crime purely instigated by South Africans, but on evaluation – the evidence against Dewani is lacking. It strains credibility that he could have set up his wife's killing on the hoof within a couple of hours of stepping off the plane. Shrien Dewanis is most likely suffering from survivors guilt – but he is innocent of this crime.

Video: BBC Panorama
https://www.youtube.com/watch?v=BSKdTw_5DIw

Harold Henthorn

Rocky Mountain National Park 2012

Case Summary: Dr. Toni Henthorn, wife of Harold Henthorn fell to her death while hiking on a wedding anniversary celebration. Harold texted Toni's brother about the "accident" announcing her death with a "she's gone". The brother suspected foul play after Harold gave three different accounts to Toni's family of how she fell.

Investigators felt the same when they found a map in Harold's car marking the exact spot where she fell with an X. Harold stood to get an insurance payout of $4.7 million from his wife's death

The Investigation: It became apparent that Harold was a controlling and demanding husband who would not allow his wife to talk to friends and family without him being there. One of Toni's work colleagues said that he carried a fixed "perma-grin" which they found creepy and unsettling. He claimed to be a high powered entrepreneur who made lots of money as a fund raising consultant for charities, but it was discovered that in reality he had earnt no money at all in 20 years.

The investigating police were then tipped off about the death of his first wife, who also died supposedly by accident. Lynn Henthorn died when their Jeep fell on top of her while she was helping her husband change a wheel on an unlit road late at night. That sounded questionable in itself and further scrutiny gave rise to more suspicions, not least his conflicting accounts of what happened. To one policeman he said that he tried to save her life by jacking up the fallen Jeep and pulled her out. But to another officer it was a passing stranger helping out that lifted up the vehicle. Harold Henthorn also changed his wife's insurance policy shortly before her death and got a pay-out of $600,000.

The Court case: The defence did not call a single witness, relying on Toni's fall simply being an accident, and there was too much reasonable doubt to suggest otherwise. However Harold Henthorn was found guilty of first degree murder and is now serving a life sentence. He launched an appeal citing that the death of his first wife should have been ruled inadmissible, but the appeal was denied.

If he didn't do it who did?: Except that both deaths were accidents, there are no other theories.

Comment: There is little doubt that justice was served here. His strategy of Marriage – Life Insurance – Murder worked well the first time, but had it been properly investigated, Toni Henthorn would have been saved. **This is why all sudden deaths must be thoroughly examined – even if they appear prima facie to be accidents or suicides.** (*Ferdy's Note – this is Matt's pet cause*).

Video: The Accidental Husband CBS 48 Hours

I need to stress, and I am sure that Matt will agree, what you have read are just case sketches. How can you possibly adequately cover the OJ Simpson case in 350 words? For a fuller understanding, it is recommended you read the books and watch the videos listed at the end of each synopsis.

From reading the above, you will have noticed a number of parallels, but how useful is an exercise like this in helping with the insight into our case? Harold Henthorn may have murdered his wife twice – but does that mean that this is what has happened in our case? Yes it does appear that Sam Sheppard was innocent and the victim of police tunnel vision, but how does that have any bearing on PJ James? While it's fascinating to look at the famous cases in the archive, each case before us must be judged on its own merits, and not be influenced by what's gone on before. However one thing is certain – this list of celebrated 'Did He or Didn't He' cases is about to make way for a new entry.

The Crown Versus PJ James trial is up next…

Chapter 12 – The Ballad of Salisbury Psychiatric Hospital

Date: Saturday 13th October
Time: 10:00
Location: Walton on Thames

I immediately recognized the face and there was a familiar ring to the Lancashire accent. I'd seen him on television but couldn't remember from where.

"I am here to talk about the very real danger of a terrible miscarriage of justice, and about a lead investigator with a chip on his shoulder as wide as the arse of a hippopotamus." Was that a joke? I wasn't sure. But I was certain who he was referring to.

The man continued: "Right from the start this policeman took a dislike to my friend PJ and, overlooked all the evidence that was staring at him right in front of his nose."

The man in the YouTube clip gave an overview of the case, coming to the death of Eduardo -"This suicide note was virtually a telegram announcing his guilt. That's what the Sussex police concluded – and yet this Surrey Police copper, this so called public defender, ignored all of that and went on a witch hunt gathering evidence on my friend. There is not one shred of evidence that links PJ to any of these crimes, and yet this copper has twisted things around to try and prove that he killed both his wife and her ex-husband

"He is supposed to have strangled both of them to death, and yet there are no marks or scratches on his body or signs of any struggle. There is no CCTV, no DNA – nothing that links PJ to this horrible crime. He even has a cast iron alibi – he was miles away in Oxford – for both times when the deaths occurred.

"Why is this policeman doing this? Does he really hate Shipton Village that much? Or is he just a bitter and twisted individual who takes pleasure in terrorising innocent people?

"I've known P.J. James for the longest time. He is a sweet and gentle kind man, though he can be a hard taskmaster on the set. He would not hurt a fly – and he is no more capable of killing someone than a hippopotamus is of joining the Bolshoi Ballet."

Was that another joke? I later learned that this comedian was known for doing a whole routine on hippos.

"PJ James has never killed anyone. PJ James is innocent. This Injustice must be stopped."

The YouTube clip had been uploaded two days before, and had 2,312 views.

I was going to ask the wife about the identity of the celebrity but thought better of it. Her opinion of me would only sink even lower after seeing me being slagged off by someone famous. Surely this YouTube clip was going to prejudice the trial. Despite it being a Saturday morning I got on the phone to our lawyer. Our lawyers are paid enough. The green braize vampire Clive Hendy answered, but did not see any urgency – "we can discuss this at our meeting on Tuesday."

So the trial for the murder of Ligia Valente and Eduardo Pinheiro had been set to take place in November. There had been a number of major developments since the arrest that had consolidated our case.

First off, Zico had made contact with Gabriella Guimares aka GG, the woman who had been on a date with Eduardo the night of the murders. Remember I had tried to speak with GG on the phone, but the language barrier had come between us. Zico had taken the initiative to find her in Sao Paolo and spoken with her in Portuguese. Critically Zico had established that GG had witnessed the call Eduardo made to Ligia's phone on immediately getting the text.

GG was sat facing Eduardo at the restaurant and saw the look of alarm on Eduardo's face as he read the text. Eduardo called Ligia up immediately – and GG heard the voice on the other side. She wasn't sure whether Eduardo had the call on speaker phone, or he was just very loud, but

180

nevertheless she confirmed THE VOICE WAS MALE AND SPOKE ENGLISH WITH AN ENGLISH ACCENT.

This was truly, as Matt would say 'Gargantuan', and backed up the theory that Ligia was possibly already dead and the text was a ruse to lure Eduardo to Asgard.

In fact we considered this so important, the Surrey Police paid for me to go to Brazil to record her testimony. They even paid for a Portuguese translator.

But this was no luxury jolly. I flew economy and the budget only allowed me to stay one night in a three star hotel in the rougher part of Sao Paolo. I was hoping to take in a football match, but there was no time for any leisurely activities. We videoed the interview, played it back to a second translator who confirmed she was saying what we thought she was saying, and I flew back home in the early hours.

Next was a bit of cell-phone analysis on Eduardo's phone. Dorothy 'Dot' Mailer our mobile phone forensic expert concluded that the "What about him? X" text that was sent out at 10.33 and the one minute later text that read "I am coming over now" had both pinged off the same cell phone tower. That tower was in West Byfleet – half a mile from Asgard. This helped my hypothesis that the whole text exchange between the two phones took place in the same house – Asgard – with both Ligia and Eduardo already dead.

Remember 10.30 was the time Rose Barraclough said that a visitor had arrived at Asgard because Willoughby the cat had appeared in their garden.

The other development was that I had ordered a raid of Dougal's garden shed studio and seized the footage on the documentary he was making about the life of PJ. The Witchfinder General was fuming and threatened to sue us – and have us burnt at the stake.

I watched the footage closely, all six hours of it. It contained nothing but PJ talking to the camera, doing take after re-take. I was disappointed not to find anything incriminating, just PJ whining away in his grating nasal mockney accent. It was like watching endless in depth interviews with Blur in maudlin post-party comedown mode. Droning on about how much he missed Ligia and how badly he was being treated by the police in general and me in particular. What it did reveal was that PJ was an awful narcissist.

A nice bit of helpful testimony came in the form of Fred the neighbour. He called me up, saying – "I don't know if this helps" in his black pudding accent. "But when I first saw him on that Tuesday I was looking out the window and he was standing in his drive way – he looked perfectly calm, keeping completely still – like almost bored, like he were waiting for the plumber. Then ten minutes later I'm in me workshop and I hear him shouting and screaming 'She's dead!' over and over when the police woman arrives."

We had some tantalizing evidence, in the form of a White Pontiac being picked up on three CCTV cameras in Oxford at 0.30 am on the Saturday morning of the 17th March. However none of the cameras were able to pick out the number plate, just one unidentifiable person visible in the driving seat. It exactly fitted my time-line of when PJ would be driving out of Oxford to Winchelsea but sadly was conclusive proof of nothing.

Now after GG's testimony my favourite break-through came in the form of a phone call from Chun-Ja to say this. "I will testify. The truth is the truth." With her evidence about the highly questionable death of PJ's first wife, Matt and I were highly confident of a conviction.

> **PJ's audio log – Monday 15th October**
> Ligia's loss was so devastating to me, that at first I really didn't care if I spent the rest of my life in prison, as I am only just about existing. But then again – why should I be punished for something I haven't done?
> Straight after my arrest and being charged, I was put on remand in Wandsworth prison. A god forsaken, terrifying place. Brutality and sodomy echoed off the walls. Never in my life did I think I'd end up in a place like this. I couldn't

help but think of how upset my dead parents must be, watching me from heaven.

How inevitable is sodomy in prison? I was dreading to find out. I kept telling myself – do not show any fear. So as I walked around, I was trying my best to look hard. Not something I find easy to pull off.

I spent a lot of the time in the gym and got talking to a few of my fellow in-mates. One of them, an older chap named Bertie – doing time for murder and robbery – seemed like a decent sort. A good honest thief. He seemed to want to take me under his wing, but I was wary. It could all be a trap. All the time I felt like shouting out loud – "I SHOULD NOT BE HERE."

Thankfully, after 10 days, my lawyer got me transferred to a high security psychiatric hospital.

Jennifer Janus had got all the medical people who I had been referred to in front of a judge, and they all confirmed my depressed mental state, and how I needed to be on constant suicide watch. The judge was talking about sending me to Broadmoor, which I didn't like the sound of at all. Isn't that where they send people like the Moors Murderers and the Yorkshire Ripper? In the end it was agreed I was sent to a smaller, lesser known facility near Salisbury. So here I am.

It was here that I got to sit down and look over the full disclosure file of the police's investigation into me. I got to see what this Ferdy policeman had been doing all this time, and the tortured logic of his case against me. At first I was enraged, but then I was encouraged.

Because if this is all they've got, then it looks good for me. No jury in their right mind would convict someone on the basis of this.

From reading and re-reading, it became clear that DCS Ferdy had been swayed by talking to Zico. For obvious reasons, Zico did not want to accept that his father had killed his mother, and his mistrust of me as his step father meant he wanted to believe I was the guilty one. I completely understand that. I can empathize. But a policeman's job is not to let themselves be overcome with emotion. Their job is to look at the facts objectively.

These full disclosure documents show that straight after the Sussex Police's announcement that Eduardo committed suicide, DCS Ferdinand decided to reject it and instead went on a fact finding mission about me.

You can pull up any facts from anybody's life and put them under the microscope, and you will doubtlessly find things that are anomalous that make them look guilty.

Calling my cat Willoughby is just an example. He was named after Willoughby & Ward the insurance company that sent me the pay out cheque after the death of Kelly, my first wife. The truth is, naming my cat was just a random choice. I was devastated by Kelly's death, but the insurance pay out helped pay for Asgard and allowed me to work on low pay in television for about 12 months, which helped set up my career as a TV director. The Willoughby & Ward cheque made that all possible. It was very welcome and so I thought I'd call the cat Willouhgby. It wasn't callous or evil. I just liked the name Willoughby. If I'd named the cat after the location where Kelly fell – now that really would be ghoulish.

The report talks about the state of my marriage. Yes – Ligia was drifting away from me, and our marriage was not in a good place when she died. But the dubious company she had been keeping was clearly behind the story of her death. Not her stay-at-home husband.

Then I looked at the so-called evidence they had gathered about the death of my first wife – Kelly. All this stuff about it being my idea to choose that location to go on holiday when I told the police it was hers. This is how it happened – having just paid up a massive deposit on a house (not forgetting stamp duty) using up all our savings, Kelly and I decided we could only afford a holiday in the British Isles that year. She asked me to come up with some proposals, I put forward a number of options, about six in all, which included Cumbria and Kelly chose Cumbria. I would have much preferred the Norfolk broads.

About the mobile phone in Kelly's pocket – I was so shocked I am not sure what happened when she fell. Was she taking a photograph, or had she just taken the photograph? I can't be sure, but it's not evidence – until you've been through what I have, you can't fully understand the state of confusion you go through. Maybe she lost her balance when she was putting the phone in her pocket. I can't say.

Then there's all this nonsense about my whole alibi being exposed because the records of the Hotel Malmaison show I made the telephone booking at 10pm. Yes I did call the hotel at that time, but my call was not to make the booking. That booking had been made by me many hours earlier in the afternoon.

My call to the hotel at 10.00 pm was to find out when breakfast was being served. I was calling from outside a pub in Oxford. It might seem strange, but I had been walking around the streets of Oxford on my own and I wanted to talk to someone. I had booked the hotel room at 4pm over the phone and obviously it wasn't until several hours later that they finally processed the payment.

Then we have that identity parade and the shaky testimony of that Cock Malling lady – Petra Grover. They clearly showed her a picture of me, and she just obliged the police by telling them what they wanted to hear. I have a very noticeable dimple on my chin and none of the other men in the identity parade did. So all DCS Ferdy had to do was tell her that they were looking for a man with a dimple on their chin, and influenced her that way. It was a total set up.

Everything that DCS Ferdinand was using as facts against me I had perfectly good explanations for. He had tunnel vision and just had it in for me.

I wrote down my lengthy list of points and gave them to my lawyer. She seemed very positive that I would get acquitted.

Date: Tuesday 16th October
Time: 10:00
Location: Offices of Chapman Hendy, Kingston on Thames

Holding the legal reigns in our case was Chapman & Hendy's top man, Clive Hendy, who hosted a series of meetings at his offices. This particular meeting was held three weeks before the scheduled trial date.

Since Saturday, the celebrity "PJ is innocent" YouTube video had gathered 20,000 more clicks. I had since discovered that the celebrity's name was Terry Snape, a comedian from Fylde near Blackpool, who had moved onto some "serious" acting by taking a role on Shipton Village.

Clive Hendy acknowledged that this video was detrimental to our case, and might influence the jury and said he would speak to the judge to have it removed as "a matter of urgency." This irked me as I had called him on Saturday morning as soon as I had seen the video, and he had been postponed doing anything about it until this Tuesday meeting.

We then had a long session overviewing our case. Hendy put up a flipchart and we boiled the case down to two columns – one listing the good facts that helped our case, and the other column listing the bad facts that helped PJ. After an hour of brainstorming we had this:

Good Facts	Bad Facts
We can put him at Winchelsea Station 5.30 Saturday morning . Eye Witness.	Sussex police had first look at a lot of the evidence of the Eduardo crime scene.

186

PJ alibi shaky. He phoned in his hotel booking after the time we think Ligia was killed.	The conclusion of the Sussex Police. We are contradicting them.
The trophy, possible "attack weapon" has been moved from West Byfleet to Rye.	Can't conclusively prove the trophy was used.
The toolbox on the pedal. Most suicides of this type use the suicidee's own foot. Was Eduardo already dead?	A complicated guilty narrative. May seem far fetched. The jury are going to have to concentrate.
The serious head injuries on Eduardo. How could he drive? Signs of Asphyxia. Broken Hyoid bone.	Eduardo's "suicide" note.
The strange death of his first wife.	What PJ said to WPC Muldrew as first respondent. "Fell in with a bad crowd."
GG's testimony that Eduardo spoke to a male when he called Ligia's phone	The cocaine in her blood stream.
How did PJ know it was Ligia in the freezer without removing the bag, and unzipping the sleeping bag?	
The final text correspondence between Ligia and Eduardo are in English. Suggesting that they did not write the texts.	
The final texts from Eduardo came from a West Byfleet cell tower.	
He comes across as a Narcissist in the video.	He comes across well in the video.
Willougby the cat came into the Barraclough's garden at	

10.30 and not 9.30 – suggesting a stranger did not come into the house until then.	
PJ not working. Getting Ligia to pay £750 a month into a non-existent mortgage. **Is that fraud?**	
Eduardo's car possibly being in Oxford. (CCTV)	CCTV not good enough to give us a number plate of the White Pontiac in Oxford.
The blow fly evidence suggesting Eduardo was already dead at 4am when the burglar alarm was turned off.	
The marriage between Ligia and PJ has broken down. The bitter row at the vets.	No known domestic violence in the marriage.
The Chloe Lund story.	Chloe Lund may not be prepared to come forward and testify.
	Much evidence on Kelly's death is hearsay eg. Jung Ra

On the flipchart our case looked strong with the good facts far outnumbering the bad facts. But Hendy stressed that our burden was to prove our case beyond reasonable doubt. "That is a very, very high bar."

We were, of course, required to hand over to the defense all the documentation we had on our investigation. This will give them plenty of time to think of something to counter all our claims, but I brought up what I thought could be a curve ball. As in something we can say in court, that's not in any of our documentation. This means the defence will not have time to concoct a story, and so they would have to counter the claim on the hoof, or leave it unchallenged.

I was talking about how did PJ know it was Ligia in the freezer? He did not remove the dustbin bag and unzip the sleeping bag. Because if he did, he would have put the bags back on and zipped up the sleeping bag. This question was not mentioned anywhere in the files available to the defence for full disclosure. Roy could mention it in his presentation on the stand, and then Clive Hendy could drive the point home in his summing up. PJ could say he assumed it was her because she had gone missing. But wouldn't anybody finding someone dead in their freezer make sure it was their wife? He had no way of being sure it was her without unzipping the sleeping bag and pulling off the two dustbin bags.

I explained to Clive Hendy that we needed to get across that the marriage between Ligia and PJ was fractured. That's why we needed to call the vet's receptionist who witnessed them having a blazing row the day before we believed she was killed. While the neighbours heard them rowing, this woman had a front row seat. Andy Goddard's evidence on Ligia is hearsay – but may be allowed as Ligia is not alive to present the evidence for herself.

I told them I wanted to present to the jury two time-lines – what we know about PJ, and Ligia's movements. I was going to give them the facts that we know for sure. Ligia's timeline will be verified by witnesses and digital evidence.

"My colleagues Roy and Rupal would go into forensic details with their testimonies, but I will give it an overview."

Hendy chipped in. "Ah! Do not refer to them as colleagues in the witness box. It makes it appear that you are all buddies on the same team."

"Roy and me are certainly not buddies."

"OK nevertheless, we need their evidence to appear completely independent and impartial."

We talked about the death of his first wife, to which Hendy said something I didn't like – "I better warn you – the judge may rule the fact that his first wife died mysteriously as inadmissible. But if it gets let in, we can call the copper you met in Manchester."

I mentioned that Jung-Ra had offered to testify. "That's all very well," said Hendy "but her testimony is hearsay and we will most likely not be able to use it in court. We would need the testimony of the sister."

That might prove tricky.

I had heard from Matt that DCS Christopher Harris of the Sussex Police was nicknamed "Slack" Harris by his colleagues, presumably because of his lacklustre detective work. Because we were contradicting his conclusion on the death of Eduardo we could use this to weaken his credibility on the stand. Hendy was reluctant, saying it was "bad form" for the counsel of Surrey police to mock and undermine the credibility of a neighbouring police force.

We had a long discussion about whether to put the video seized from Dougal the Witchfinder General into evidence. To me, it made PJ look repulsive, and clearly lying about being traumatized by the death of his wife. While the rest of the team thought differently. Hendy said, "The problem is he comes across quite well in the videos. He's got a charm about him. The danger is that some jury members will warm to him." In the end we decided against putting it in as evidence.

We had a bit of a heated exchange over the evidence of Willoughby the cat. To me it was significant that the cat, who was known for running into the neighbour's garden whenever strangers came to Asgard, did it at 10.30pm and NOT 9.30pm.

Hendy was dismissive of this, saying, "shall we call Willoughby the cat to testify on the stand?"

Despite my annoyance, I patiently explained that what was important was that somebody must have driven Ligia home – she couldn't have got there on her own from the off licence at 9.24 to turn on the Spotify playlist at 9.32. She can't have been alone in the house then because the neighbours heard her rowing with a male. Willoughby the cat stayed in the house, supporting the theory that the person Ligia was rowing with was PJ. A stranger did come to the house at 10.30 because that was when Willoughby appeared in their garden.

"Yes but the person Ligia was rowing with could just have been someone else that the cat felt comfortable with," countered Hendy, annoyingly playing the devil's advocate, which of course is his job.

"OK – yes," I conceded "but it still backs up my proposed version of events."

"And it pre-supposes that Willoughby is totally consistent in this behaviour of his, he may have run into someone else's garden, or he may not run every time a stranger enters the house." "Listen this is good evidence, it's got to go in." I asserted.

"OK – but we have to be careful how we present it. It could give rise to levity and mocking from the defence. What with the evidence of Brandi the Cadaver Dog, people could say that the Surrey Police are relying on a herd of animals to do their detective work."

"They do," I said.

PJ's video log – Tuesday 16th October

I am unfit to face trial. My depression is overwhelming, exacerbated by having to exist in incarceration.

They had me sectioned into this place they call a high security psychiatric hospital, but in reality it's still a prison. Bars on the windows, the slamming of the heavy metal doors, the sound of clanking keys and shutting locks, the weirdos wailing out, slopping out in the morning, waking up to the sounds of sodomy. Whatever happened to the notion of being innocent until proven guilty?

I am being given regular counselling sessions, but it's clear these counsellors are detached, just there to tick a box. In no way are they helping me alleviate my grief. But the visits from Terry Snape are a godsend – and that YouTube video of his was a cry of sanity in amongst this wilderness of madness. He's done what I thought was

> impossible. He's managed to cheer me up.
> And what could I possibly do without my sister Samantha? She has always been a rock.
> And of course I really appreciate your visits Dougal and I am so glad that the hospital are now finally allowing us to film these interviews. I know you and Terry keep saying, "When you get off this, it's going to make one hell of a good documentary." But I can't think about that right now.
> Both my parents were gone a long time ago, but I think of them every day. And of course Ligia is forever in my thoughts. She's up there too, sending me strength.
> Ligia sent me a message. She told me that I need to put everything in perspective. Yes I am going through much suffering, but I've met people here who are going through much the same. She tells me that I need to stop thinking like a victim. I need to start thinking positively.
> In November I will be free. I have to believe this.

Date: Wednesday 17th October
Time: 10:00
Location: Kingston Crown Court

"My client cannot possibly face a trial. He is unfit and still suffering from the most severe depression." Proclaimed Jennifer Janus. All eyes in the court house turned to look at PJ stood next to her. He was puffing out his face, and making his eyes look all misty, creating a mask of cartoonish theatrical gloom.

I couldn't help it, I let out a laugh and loudly shouted a "Leave it out."

I was thrown out by the judge for contempt.

In my absence, Jennifer Janus then brought forward a psychiatrist to back this claim up, and a list of all the pills PJ had been prescribed.

I waited outside the courthouse, and presently Hendy came outside to tell me that the Judge had refuted the unfit to trial claim. The trial was still on for November. He would have high fived – but that doesn't fit with Hendy's style of sobriety.

Clive Hendy ran through the court's other decisions – two of them good and two of them really fucking bad.

The two good ones – The You Tube clip was be taken down immediately and the defendant was "admonished" for arranging to have it put up. In Jury selection, members would be refused who had seen the video. The other good news is that PJ was refused bail and he was to remain at the psychiatric hospital.

The bad ones were sledgehammers to our case. The judge ruled that the **death of his first wife was inadmissible**. The defence argued that PJ had just been unlucky and that the court's official verdict was accidental death. By allowing it into evidence would cast doubt on a prior legal decision, when this case should be judged on its own merits, and not prejudiced by previous events. The judge agreed and furthermore issued a super injunction on the press to not mention the death of the first wife.

Hendy then told me that somehow the defence knew that we had put a wire on Samantha and they were demanding those recordings were handed over to them as part of the full disclosure. How did they know about that? Samantha must have told him – how else?

This had not been a good day in court. To me, making Kelly's death inadmissible was a much bigger blow than the victory of getting the YouTube clip taken down. With Jury selection we could have just chosen people who hated that comedian.

> **PJ's audio log – Friday 20th October**
> I had a day long, highly productive, meeting with Jennifer Janus my lawyer, and we went over our case with a fine tooth comb. We did a flipchart exercise of listing the good facts versus the bad facts.
> Jennifer concluded that the prosecution's narrative was convoluted and so there was way too much reasonable

doubt.

How was it possible that I could come up this intricate plot to kill Eduardo and make it look like a suicide, when there was no evidence of any pre-planning?

Yes the blow fly evidence might prove that Eduardo was already dead by the time the burglar alarm was turned off at Rye. But there's no proof that it was me that turned it off.

Yes there might be splash back blood on the ceiling in Asgard – proving that Eduardo was attacked there. But no proof that I did that.

I wanted to ask my lawyer if she believed in my innocence. But I didn't dare. I needed to fully trust her, and if she equivocated about my innocence, it would make me doubt her. It's too late to change lawyers now. I asked Dougal to do a bit of research, and he discovered that Jennifer Janus had a formidable reputation, and was known to be a great performer in the courtroom. I was in good hands. But I wanted her to believe in my innocence, she certainly seemed to.

What had been bothering her was that the death of Kelly might prejudice the jury, and we were both delighted with the ruling that the death of Kelly was inadmissible. It gave me hope that there is some form of decency in the British legal system.

I really hoped that DCS Ferdinand being thrown out of court for contempt would in the end count against him. He really is a nasty piece of work. What kind of person mocks somebody in their grief?

Losing two wives – it was just bad luck – it happens. People can be involved in two fatal car crashes in their lifetime, they can lose two best friends to cancer. Tragic co-incidences happen all the time. As my lawyer said, the prosecution must prove this case, and not base it on innuendo about what happened years ago. Besides – the inquest ruled Kelly's death an accident.

Despite all the medical experts my lawyer presented,

> the judge still decided I was fit to face trial.
> Jennifer Janus had at least arranged that I could remain here at the psychiatric hospital. The staff here tell me that if I'm found guilty I will most probably serve my time in a proper prison which will make this place seem like a holiday camp.
> Well Ok let the legal battle begin.

Date:	Tuesday 23rd October
Time:	10:00
Location:	Offices of Chapman Hendy, Kingston on Thames

"You need to dress smart, but not too expensive." Clive Hendy was giving me his pre-trial pep talk. All my suits are off the peg Mr. Byrites, so I was alright there. "We are NOT going to give them your own personal journey of the investigation. We need to make your testimony as impersonal as possible. "So you must NOT directly accuse PJ of the crime, or attack his personality. You must leave that to me. You must be seen to be impartial, detached even, as if you are following this all to its logical conclusion. But you leave it to me to spell out that logical conclusion.

"And don't try to be funny. I've heard you do that in the past – and it's not worked well."

"Well I beg to differ. At my last trial, the jury warned to me – they laughed at some of my humorous asides......"

"No. We don't want them to laugh. We want them to believe you. That's why you must NOT try and be funny – it comes across as being flippant. You must convince the jury that you are level headed, unbiased, and that you decided to charge PJ by only looking at the facts.

"What the defence will do is put YOU on trial. That will be their strategy. That you had it in for their client and by trying to be funny will make it seem that you are frivolous and reckless with justice. You need to be prepared that the defence will try and destroy your character. They are going to lay into you Do NOT rise to the bait.."

"Yes I am prepared for that."

"No I mean they are REALLY going to lay into you."

"Look I've done a couple of murder trials before. I know the score."

"No – the cross-examination that you will get in this trial at the hands of Jennifer Janus will be on a whole other level. So that's why we need to rehearse you thoroughly so you can handle whatever she throws at you, and you don't wilt on the stand like a Mars Bars in a deep fat fryer. The key to winning cases is to drive the point home to the jury. It's all about Repetition. Repetition. Repetition. The key is repetition of the message – but also to try and not make it repetitive. Sounds ridiculous? It's all about saying and framing it in a different and interesting way each time.

"So I will say things in my opening statement, you will say them in your testimony, and here's the hard part – you will try to re-enforce them when you are being cross-examined. I will try my best to get the witnesses to say the same thing, and finally I will re-enforce the message in my summing up.

"We anticipated that they will go heavy on the fact that cocaine was found in Ligia's blood stream and try to imply that her murder was linked to that and the supposed "bad crowd" she was hanging out with. We know that they will try to show that you did not properly follow up all the other leads of investigation."

"OK let's go for a rehearsal."

I spent two hours doing the mock-trial. I thought I did well, and so did Hendy, but the whole process only served to make me feel even more apprehensive about what was to come.

> **PJ's video log – Tuesday 23rd October**
> I told Jennifer Janus I was going to take the stand. I wanted the jury to hear in my own words my proclamation

of innocence. I wanted them to hear the pain in my voice as I talked about my loss over Ligia, and how I could never harm her. I did not want to hide behind my counsel.

This is why I am doing these videos. So people like you can hear my side of the story in my own words and my own voice.

Jennifer Janus listened to me, and after I had finished speaking told me that taking the stand was out of the question. Defendants should only ever take the stand as a last resort, and past cases show that they seldom end well. An accomplished and rigorous cross examiner will make Winnie The Pooh look like Ted Bundy by turning every vague answer into an admission of guilt, the slightest contradiction into a smoking gun. Instead my defence would focus on laying into the lead investigator.

That's why her jury selection strategy would be to try and pick people with a rebellious non-conformist streak, the sort of people who would readily believe that a policeman would abuse their power. She was going to rip DCS Ferdinand apart in the stand. Big time.

I was really looking forward to seeing that.

Date: Monday 5th November
Time: 10:00
Location: Kingston Crown Court

I sat out the preliminary part of the court hearing where the jury selection was made. Our counsel was keen to not get a jury member who had seen Terry Snape's YouTube appeal or were ardent fans of Shipton Village. I didn't think that made any difference. To me a level of intelligence was important. This was a complicated case, and we needed a jury that was able to concentrate. We didn't want a docile and naïve jury person letting PJ off because he looked nice.

I was still smarting from the judge's decision to make the death of Kelly Hill inadmissible. I thought about leaking it to someone, and then getting that someone to leak it to the press, but they were gagged from mentioning it anyway. But a local paper journalist, for instance Jane Barrow at the Surrey Star, would publish something like that without checking.

I decided against it, not only could the judge then throw out the case, it could also get me into some career ending trouble.

Another annoying legal snag – The TV company that produced Shipton Village put their oar in by raising an injunction to prevent the name of Chloe Lund being mentioned in the trial in the context of her complaint about PJ. Their reason being that they did not want the image of the show tarnished by a sexual harassment story. We were allowed to mention that he got sacked, but not allowed to mention the name of the high profile complainant.

Meanwhile I rehearsed my testimony over and over with Matt. We both thought we had a pretty rock solid case – but I was still bricking it.

> **PJ's audio log – Monday 5th November**
>
> By now the national newspapers had all covered the story, and with that I started getting letters. Weird letters, proposals of marriage, offers of conjugal visits, from these bizarre women. I did not reply to any of them.
>
> I never wanted any fame or notoriety. That's why I chose to stay behind the camera. So the trial is about to begin. I am to sit in the dock, watch the proceedings and say nothing. It doesn't feel right. I am constantly on edge. Not getting any proper sleep.
>
> Back at the hospital-stroke-prison, a hippy inmate who calls himself Wally suggested I start meditating.
>
> "It will do wonders for your psychic healing mate."
>
> So I tried it. I was supposed to be thinking of nothing – letting my mind go blank, but all these visions came into my mind like I had no control over them. And these visions made sounds. They had voices. I saw a vision of my father, who has been dead now for nearly 20 years, and he smiled at me and said "you'll be fine mate."

The next day at breakfast, I was talking to Wally the hippy in the refectory and I told him the meditating was helping, though it was giving me strange visions. He said, "you'll be fine mate" in the exactly the same way my Dad had said it.

It freaked me out a bit, but it also made me feel reassured, that there were cosmic forces I did not understand that were looking out for me.

Chapter 13 – The Trial

Date: Tuesday 6th November
Time: 10:00
Location: Kingston Crown Court

When it comes to a murder case – there is only one truth – they either did it or they didn't. You can't have alternative facts. You can't agree to disagree. The courtroom is the arena where this truth is argued out and finally established. Hopefully.

"Just the Daily Mail and the Telegraph in. I thought we'd get more of the nationals than this," whispered George the hairy-nosed black robed court usher, as he led me to my seat in the press gallery. I was on friendly terms with George, so he always let me have a good courtroom seat. Jane Barrow of the Surrey Star was of course there, and for some reason took her seat next to mine.

"I am looking forward to this," said George "been a while since we've had a juicy murder case at the court. It's a big 'un this. I guess you're quite nervous."

"Indeed I am George," I confessed "I am going to have to sit in that witness box and get cross examined by Jennifer Janus."

"I am supposed to be impartial – but good luck."
He gave my arm a gentle squeeze.

Courtrooms are designed to intimidate the public. The dark mahogany, the large imposing insignia, the pounding of the gavel, the sombre tones from the judges to the ushers, are all there to strike fear in the heart of the ordinary citizen – not just the guilty, everyone. Even coppers like me.

The only people at ease in this environment are the senior legals – the judges and barristers. People like Clive Hendy who walked in with his assistant. He gave me a re-assuring nod as he passed. Next came the defence counsel. Jennifer Janus came in with a flotilla of three young assistants. I looked the other way. Then the police brought in the man of the moment – the handcuffed accused and sat him in the dock. PJ had brushed up for the occasion, with neat hair and a dark blue Paul Smith suit. The main public gallery was in a raised area behind the dock, so they cannot see the defendant. But being in the press gallery I could watch him from the side, but only in profile, as PJ just looked ahead, never in my direction.

This is how the Kingston Crown Court is laid out:

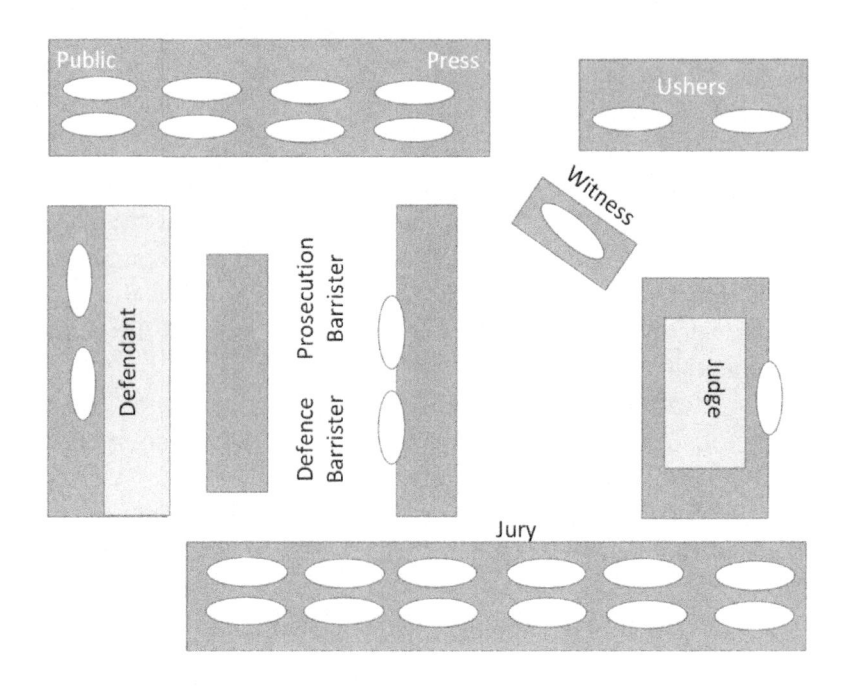

Albert the usher called everyone to order in his best solemn voice and announced the judge. We all rose, and I felt a tingle as the trial was about to begin.

As you are probably aware, court cases have a long pre-amble before the business proper starts. So let's fast forward all of that. What I have for you are the highlights taken from the court transcripts, with the occasional annotation from me:

Prosecution opening statement

Clive Hendy – There is no such thing as a typical murder trial, but this one requires an extra amount of attention. I need to prepare you ladies and gentleman of the jury – you are going to need your highest powers of concentration to fully understand the evidence presented to you. And when you do – you will be rewarded by seeing the truth of this case.

But at the same time we must never lose sight of the tragedy.

(A picture of Ligia is projected.)

By all accounts Ligia was a warm and wonderful person – outgoing and sociable.

On the night Ligia died, she went for an after work drink with her colleagues, which she did often. But this particular social gathering was alloyed by the news earlier that day that their jobs had been put at risk. Ligia was naturally concerned about her financial future, as PJ her husband had not worked for two years.

So this was most likely troubling her when she got home at 9.30 that evening. She put on some music, this was heard by the next door neighbours, but then a bitter row ensued between Ligia and PJ – also heard by the neighbours – and we will show you that PJ struck her with a heavy trophy that was on the mantelpiece.

The blow would have knocked Ligia unconscious. Looking down at his wife prostate on the ground bleeding from her head wound, PJ realized there was no turning back. He did not want to face the consequences of her regaining consciousness.

So he put a plastic bag over her head and hit her one more time – and with her comatose, the defendant strangled her. When she breathed her last breath we believe he turned down the volume of the music playing because he needed to think. The neighbours' testimony is that the volume went down at around quarter to ten, and it is here where he hatched his plan. If there is a murderer's text book, it would tell you that if you want to get away with murder you need to put someone else in the frame. But PJ didn't need to read this text book. This knowledge is firmly in the public domain. It's common sense if you've ever thought about it with any seriousness.

So after 15 minutes of planning the accused then used Ligia's phone to lure the ex-husband Eduardo to his home. The plan being to lay down a false trail to make it look like a suicide – and that Eduardo had killed Ligia.

He then put Ligia in a sleeping bag and into the freezer. Why the freezer? Because that would mess around with being able to establish a time of death. Because as many of you are aware, establishing a time of death is often based on the body's temperature when it is found.

After he chose his course of action, PJ called the Oxford Malmaison and booked a room, paying for it over the phone to make it appear that he was checking in then and there and in person. He then replied to Ligia's earlier text request to be picked up at West Byfleet station 'I am in Oxford remember?'

Next PJ used Ligia's phone to text Eduardo Pinheiro. Ligia was often exchanging texts with Eduardo her ex-husband, often to do with arrangements about their son Zico. But all the previous genuine text exchanges were in Portuguese. This one text from Ligia's phone was sent in English. 'I MUST SEE YOU NOW.'

That's because that text was not from Ligia.

On receiving the text, Eduardo immediately called Ligia and PJ answered Ligia's phone. We know PJ answered because Gabriella Guimares, otherwise known as GG, the date who was with Eduardo at the time, testifies to hearing a male voice.

We cannot be certain exactly what PJ said to Eduardo but it is likely to be something along the lines of – Ligia is very ill and she needs to see you immediately.

This is why the cushions on the bed in the spare room were put under the covers so that in the half light it would look like someone lying in bed.

When Eduardo arrived at the house, it's possible that PJ got Eduardo to write something down on a bit of paper – I am so sorry – in Portuguese. PJ got him to do this so it can be used as a fake suicide note.

PJ then leads Eduardo upstairs telling him that his ex-wife was in the bedroom. Once in the bedroom PJ struck Eduardo from behind with the same heavy object he used to kill Ligia. We know this from the splash back blood on the ceiling of the bedroom. He then used the same method to kill Eduardo. After knocking him unconscious – strangling him with a plastic bag over his head.

He strangled him face down making it impossible for Eduardo to raise his hands in his defence. We found abrasions on Eduardo's wrists. So it's possible handcuffs were used. This is how PJ managed to commit these murders without sustaining any injuries.

He then dragged Eduardo's 88kilo body down the stairs and put him in the boot of Eduardo's car. We know this because there was a trail of fibres consistent with Eduardo's sweater and trousers that went all the way from the bedroom to the front door. We know he was put in the boot because we found decomposing cells belonging to Eduardo.

Taking Eduardo's phone he then concocted a text exchange. Again all in English – which is why we know it was a fake text conversation between two people who, by now, were both dead.

Then, with Eduardo's body in his car, he drove to Oxford to check into his room and set up and alibi. He drew out some money from an Oxford ATM.

He then drove Eduardo's car, still with the dead body in the boot, to his second home in Rye – not using any motorways to avoid the CCTV.

We do however have 3 sightings of a White Pontiac in the Oxford area at this time, although unfortunately we cannot make out the number plate.

The burglar alarm at the house at Rye was turned off at 4am in the garage, so that's when we think he arrived.

The forensics in this case will provide entomology evidence that tells us that Eduardo was already dead at 4am – as blow flies had already hatched their eggs in his head injury and eyes. He had died some three hours before and the flies had begun hatching when the body was in West Byfleet.

Both murder victims were rendered unconscious and suffocated. We will show you the weapon used to knock them out – and how that weapon was moved from his house in West Byfleet and was found at his second home in Rye – having been soaked in bleach. He could have disposed of the trophy, but it is one of the few accolades that the defendant has won in his career in television.

The forensic trail tells the story that Eduardo Pinheiro, instead of committing suicide, was in fact killed in the house in West Byfleet.

So then PJ set about creating the scene of a fake suicide in his garage in Rye. He sellotaped that note on the window – the one that Eduardo had written before. He connected up the exhaust pipe with some garden hose tubing and placed it inside the narrow opening in the car window. He turned on the ignition and then placed a tool box onto the accelerator to keep it going until it run out of petrol. We will show you a video demonstration of how this was done.

The assumption that Eduardo killed Ligia and then committed suicide is false. Eduardo could not have committed suicide for the following reasons -

1) He could not have turned off the burglar alarm at Rye at 4 am Saturday morning. His time of death is assessed as <u>before</u> the burglar alarm was turned off.

2) His concussion and head injury would have made it impossible for him to drive his car to Rye.

3) The text correspondence with Ligia is false. Why was it not in Portuguese?

After setting up the suicide scene in the garage in Rye, PJ now needed to get back to Oxford. He had no car, he couldn't get a taxi as that would lead to a transaction trail. So the only way was to get a train and paying the fare by cash, using the money he drew out from the Oxford ATM. The nearest station was Rye but that was a main station with lots of CCTV. Three miles away was Winchelsea which had less CCTV. So he jogs there – but he has a problem. It was 5.30 in the morning and the ticket office was closed, he had to buy a ticket from a machine which was card only.

As luck would have it, a woman was there buying a ticket and he got her to buy his ticket and he gave her the cash. That woman positively identifies PJ as the man giving her the cash to buy the ticket and you will hear that woman's testimony in this court house.

PJ got back to Oxford at around 9am in time for breakfast. He spent the whole week-end providing us with a whole bunch of receipts to prove he was there. But critically none in the time frame when Ligia and Eduardo were killed.

PJ gets home on Monday. He may have used that day to clear up the crime scene and lay down his alibi – and chooses Tuesday afternoon as the time to find the body of Ligia.

After opening up that freezer door – as an aside we are not certain that he actually did open the door – but after supposedly opening it, he calls the police, and right from the outset the accused put up a wall of silence refusing to answer any of their questions...

Jennifer Janus – Objection your honour, my client has the right to silence, and no guilt should be inferred from invoking it.

Clive Hendy – I am not inferring any guilt, merely stating fact.

Judge – Over-ruled. Please proceed.

Clive Hendy – The accused refused to answer any questions. Providing only one written statement as an alibi of where he was when Ligia was killed.

While the accused has been very clever in covering his tracks and making the evidence point to another killer of his wife, there is an inevitable trail pointing right back to PJ. We will demonstrate that to you with forensic, digital and eye witness evidence.

To uncover the truth we must scratch beneath the surface of the claims in PJ's alibi statement. By doing this we will demonstrate how PJ was at certain places at certain times in order to do what he did, contradicting his official statement.

The accumulation of evidence proves beyond a reasonable doubt that PJ James is guilty of murder on two counts. We will provide that proof in meticulous detail in the days ahead.

Defence opening statement

Jennifer Janus – Wow! Somebody has a very fertile imagination. Someone has watched and read rather too many farfetched murder mysteries. It would be funny if it wasn't hurting an innocent man – PJ James. Not only is my client suffering from the trauma of finding his wife, his soul mate, dead – but within days he also had to deal with the stress of a lead investigator out to get him and accusing him of the most heinous of crimes – while ignoring all other leads and lines of enquiry.

In the prosecution's case you will hear a giddying amount of evidence that will make your head spin. Cadaver Dogs, Blow Flies, Fibre Trails…

But do not let yourself be bedazzled by the BS. Very often the most logical and immediate solution is the true one. That is what we have here. The Sussex Police who investigated Eduardo Pinheiro's death concluded within days that he had committed suicide, most likely from the guilt of killing his ex-wife Ligia, who he had met up with earlier that evening. Eduardo was a troubled man, plagued by the guilt of a previous death – the death of his son in a car crash in which he was the driver. He had been receiving treatment for depression.

My client realized immediately he would be a suspect, and even though he was in a state of shock decided the best thing to do was to exercise his right to silence. No inference of guilt should be made from that. He has the right to remain silent – and it is down to the prosecution to prove his guilt beyond a reasonable doubt.

We believe the eye witness at Winchelsea was "groomed" into identifying PJ at Winchelsea station.

The defence claims that Detective Chief Superintendent Ferdinand did not follow through on the evidence of the drug gang. Just because the Romanians turned out to be a false lead doesn't mean that a drug gang was not involved.

The defence will also show there was no sign at all of any pre-meditation or planning. You do not make up a complicated murder plan like the one proposed by the prosecution on the hoof.

Ferdy aka DCS Ferdinand the lead investigator for the Surrey Police had a problem with PJ and let this colour his judgement. He was blinkered to all the other evidence and just focused on trying to find my client guilty.

This is the statement PJ made the day after his wife was discovered dead.

(She then reads out PJ's formal statement. If you want to read it again it's on page 33. Hendy told me that he considered the opening statement in a trial more important than the closing one, as it's vital to win the jury members over to your side as early as possible. Very often, as a long court case reaches a close, the jury have already made up their mind and have switched off.

While Clive Hendy delivered his opening statement with all the gravitas you'd expect from a seasoned Crown Court barrister, I thought his opening statement was muddled and long winded which gave the Jennifer Janus the opportunity to start off with that "Wow! Somebody has a very

208

fertile imagination." I think Hendy gave the jury too much too early – an overload of information.

Despite my stage-fright I was looking forward to delivering my testimony where I was hoping to put clarity to our claims by showing the jury some of my charts. I was on the next day.)

Date: Wednesday 7th November
Time: 10:00
Location: Kingston Crown Court

Prosecution Witness – DCS Ferdinand

Clive Hendy – What do you know of Ligia Valente's movements in the days leading up to her death?

DCS Ferdinand – *(I had to pretend to be thinking about this before answering, to give the impression this wasn't rehearsed.)* In the days leading up to her death she went to work as normal. From Monday through to Friday we have her work colleagues and work emails to verify that. We know that on Thursday morning, the day before we believe she was killed, she went with PJ to the vets with Willoughby – that's the name of their cat – who was suffering from anaemia. A heated argument took place over the vet's bill between PJ and Ligia. We know this because we spoke to the lady on the reception desk. After the vet, she got the train to work.

We know that on the Friday afternoon at work she was told that her job at the Events company was put at risk of redundancy. Her whole department was put at risk, so after work she went for a drink with her work colleagues – she bought a bottle of wine – and a work colleague, Andy Goddard, bought another bottle about half an hour later that they shared.

Clive Hendy – What did you find from her email correspondence?

DCS Ferdinand – The two people she corresponded with the most, were Eduardo her ex-husband, and her son Zico. All the emails to these two people were always in Portuguese.

209

Clive Hendy – Why is that important?

DCS Ferdinand – Because the only exception to that was her final texts to Eduardo which were in English. That's why we believe these were sent by the killer.

Jennifer Janus – Objection your honour, the witness is speculating.

Judge – Sustained. Kindly refrain from speculating. Just give us the facts.

DCS Ferdinand – Sorry. Your honour.

I'd like to show you a chart of Ligia's movements if I may.

This chart went up on the big screen:

Time	Activity	Verification
18.31	Ligia is at the Marquis Pub, Covent Garden	bank card + witness
20.34	Ligia sends text to PJ requesting pick up at train station	PJ's phone
20.53	Ligia boards train at Waterloo	Station CCTV
21.21	Ligia alights train at West Byfleet	Station CCTV
21.27	Ligia is at West Byfleet buying wine	bank card + witness
21.35	Ligia is at home playing the Spotify play-list	Laptop forensic
21.36	A row ensues	Witness – next door neighbours

On the day we believe she died, we know for a fact that she was in West Byfleet at 21.27 because she bought a bottle of wine at the off licence by the station – and she somehow managed to get home at 21.35 – because she activated her Spotify play list.

Clive Hendy – How could she have got home so quickly? In eight minutes?

DCS Ferdinand – Exactly. She couldn't have got a taxi – because none of the local firms have any records of any fare picking her up from the station to anywhere near her house, and she didn't get an Uber, because they have a collective database and Uber also confirmed that they had taken no fares from the station to anywhere near her home.

So in order to get from West Byfleet to her home two miles away, she either ran very fast or got a lift. Looking at

PJ's phone records, she would often text him with a time of her train coming in, requesting a lift from the station. PJ would acknowledge these texts with an OK, but on this Friday he replied hours later, at 21.55 – at a time we believe Ligia was already dead.

Now it's possible that she was in fact picked up by PJ and he did send a text acknowledgement but then deleted it. We saw that the defendant had downloaded SafeWiper. That's an app that allows you to delete texts irreversibly and without a trace. He downloaded this app on the Sunday – two days after Ligia's death.

Jennifer Janus – Objection! Come on! The witness is speculating again.

Judge – Sustained.

DCS Ferdinand – Sorry your honour. But this needs to be stressed – Ligia sent her text to PJ at 20.34 to be picked up at 21.21. PJ's reply about Oxford came out at 21.55 – that is close to an hour and a half after receiving the original text, and a full half an hour after she was requesting to be picked up.

Clive Hendy – But maybe he was in Oxford and only received the text just then.

DCS Ferdinand – No. Because we got hold of PJ's phone and it shows he received the text on his phone at 20.34. And the reply couldn't come any earlier because it was actually sent on his phone at 21.55.

Clive Hendy – What did you find at Asgard – the crime scene?

DCS Ferdinand – We found a glass in the cupboard with residual traces of the Chablis that she bought at the off licence. So it appears she got home and poured herself a glass of wine, and so it also appears someone poured the glass of wine away and put it in the cupboard.

It appears also that someone cleared up the scene. Blood was wiped away, though we were able to locate what was left of the blood through Brandi the cadaver dog.

My colleagues, sorry, other witnesses, Roy and Rupal will be able to take you through all our forensic findings.

Clive Hendy – You got a warrant to search's PJ's PC and phone. What did you find?

DCS Ferdinand – It was clear that their marriage was in a bad place.

Jennifer Janus – Objection.

Judge – Over-ruled.

DCS Ferdinand – In a bad place. By studying the text and email correspondence – there was a coldness, a distance between them. Never any affection. Just one kiss in a text at the end which we think came…Ok sorry…

I'd like to show the text messages if I may.

(A graphic of the text exchange between Ligia and PJ was shown.)

They were regular disputes over money, and it was clear that PJ not working was causing Ligia a lot of stress.

Also the circumstances of his sacking really upset her. PJ was sacked after complaints from a member of staff – a woman – involved in the show Shipton Village. So there was no chance of him being hired again by the show.

Jennifer Janus – Objection your honour – the witness is talking about a Human Resources matter which is of no relevance and is not yet resolved.

Judge – Over-ruled. This is relevant.

DCS Ferdinand – Thank you. Ligia read an email outlining the reasons why he was sacked and the nature of the complaint – that he was hassling a female member of the team – and naturally she was very angry.

Let me show you the email correspondence where Ligia says this.

Judge – Before you show it to the jury. I need to make sure. Has it been redacted?

DC Ferdinand – It is redacted your honour.

I projected up this email exchange:

You fucked up the Shipton Village job – by perving over ■■■■■■■■■.
I was NOT perving over ■■■■■■■■■ it

212

> wasn't like that.
>> How was it then? You were special friends? Is that why she insisted you were kicked off the show?
>> She didn't insist I was kicked off the show. SHE TOLD ME HERSELF!!!!!

DCS Ferdinand – As you can see from this email exchange, Ligia actually contacted the woman – the redacted woman – and she confirmed that PJ was inappropriate with her. So Ligia's resentment of PJ came across in their texts and emails. Which were generally about paying bills – feeding the cat, picking up dinner, and getting a lift from the station.

Clive Hendy – What did you find by going into bank records?

DCS Ferdinand – We found something rather amiss. PJ had arranged that Ligia pay £750 a month supposedly to contribute to the mortgage of Asgard.

I have this email from PJ – 'Don't worry – the Mortgage is going through fine. I am paying my half with the savings from the Shipton Village.'

This is an outright lie. When we delved into his financial records PJ owned Asgard outright. He was a cash buyer in 2007 after he got a massive pay out after the death of....a relative. (*Note – I had to resist the temptation to say he had bought the house after the insurance pay out from the death of the first wife.*)

So there was no mortgage. PJ was getting Ligia to pay him £750 a month for a non-existent mortgage and the money was just for his benefit. It's possible Ligia discovered this that night. That would be enough to trigger a bitter row.

Jennifer Janus – Objection – More speculating.

Judge – Over-ruled.

DCS Ferdinand – The neighbours Fred and Rose Barraclough said they often heard rowing – and they did on the night we believe Ligia was killed. We did an audio test in the Barraclough's kitchen and discovered that raised voices could only be heard coming from Asgard – Number 5 – the house

213

directly next to them and not from any of the other houses nearby. These test results we can provide. Then the rowing stopped suddenly and then so too did the music.

Clive Hendy – Would you like to show us the video of your interview with PJ on the day she was found dead?

DCS Ferdinand – Yes I can, but it's rather boring.

They play back the first interview tape.

DCS Ferdinand – The police interviewed PJ 4 times – and the only words he ever said to any of us were 'No Comment'.

But of course that is his absolute right.
(I said this trying to add a touch of sarcasm.)

Date:	Thursday 8th November
Time:	10:00
Location:	Kingston Crown Court

As Jennifer Janus stood up to do her cross-examination, my heart went a-flutter. In her thick war paint make-up, she looked fierce and ready to rumble. I was in for a bumpy ride.

Cross–examination

Jennifer Janus – Ligia visited Brazil in September 2017. Did you know about that?

DCS Ferdinand – Yes. She visited her relatives. Eduardo's family.

Jennifer Janus – There was reason to believe she brought back with her a quantity of drugs.

DCS Ferdinand – I found nothing of the kind. Trawling through her emails, her contacts, nothing at all.

Jennifer Janus – She's not likely to announce that she's smuggling drugs in an email is she?

DCS Ferdinand – No. But we found no coded emails, or any contact with a third party that she had arranged anything.

Jennifer Janus – But you did not have access to her phone?

DCS Ferdinand – Well we had the phone, but it was frozen so we couldn't get any data from it.

Jennifer Janus – So the trafficking arrangements could have been made on that.

DCS Ferdinand – Maybe. But as I say – we found no evidence of any drug trafficking arrangements. And normally people do that sort of thing for money. We found no payments…

Jennifer Janus – Drug payments are normally in cash…

DCS Ferdinand – Not always. But there was no spending spree… I can't presume she's dealing with drugs. The evidence available to me showed no sign of it.

Jennifer Janus – The autopsy found traces of cocaine and alcohol in her system. Is that correct?

DCS Ferdinand – Yes. But can I add that the autopsy did not find any heavy sustained use of cocaine. Just recent use of cocaine.

Jennifer Janus – So she was a light cocaine user?

DCS Ferdinand – Yes.

Jennifer Janus – So that makes it alright?

DCS Ferdinand – No. But it means she was not a raging coke fiend.

Jennifer Janus – Who was supplying cocaine to her?

DCS Ferdinand – We identified someone who we think had supplied it to her. As in giving her a line at the pub.

Jennifer Janus – That person is Andy Goddard.

DCS Ferdinand – Possibly.

Jennifer Janus – Andy Goddard was also the person plying her with alcohol. Correct?

DCS Ferdinand – No he was drinking with her. She bought a bottle at the pub and then he bought a bottle of the same type at the same pub.

Jennifer Janus – A neighbour reported seeing a group of four men inside a white van around the corner from the house where Ligia was found – is that right?

DCS Ferdinand – No. It was three men the witness saw in the van. He said that one of the men had a tattoo. A tattoo with a distinctive 8 point star tattoo. We did a public appeal to find the owner of that tattoo.

Jennifer Janus – You met the Romanian gang in the pub. Is that right?

DCS Ferdinand – Yes – but they aren't "a gang" – they just work together in a flooring company. The man who owns the company is Dan Lupescu and I met with him and his team. I wanted to make the first interview informal because I didn't want them to clam up – and them give me the "No Comment."

Jennifer Janus – So your interviewing of them was a loose laid back affair.

DCS Ferdinand – Well they were very forthcoming – they answered all my questions. Mr. Lupescu showed me his order book – plus their forward bookings. They were working flat out. If they were drug dealers or paid assassins, they was very little time for any of that.

Jennifer Janus – You did not think that some of those entries were coded?

DCS Ferdinand – Yes – so we checked every job on their order book, and they were all private individuals and bona fide tiling jobs. Pictures were taken of the work they did. Most of the jobs got trust a trader reviews.

Jennifer Janus – Did you check them all yourself personally?

DCS Ferdinand – No I didn't Huey, Dewey and Lewey did that.

Jennifer Janus – Who?

DCS Ferdinand – That is my research team. My nickname for them. But I did personally speak with the woman who had hired them on the night in question. The Australian woman who lived on the street next to the crime scene. So unless the woman was also in on the hit of Ligia – I had to rule them out.

Jennifer Janus – And with that you ruled out the whole drug gang line of investigation?

DCS Ferdinand – No I did not – but once I ruled out Daniel Lupescu and his tilers who were parked nearby I had no other evidence of any gangs being involved. None at all.

Jennifer Janus – But you stopped looking for any drug gang?

DCS Ferdinand – No I did not stop looking, but there were no other leads to take us in that direction.

Jennifer Janus – What about when Ligia went to Brazil? It is believed she had been a drug mule, taking drugs from South America into the UK. It is also believed she held back some of the drugs, which is why the drug gang were after her.

DCS Ferdinand – Well who believed this? Who's speculating now? What evidence do you have?

Jennifer Janus – PJ suspected her of doing this.

DCS Ferdinand – Well PJ never told me about this, and I did not hear it from anybody else. There is absolutely no evidence of this. Her trip to Brazil was to see Eduardo's relatives in Sao Paolo – nothing suspicious was found.

Jennifer Janus – You met with Andy Goddard is that right?

DCS Ferdinand – Yes I did,

Jennifer Janus – And Andy Goddard was the man who was with Ligia on the day she is believed to have been killed.

DCS Ferdinand – That's right.

Jennifer Janus – And you chose not to consider him as a suspect.

DCS Ferdinand – Of course I did. I raised a warrant to search his flat on Day3 of the investigation.

Jennifer Janus – And what did you find?

DCS Ferdinand – We found nothing in his flat that was relevant to this case. But he remained a suspect.

Jennifer Janus – Did you find anything else?

DCS Ferdinand – Not anything that would help us find Ligia's killer.

Jennifer Janus – PJ said that he had reason to believe that Goddard had been supplying Ligia with cocaine.

DCS Ferdinand – Maybe. PJ never said this to me. But supplying someone with cocaine, is not the same as killing them.

Jennifer Janus – What? But it means they move in illegal circles. Were you aware that this Andy Goddard had feelings for Ligia?

DCS Ferdinand – Yes I did. He told me. On the record.

Jennifer Janus – It's in the transcript of your interview with him.

DCS Ferdinand – Yes. As I say – on the record.

Jennifer Janus – Would that not make him a top suspect?

DCS Ferdinand – Yes it did. Very much so. That's why I said to him at the time something like 'that's the top reason for killing someone.' That's also on the record. But I ruled him out – because we know for a fact that Ligia was on the train to West Byfleet at 20.53 and she bought a bottle of wine at West Byfleet at 21.27.

In that time Andy Goddard went back to his flat to create a digital trail of activity on his computer at home.

Jennifer Janus – How can you be sure it was him creating that digital trail?

DCS Ferdinand – Because the social media postings and comments and sites he visited were all consistent with his previous activity.

Jennifer Janus – But someone could have been posing as him, and doing it before. Instead – maybe Goddard followed her home? Maybe after getting the brush off from her?

DCS Ferdinand – That is a possibility – but no evidence of that came forward.

Besides we picked up Ligia on the CCTV at Waterloo station and West Byfleet. We actively looked for someone following her – considering Goddard as a possible suspect. But we found nobody that appeared to be following her. We counted around 20 people getting off at West Byfleet station and identified them all.

Jennifer Janus – But it's still possible someone was following her?

DCS Ferdinand – Not picked up by the CCTV. But – yes it is. But highly unlikely.

Jennifer Janus – You raided the offices of TV Producer Dougal MacPherson. Why did you do that?

DCS Ferdinand – PJ had asked him to film some interviews with him, to tell his story – I needed some information on him as he was refusing to answer any of my questions.

Jennifer Janus – Objection. Your honour. He is inferring guilt.

Judge – Over-ruled.

DCS Ferdinand – This is exactly why I ordered the seizure of that video. PJ had not said one word – one word to me. Apart from No Comment. All I had was a typed up statement given to me by you – his lawyer.

Jennifer Janus – Why did you not put that video footage into evidence?

DCS Ferdinand – It's just him droning on about how the world is against him. It's deeply tedious – and we didn't want to bore the jury.

Jennifer Janus – Do you watch Shipton Village?

DCS Ferdinand – How is that relevant?

Jennifer Janus – Of course it's relevant. My client is a director on the show.

DCS Ferdinand – Well actually no. He was thrown off the show. Chloe Lund....sorry......

That's why he hadn't worked on the show.

Jennifer Janus – You took an instant dislike to my client. Because to you he is a successful person and represents a world that you are excluded from.

DCS Ferdinand – What world would that be?

219

Jennifer Janus – A world of glamour.

DCS Ferdinand – (I laugh).I did not –…That's right – I so wish I lived in a world of glamour …I'm so jealous…(I checked my sarcasm)

It's a world of glamour that he was also excluded from – after all he got the tin tack from Shipton Village and his friends in showbiz cut him off. He was never going to be invited back and he hasn't worked in television since.

Jennifer Janus – There you are. You are motivated by spite.

Judge – DCS Ferdinand please adopt a more appropriate tone.

DCS Ferdinand – Apologies your honour.

Jennifer Janus – So you need to answer my original question – do you watch Shipton Village?

DCS Ferdinand – No.

Jennifer Janus – You hate the program.

DCS Ferdinand – Well how can I hate it? I've never seen it.

Jennifer Janus – Does celebrity smugness annoy you?

DCS Ferdinand – Not especially. I am not a fan of smugness though.

Jennifer Janus – Does your wife watch Shipton Village?

DCS Ferdinand – How is that relevant?

Jennifer Janus – You seem so keen to put the spotlight on PJ's marriage. How about yours?

DCS Ferdinand – Well my wife's not dead in a freezer. If she was, I would expect someone to put my marriage in the spotlight.

Jennifer Janus – Ah! The flippant Detective Chief Superintendent Ferdy is coming out now. So this is all a big laugh for you isn't it?

DCS Ferdinand – Absolutely not. I take my job very seriously.

Jennifer Janus – Then why aren't you answering my questions? Does your wife watch Shipton Village?

DCS Ferdinand – I have no idea if she watches it or not.

Jennifer Janus – Why do they call you the laughing policeman?

DCS Ferdinand – I had no idea they call me the laughing policeman. Who calls me that?

Jennifer Janus – The word gets around. You are Ferdy the laughing policeman – the man who likes to have a laugh on the job.

DCS Ferdinand – Well I'm not having much of a laugh now.

Jennifer Janus – How many homicides do you investigate a year?

DCS Ferdinand – Well I'd say 5 or 6 a year.

Jennifer Janus – So you're not really that used to dealing with murder cases then.

DCS Ferdinand – Well thankfully homicides in Surrey are quite rare.

Jennifer Janus – So you're hardly experienced and seasoned.

DCS Ferdinand – I am experienced in all sorts of crime – including homicide.

Jennifer Janus – What made this case different from your previous cases?

DCS Ferdinand – All the cases are different in their own way.

Jennifer Janus – And how is this one specifically different?

DCS Ferdinand – The body in the freezer was an attempt to mess around with establishing the time of death. Most other murders don't have that level of planning.

Jennifer Janus – So this murder was planned. That contradicts that you think she was killed on the spur of the moment by a row.

DCS Ferdinand – No because the planning was made after the killing. That's why the music was turned down – to concentrate and hatch the plan.

Jennifer Janus – Can I suggest that this case had more of a mystery element to it than the murder cases you are used to? It's more of a whodunit.

DCS Ferdinand – No. I investigated a case last year the Slaughter on Thames case – that was a real whodunnit. You might have heard about it.

Jennifer Janus – Can you tell me about the first time you met Ligia's son Zico?

DCS Ferdinand – *(This question threw me. We did not anticipate them asking questions about Zico.)* I met him later on the day after Ligia was found. We had to track him down first to notify him.

Jennifer Janus – He must have been extremely upset.

DCS Ferdinand – Absolutely – what made it worse is that he had to identify Ligia's body. That's because PJ refused.

Jennifer Janus – Right. So you bore a grudge against PJ for that.

DCS Ferdinand – *(I did not rise to the bait)*. No. I just thought it unfair. PJ had already seen Ligia dead, it was horrible that the son had to identify his mother's body. He shouldn't have had to see her like that.

Jennifer Janus – And after that, Zico stayed in constant contact with you throughout the investigation?

DCS Ferdinand – I kept him updated about the investigation. No more than that.

Jennifer Janus – We have evidence of you meeting with Zico. And an on the record interview where he attempted to smear the name of PJ.

DCS Ferdinand – He was just telling me he didn't like PJ.

Jennifer Janus – So Zico influenced you in accusing PJ. Because he did not like the narrative of his mother being killed by his father.

DCS Ferdinand – No not at all. What influenced me was the evidence – nothing and no one else.

(That was it! I blew a massive huff of relief as I stepped down from the witness stand. Jennifer Janus was a fearsome

harpies, glaring at me malevolently as she fired off her questions. But I did not wilt. My Mars bar remained solid and upright against the hot grease of her fryer. I was on the stand for two days – ten hours in total. Having run my court room marathon, I felt drained and was hoping that my anxiety would now subside. Sadly no. I still felt the knot of nerves in my stomach as I sat and watched the rest of the trial as a spectator in the press gallery.)

> **PJ's audio-log – Thursday 8th November**
>
> I was hoping to see Jennifer Janus demolish Ferdy on the stand. Make him break down and admit to faking evidence, and the judge would throw the case out, and I could go home. But that was probably expecting too much.
>
> But Jennifer Janus was very pleased with how it went, and if she's happy – then so am I.
>
> So strange to spend the whole day sat in the dock of a court room. I don't recommend it.
>
> I am raised up for all to see, but the main public gallery is behind me, so I can only sense the eyes burning into the back of my head. I know Sam is there, my loyal sister, who's taken unpaid leave to give me moral support. But I can't see her. There is the press gallery to my left, where that bastard Ferdy sits, so I avoid looking over there at all costs. I don't know where to look, so I spend most of the time just looking forward, or at the person speaking at the time. Occasionally I would catch the eye of a jury member to the right of me, and they would quickly look away. I just hoped our eyes locked long enough, for me to send a signal to them saying, "I am human. I am not a monster. I did not kill my wife. I am innocent."

Date: Friday 9th November
Time: 10:00
Location: Kingston Crown Court

Prosecution Witnesses

As I took my seat in the press gallery, Jane Barrow slid next to me asking – "On the stand you said the name of the actress Chloe Lund. What was all that about?" I brushed her away with a "I can't tell you."

On the order of play today we had the following prosecution witnesses:
- Rupal Chakrabharti with the video evidence of Brandi the Cadaver Dog.
- Roy Hughes
- WPC Muldrew
- Rose Barraclough
- Fred Barraclough
- Andy Goddard

Rupal Chakrabharti

(Rupal is usually quite lively and engaging, so I had high hopes for his testimony.)

Clive Hendy – What is your area of specialism?

Rupal Chakrabharti – I am a blood splatter specialist analyst, I concern myself with the physics of liquids. But I am also here to tell you about the evidence provided by Brandi the cadaver dog.

Clive Hendy – Can you explain to the jury what a cadaver dog does?

Rupal Chakrabharti – Brandi the Cadaver Dog has been trained to detect where dead tissue has been secreted. Simply put – Brandi can smell death. A dog's sense of smell is 1,000 times greater than ours and Brandi can locate where decomposition has been, which means he can locate body parts, tissue, blood and bone. He can also detect residue scents, meaning that he can tell if a body has been in a place, even if it's not there any more.

But what Brandi does is not evidence or proof of anything in itself. What he does is point the forensic team in the right direction to where forensic evidence can be found.

For instance with the first crime scene, it is a large house, and it would take a very long time to run a Luminol test

224

all over the house, but Brandi was able to tell them where to look. He saved them a lot of time.

Clive Hendy – OK for the jury – Luminol is a chemical that shows up blood if it's been cleared up. OK. How long does a dead body need to be in a certain spot in order to leave a scent for the cadaver dog?

Rupal Chakrabharti – Ten minutes approximately. We have tested Brandi on this – many times. I could arrange for a demonstration in this courthouse, it is very impressive.

Clive Hendy – No there's no need for that. Unless the jury requests it. But you can show us the video of him finding the kill location in the house.

(The lights were dimmed and a video was shown of Brandi doing his stuff in Asgard. It brought back fond memories. When Brandi found the spot by the mantelpiece and did his bark and appears to be smiling, the jury gave a warm laugh.

Rupal then showed a second video from the work done on Eduardo's Pontiac.)

Rupal Chakrabharti – So that's how we found much residual tissue in his car. You may say – it is the car of Eduardo Pinheiro so it is normal to find his DNA in his car. But so much of it in his boot?

Clive Hendy – OK let's talk about the blood splatter in this case.

Rupal Chakrabharti – Ah Yes! We have three in this case.

I will first talk about each blood splatter location and then the blood splatter itself.

(The man was about to enter hog's heaven!)

Location 1 – was close to the mantelpiece. This has been cleared up, wiped away with something like a J cloth, so just traces remain. What we see here is not a splash from wiping, but residual of blood picked up by the Luminol.

The blood belongs to Ligia James and the direction of this splatter gives us an indication of where she was standing and where her attacker was standing when she was struck.

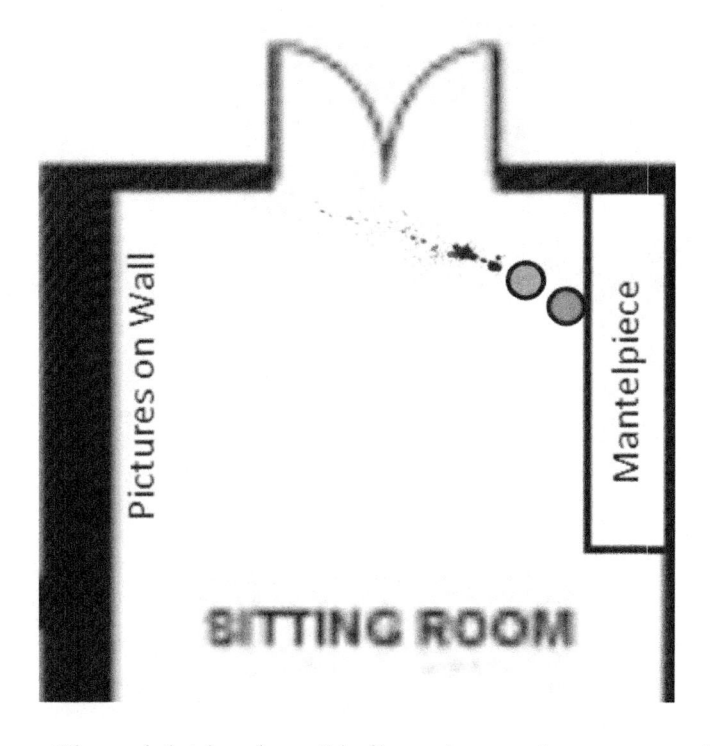

[Floor plan labeled: Pictures on Wall, Mantelpiece, SITTING ROOM]

The red dot is where I believe the attacker was standing and the blue dot is the victim. More would be found on the cloth used to wipe the floor. But the cloth was never found.

It seems that the victim was hit once. The victim had two head injuries so it appears they were hit again with their head inside a dustbin bag. The body was found with their head inside two dustbin bags. The inner dustbin bag had a tear in it, indicating that second blow was made with that dustbin bag on the head.

Clive Hendy – OK – let's look at Location 2.

Rupal Chakrabharti – Yes Location 2 is the ceiling of the spare bedroom.

Pillows arranged to look like a body

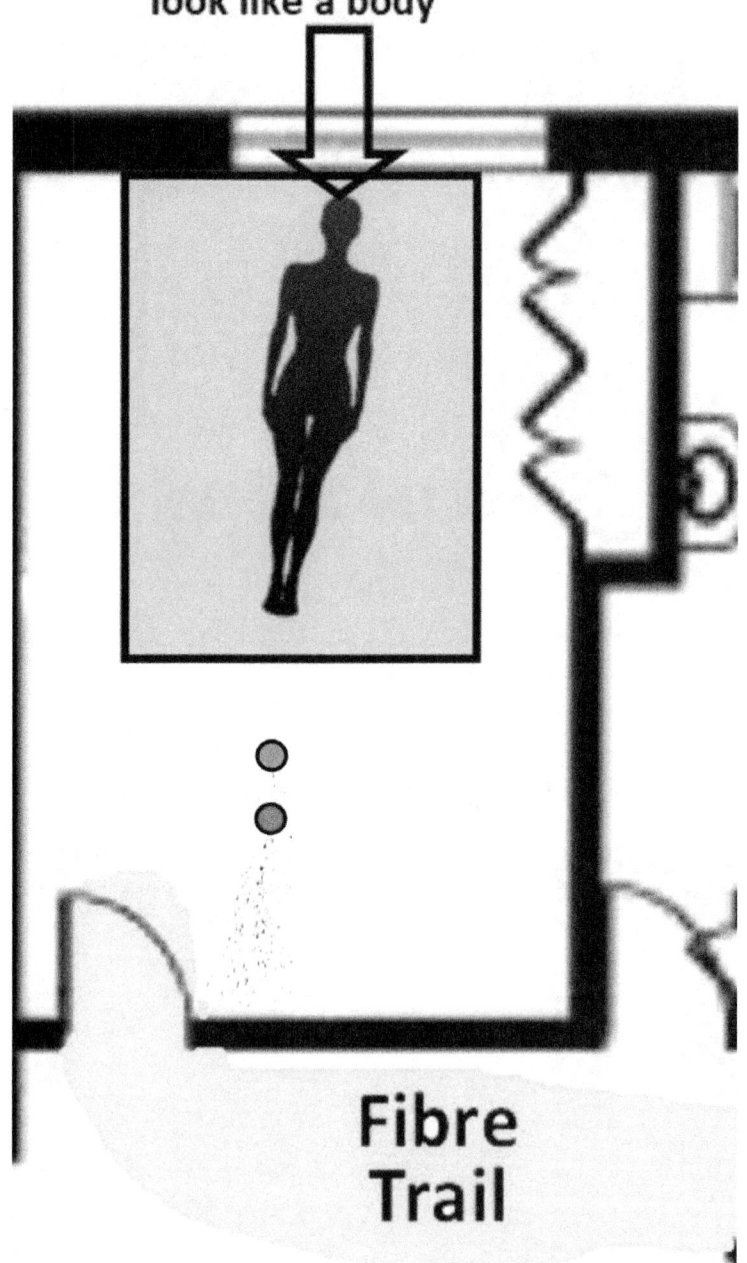

Fibre Trail

In this diagram the red dot is where we believe the attacker was standing and the blue dot is the victim. This blood appears to be splash back from hitting someone and creating a cast off when the weapon is pulled back. This blood was not wiped. The blood was tested and found to be that of Eduardo Pinheiro. We also found some wiped blood on the floor. The same cleaning agent was used. Brandi did not sniff this out in his first visit to the house because he was given Ligia's scent to pick up and not Eduardo.

Clive Hendy – You did not find much blood in front of the victim, why's that?

Rupal Chakrabharti – Yes In Location 2 – while there is splash back there is very little forward spray. My conclusion is that this blood went onto a rug or a blanket and this was disposed of. Because of the splash back I conclude that the victim was struck twice. I cannot determine the height of the assailant because their arm would have been raised

Clive Hendy – OK – so why was there no splash back found in Location 1?

Rupal Chakrabharti – We found no splash back around Location 1 – not even with Luminol – that supports my conclusion that the victim was struck just the once – and the second blow was when the victim's head was inside a bag.

Splash back is caused when the assailant raises the weapon to hit a person a second time.

Clive Hendy – OK let's look at Location 3.

Rupal Chakrabharti – <u>Location 3</u> – is the garage in Rye and the blood is on the headrest of the driver's seat of the car. The blood is from Eduardo Pinheiro. This is not surprising as it was his decomposing head that was found on the head rest. *(A slight laugh from the jury).*

The blood was dried and not wiped. This third one is not splatter, it is not coming out of someone at speed. It is merely a blood stain. It has seeped down from his head injuries

<u>Cross-examination</u>

Jennifer Janus – You say that Brandi told you there had been a dead body in the boot of Eduardo's car.

Rupal Chakrabharti – Yes.

Jennifer Janus – And Eduardo's DNA was found in the boot, but that's not surprising as it's his car.

Rupal Chakrabharti – Yes.

Jennifer Janus – Is it not possible that it was Ligia's dead body in the boot?

Rupal Chakrabharti – Possibly. But Brandi went there after being given Eduardo's scent.

Jennifer Janus – But it is possible.

Rupal Chakrabharti – Yes.

Jennifer Janus – No further questions.

Roy Hughes

(Roy can be rather boring on the stand. He has a habit of rattling off the facts and observations like he's reading a train timetable. So we needed Hendy to liven him up, and underline what he was saying to drive home to the jury the importance of what we were telling them.

Roy's testimony began with projecting a series of photographs from the crime scene. This was crucial for making our coup de grâce point of how did PJ know it was his wife dead – without unzipping the sleeping bag and removing the two bags.

Photograph 1 – a zipped up sleeping bag through an open freezer door. Unseen is Ligia's body inside the bag.

Photograph 2 – the sleeping bag is unzipped. The head covered in a black dustbin bag, with signs of clotted blood.

Photograph 3 – A grizzly sight of icy blue and vermillion. Gashes in her head, blood in her eyes. It drew gasps from the jury and the gallery. I looked away. Then I looked at PJ in the dock. He was looking down with his head in his hands.

I remembered crying when I first saw that. I had since seen the pictures a few more times, but I had not grown insensible. It still affected me.

229

Photograph 4 – *the head of Ligia in the morgue, cleaned to demonstrate the two head injuries. I could not look at this either.*

Roy explained that Photograph 1 was the very first thing he saw before touching anything. In order to establish that a body was actually inside the sleeping bag he had to unzip it. Then to establish the identity of the person he had to pull off the two dustbin bags.)

Clive Hendy – So you examined the body. What did you assess to be the cause of death?

Roy Hughes – Asphyxiation. The head injuries that you saw caused her bleeding and rendered her unconscious, but that's not what killed her.

Clive Hendy – How can you be so sure?

Roy Hughes – There were purple marks in the lungs – and also in the eyes. These are the signs of petechial haemorrhages which you get when you die from strangulation. We also found foam in the victim's airways as they struggle to breathe and mucus in the lungs. We also found an enlarged heart – all consistent with a death from asphyxiation.

Clive Hendy – So the blow to the head may have been used to knock her unconscious – and then she was subsequently strangled.

Roy Hughes – Yes – and it appears that she was strangled with the dustbin bag over the head.

Clive Hendy – Why do you say that?

Roy Hughes – Because of all the head injury blood that was inside the bag. On the inner side.

Clive Hendy – Do you think this was done so the killer would not have to look into his victim's eyes?

Jennifer Janus – Objection your honour. It's asking the expert witness to speculate.

Judge – Sustained. Mr. Hendy you should know better. Strike the question from the record.

Clive Hendy – Sorry m'lord. Can I ask about trying to establish a time of death?

Roy Hughes – Normally you can assess the time of death by the body temperature, but putting the body in the freezer made that impossible. However we were able to work out a time frame by the state of her mobile phone.

Clive Hendy – How did you do that?

Roy Hughes – Her mobile phone cracked. Now most smart phones can last a couple of days in a freezer before cracking. So we ran numerous tests on that Nokia brand of phone and that specific model and they always cracked after 76 hours. Never before.

That way we were able to work out that she was put in the freezer at a time before 9 am Saturday.

Clive Hendy – What else did you find at the crime scene?

Roy Hughes – In the garden we found the shed unlocked and the key still in the lock. We found a sleeping bag in there identical to the one that Ligia was found in. Indicating it was from the same set of two.

Clive Hendy – What did you find upstairs?

Roy Hughes – Upstairs we found blood on the ceiling in the spare bedroom. When we analysed the blood we found it to be the blood of Eduardo Pinheiro.

We found bleach on the floor as if it had been heavily cleaned, and what was also curious was that pillows were placed on the bed under the cover that made it appear that someone was sleeping there.

(A photograph of this was shown).

The other big thing we found was a fibre trail – two sets of fibres that ran from the spare bedroom, the landing, all the way down the stairs, and through the ground floor to the front door. It would appear that someone had been dragged from upstairs to the front door.

Clive Hendy – Were you able to trace the source of the fibre?

Roy Hughes – Yes the clothes on Eduardo Pinheiro's body were given to Zico the son. The clothes were passed onto me and we found that the fibres on the fibre trail were consistent with that.

We also found blood on the floor around the mantelpiece, which Rupal talked about in his testimony. The blood was that of Ligia James.

Clive Hendy – So it seems possible that the attack took place there by the mantelpiece.

Roy Hughes – Very possible. Yes. Almost certainly.

Clive Hendy – Someone cleared up the crime scene. Why would they need to do that?

Roy Hughes – I obviously can't answer that. That's inviting me to speculate.

Jennifer Janus – Objection…..

Clive Hendy – OK let's now move on to the second scene. The garage in Sussex.

Roy Hughes – My visit to that crime scene was secondary. Sussex Police were the first team to deal with it.

Clive Hendy – You got to examine the body.

Roy Hughes – Yes. After the Sussex Police finished with the body, they gave it to Zico the son to arrange the funeral. But before that I got the chance to examine it.

Clive Hendy – What did you find?

Roy Hughes – He had head injuries – a cracked skull. Like he'd been hit by a blunt instrument. That made it hard to believe he could have driven from Byfleet to Rye as he would have been suffering from heavy concussion.

(A picture of this was shown to the court. They also showed the picture taken by Sussex Police which had the blow flies growing out of the wounds. Squeamish gasps from the jury.)

Clive Hendy – Sussex Coroner concluded that he died from carbon monoxide poisoning.

Roy Hughes – Yes but I also found the tell-tale signs of asphyxia. The purple marks in the lungs.

(A picture of Eduardo's post-mortem lungs are shown)

I also found a broken Hyoid Bone which is found in a large number of strangulations.

Clive Hendy – Can you explain what the Hyoid bone is?

Roy Hughes – It's a U-shaped bone in the upper part of your neck.

Clive Hendy – Did Eduardo Pinheiro die from carbon monoxide poisoning?

Roy Hughes – While I found toxically high levels of Carbon Monoxide in the body – I did not find as much of it in the lungs as you would expect if the person was still alive when the accelerator was pressed down and is breathing in the Carbon Monoxide.

Clive Hendy – So you are contradicting the finding of the Sussex County Coroner?

Roy Hughes – Yes I am. I did not find that he died from Carbon Monoxide poisoning, my finding is that he died from asphyxiation.

Clive Hendy – So Eduardo's body had been used by flies to hatch eggs? What was that able to show us?

Roy Hughes – By looking at the temperatures on those days, the temperature in the garage I was able to work out when he sustained those injuries and died.

Clive Hendy – Would you like to demonstrate?

(Roy then put up the graphic to explain the blow fly evidence.)

Cross-examination

Jennifer Janus – The body of Eduardo was given to you by the son Zico.

Roy Hughes – Correct.

Jennifer Janus – He did that hoping you would come to a different conclusion about his death to that of Sussex Police.

Roy Hughes – Well I don't know about that. He just gave me the body, I didn't get any instructions.

Jennifer Janus – The Sussex Police and their Coroner thought differently about the head injuries.

Roy Hughes – They noted the head injuries in their report, but made no comment on them.

Jennifer Janus – But these injuries that Eduardo had – could have been a consequence of a struggle with Ligia.

Roy Hughes – Could be. I can only report on what the body tells me.

Jennifer Janus – No further questions.

<u>**WPC Muldrew**</u>

(We considered not calling WPC Muldrew to the stand because she was the only police force representative that PJ spoke to about the drug gang/bad crowd angle. So if she didn't take the stand and predicting that PJ would not testify, there would be no one to put forward that story.

But if we didn't call her, the defence most likely would – and then this would look as though we were holding back. So we decide it best to call her in as a witness and so then PJ's accusation would come from our counsel and not a revelation from theirs. Her bodyarmourcam footage was inadmissible. But there wasn't anything incriminating in that anyway.)

Clive Hendy – You were the first respondent?

WPC Muldrew – Yes I was. I got there on the scene 15 minutes from his call.

Clive Hendy – What did the defendant say to you when you got there?

WPC Muldrew – (Referring to her notes) – "She was doing cocaine. She fell in with a bad crowd! It has got to be something to do with that.

"I know her first husband was back on the scene. Eduardo. They'd been meeting up."

Clive Hendy – Did he ask you to check that the woman was dead?

WPC Muldrew – No he did not.

Clive Hendy – Did he appear certain that it was his wife dead in the freezer?

WPC Muldrew – Yes he was certain.

Clive Hendy – What did you do after he told you that?

WPC Muldrew – I took him next door to sit there and recover, and I sealed off the crime scene and waited for my colleagues to arrive.

Cross-examination
Jennifer Janus – You were involved in the door to door enquiries. Yes?
WPC Muldrew – I was.
Jennifer Janus – Any leads come out from that?
WPC Muldrew – The only solid lead was that a neighbour saw a white van with a gang inside, hanging around Friday evening.
Jennifer Janus – Right I believe that there was a public appeal to identify the men in this van?
WPC Muldrew – Yes. One of them had a distinctive tattoo.
Jennifer Janus – How many men did the witness say he saw in the white van?
WPC Muldrew – I think he said three.
Jennifer Janus – Was it not four?
WPC Muldrew – Could be.
Jennifer Janus – But DC Ferdinand only interviewed three men.
WPC Muldrew – Yes three men.
Jennifer Janus – Were you there when Ferdy met the Romanian gang?
WPC Muldrew – No I wasn't.
Rose Barraclough
Clive Hendy – You live next door to PJ and Ligia James. Is that right?
Rose Barraclough – Yes we're at number 3. They're at number 5.
Clive Hendy – Did you have much interaction with them?
Rose Barraclough – Not really. I used to say hello to her. Never got anything out of him.
Clive Hendy – Did you ever hear them make a noise?

Rose Barraclough – I used to hear them rowing from time to time. And I used to hear music – sometimes really loud – and sometimes not so much.

Clive Hendy – How often was the rowing?

Rose Barraclough – Dunno.

Clive Hendy – Every month?

Jennifer Janus – Objection. Leading question.

Rose Barraclough – I never kept a log. But it were quite regular.

Clive Hendy – Tell me about the last night you ever heard noises from number 5. Tell me about the night of Friday the 16th March.

Rose Barraclough – The record was playing and then it suddenly stopped. Singing Prawn, Prawn, Prawn – and then it stopped. I remember it clearly because if it was going to stay loud like that when Graham Norton came on I was going to have to go over there and ask them to turn it down.

Clive Hendy – So after the music and rowing stopped, did anything else happen of note that Friday night?

Rose Barraclough – We think they must of had a visitor at half ten because their cat came into our back garden and set off the burglar lights. He always comes into our garden when they get a visitor. Always.

Clive Hendy – And what time was that?

Rose Barraclough – Half ten. I know it were that time because Graham Norton was about to start.

Cross-examination

Jennifer Janus – When you heard the rows – you never saw the people having the row?

Rose Barraclough – That's right I was indoors.

Jennifer Janus – So the people having the row might not have been Ligia or PJ.

Rose Barraclough – Could be. But they did a test with a tape recorder – the police did all the other houses nearby – and the only house I could hear rowing in my kitchen was

236

from House Number 5. I could hear it coming from that direction.

Jennifer Janus – Yes – but you couldn't be sure it was PJ rowing with Ligia. It could have been another man.

Rose Barraclough – Yes.

Jennifer Janus – No further questions m'lord.

Rose Barraclough – Hang on a sec. I've got a question. We've been looking after their cat since this all started. Who's going to be re-impurse us for all the cat food? I mean we're pensioners.

Judge – That is not a matter for this court Mrs. Barraclough. You may leave the witness box.

Fred Barraclough

Clive Hendy – What do you remember of the day PJ found his wife dead?

Fred Barraclough – I was looking outside my window and I saw him standing there like he were waiting for the plumber. So I didn't think too much about it.

Then I hear all this wailing, and I look outside and there's a police car.

Clive Hendy – So you never heard a shout when he supposedly found the body?

Fred Barraclough – No. Only when the police turned up.

Cross-examination

Jennifer Janus – Have you ever found your wife dead?

Fred Barraclough – No of course not. She's here at t'court.

Jennifer Janus – So you can only imagine what it would feel like, and how you would react?

Fred Barraclough – Yes.

Jennifer Janus – So when you looked out of the window and saw PJ, he could have been in a daze of disbelief.

Fred Barraclough – Yes it could.

Jennifer Janus – Thank you. No further questions.

237

Andy Goddard

(We knew the defence would put Goddard up as an alternative suspect and so would be called up anyway. So we called him as our own witness so Clive Hendy could put him through some of his pre-trial coaching. Goddard could testify about the marital problems. While this is hearsay evidence, it is allowable because Ligia, the person making these statements about her marital problems, is now dead and so cannot testify for herself).

Cross-Examination

Jennifer Janus – You bought her a bottle of wine.

Andy Goddard – To share. Yes. And a third person had a glass.

Jennifer Janus – So you were trying to get her drunk. And you succeeded.

Andy Goddard – No. Not at all. She bought a bottle. A few of us had a glass, not just me and her. Then I bought another one. She wasn't that drunk.

Jennifer Janus – Cocaine was found in her blood stream. Did you give it to her?

Andy Goddard – Errr.

Jennifer Janus – Remember you are under oath.

Andy Goddard – I gave her a line. She did it in the toilet of the pub.

Jennifer Janus – In your interview with DCS Ferdinand you told him you were in love with Ligia. Is that correct?

Andy Goddard – Yes.

Jennifer Janus – And that makes you a top suspect.

Andy Goddard – Everybody who knew Ligia loved her. So that makes every one of them suspects.

Jennifer Janus – But you had special feelings for her.

Andy Goddard – I cared for her yes.

Jennifer Janus – So you must have been jealous of her husband. Resented that he was in the way.

Andy Goddard – No.

Jennifer Janus – Resented that she still had feelings for him, while she brushed you aside.

So you plied her with cocaine. To take advantage of her.

Andy Goddard – No.

Jennifer Janus – So all this stuff Ligia supposedly told you about her marriage. Was anyone else present?

Andy Goddard – No. She was confiding in me.

Jennifer Janus – Ah! So you were her confidante.

Andy Goddard – I don't know about that. She had lots of friends.

Jennifer Janus – So we've got only got your word that she said it. Maybe this is your fantasy.

Andy Goddard – Like I said earlier – the day before the last time I saw her alive, she had a massive row with PJ at the vets. Over money.

Jennifer Janus – We are expected to take the word of you – part-time DJ, a small time cocaine dealer that she was having marital problems.

Andy Goddard – You don't have to take my word for it. There are other witnesses to that.

Date: Monday 12th November
Time: 10:00
Location: Kingston Crown Court

On this day on the Prosecution Witness order of play we had:

- Hannah Wiles (Happy Pets Vets)
- Petra Grover
- Jorge Guitterez (Hotel Malmaison)
- Gabriela Guimaraes (GG)
- Dorothy "Dot" Mailer (Phone Forensics)
- Charles Hooper aka Chops

Here are the transcript highlights:

Hannah Wiles

Hannah Wiles – He did get quite shouty. I had to tell them to leave.

Clive Hendy – What was the argument about?

Hannah Wiles – He was complaining about the treatment costs, and telling her that she was being taken for a ride. But that's not true. Our fees are very reasonable, they are in line with every other vet – and as long as you've got insurance...

Clive Hendy – Thank you Ms. Wiles. Do you often witness rows at the vets?

Hannah Wiles – Once in a while. But never like this. This was on a whole other level. This was a blazing row.

Clive Hendy – Did you detect bitterness in the row?

Jennifer Janus – Objection.

Judge – Mr. Hendy you must stop asking leading questions. You know better than that.

Clive Hendy – Sorry m'lord I will re-phrase – what do you mean exactly by a blazing row?

Hannah Wiles – It was an angry bitter row...I actually got the impression...

Clive Hendy – The impression of what Ms. Wiles?

Hannah Wiles – I got the impression that they weren't just rowing about the vet bill.

Jennifer Janus – Objection – the counsel has planted the word bitter into the mind of the witness.

Judge – Sustained. Please strike from the record. Move on. Ask another question.

Cross-examination

Jennifer Janus – So when did you see the defendant after that Thursday?

Hannah Wiles – He came in on the Monday. Without his wife.

Jennifer Janus – He came in with the cat?

Hannah Wiles – Yes Willoughby.

Jennifer Janus – And he paid the bill?
Hannah Wiles – Yes.
Jennifer Janus – Without any fuss?
Hannah Wiles – Yes.
Jennifer Janus – No further questions.
Petra Grover

(Petra described to Clive Hendy how she met the defendant at Winchelsea Station and then a video was shown to the jury of the ID Parade. My nervousness raised up a gear as Jennifer Janus stood up to begin her cross-examination. I realised that so much of our case was riding on the integrity of Petra Grover's identification of PJ, and if Janus succeeded in demolishing her on the stand, it would in turn annihilate our case.)

Cross-examination
Jennifer Janus – The time of this was 5.30 am. So very early in the morning. It would have still been dark.
Petra Grover – Yes.
Jennifer Janus – In fact extremely early in the morning. Are you normally up so early?
Petra Grover – No.
Jennifer Janus – I bet you were still sleepy.
Petra Grover – Yes I was.
Jennifer Janus – You may have seen my client before, he owns a house in the area about 3 miles away. But not necessarily at that station at that time.
Petra Grover – No it was definitely him.
Jennifer Janus – But you said yourself you were sleepy – that's when people hallucinate, when images they see in their dreams they see in their waking state.
Petra Grover – No I was awake. It was him. I had never seen him before and I remember the dimple on his chin.
Jennifer Janus – It was still dark.
Petra Grover – I could still see him properly.

Jennifer Janus – Ok. So you picked him out at the identity parade after DCS Ferdinand showed you a photograph of the accused. Is that right?

Petra Grover – No he did not show me a photograph.

Jennifer Janus – But he visited your house one evening and met with you. Alone. No other policemen were present? Is that correct?

Petra Grover – Yes.

Jennifer Janus – And is it there where he showed you a picture of the defendant?

Petra Grover – No.

Jennifer Janus – So you picked him out after DC Ferdinand described the accused and mentioned the dimple on his chin?

Petra Grover – No he did not do that either.

(I was mightily relieved that Petra Grover stood up so well to the cross-examination.)

Jorge Guitterez

(Jorge Guitterez is the general manager at the Hotel Malmaison, Oxford who I met with in April. In the witness stand he told Clive Hendy that their records show that PJ's booking was made at 9.55 and it appears to be paid by card as a phone transaction.)

Cross-examination

Jennifer Janus – Did you take the booking yourself?

Jorge Guitterez – I think so, but I can't be certain. We take so many bookings, and Friday night on the front desk are especially hectic.

Jennifer Janus – Is it possible that he did the booking in person – but that booking was put through the system as if it was over the phone?

Jorge Guitterez – It is possible, but it is on our system as a telephone booking. The payment was recorded as the card holder not being present, which is why the three digit number at the back was taken.

Jennifer Janus – But it is possible?

Jorge Guitterez – What's possible?

Jennifer Janus – That the transaction took place while the client was there at the desk, but it was recorded as done over the phone.

Jorge Guitterez – Yes. Ah! But our records show that the key card was created at 12.04, and access to the room was at 12.07.

Jennifer Janus – You recall speaking with PJ James yourself?

Jorge Guitterez – Yes I do.

Jennifer Janus – What do you remember?

Jorge Guitterez – He was on the phone calling his wife trying to find out how his cat was.

Jennifer Janus – He appeared concerned about the welfare of his cat?

Jorge Guitterez – Yes he did.

Jennifer Janus – And when was this?

Jorge Guitterez – I can't be certain. I think it was the morning.

Gabriela Guimaraes (GG)

(We considered GG's testimony so important, Surrey Police paid for her flight and accommodation to appear in this trial. Her testimony was especially difficult because it had to go through a Brazilian interpreter. She told Clive Hendy that she was sat with Eduardo in a restaurant when he got a text. He seemed troubled and immediately called back. He did not go outside the restaurant. He called Ligia immediately in front of her.

Giving her testimony to Hendy she explained how Eduardo put the call on loudspeaker, she thinks, because so Eduardo could show GG that he was being straight with her, and not making an excuse to leave.

She heard a male voice but she could not understand everything that was said, because it was in English. "I just remember the word 'immediately'," she said on the stand through an interpreter.

Eduardo then finished the call. He apologized profusely to her and handed over to her £40 pounds in cash. He said he would call GG later and left. She never saw him again.

Under cross-examination GG was a veritable Brazilian Spitfire on the stand – and showed herself to be very firmly in the Eduardo-did-not-commit-suicide camp.)

Cross-examination

Jennifer Janus – Thank you. You came forward with this testimony when Zico the son got in touch with you. Is that right?

GG – Yes.

Jennifer Janus – So you wanted to help Zico with something he wanted to hear.

GG – I told Zico the truth. I did not change anything for his benefit.

Jennifer Janus – You heard a male voice? But you cannot tell me who was the male voice? It could be PJ or it could be another male voice.

GG – Yes.

Jennifer Janus – Thank you.

GG – It was an English accent. Not a South American drug gang accent. Not a Romanian accent. It was English in an English accent.

Jennifer Janus – Thank you.

GG – Eduardo did not commit suicide.

Jennifer Janus – Thank you. In your opinion.

Dot Mailer

(Dorothy or Dot Mailer is our forensic phone expert hired by Roy Hughes. I've worked with her a fair bit over the years and she is highly meticulous.

In her testimony to our counsel she showed the data on how the final texts "What about him?" from Eduardo pinged off the same mobile phone tower in West Byfleet.)

Cross-examination

Jennifer Janus – The text may have been sent from a distance away where the signal was poor and only pinged through when he got close to the house and the cell tower.

Dot Mailer – It's possible. Yes. But he was driving from London …

Jennifer Janus – No further questions.

Dot Mailer – …and on that journey it was highly likely he would have come into the range of at least one tower.

Charlie Hooper aka Chops

(We called on Chops to confirm the golfing dates to demonstrate that only PJ had been using the house in Rye in the last six months. Also that he was a no show on Sunday – casting doubt that he had planned the trip to Oxford.

Clive Hendy then showed the jury a video demonstration of how we think PJ faked the suicide of Eduardo Pinheio. It was a re-shoot of the one we did in Merton of me lifting the 1.8 metre, 88 kilo mannequin into the boot – then out of the boot and into the passenger seat. Then attaching the tube to the exhaust pipe, starting the engine, putting the tool box on the accelerating pedal and finally affixing the tubing with car fumes coming out from into the narrow opening in the car window. Faking a suicide is that easy folks, and according to Matt it happens all the time.

We got someone else to do the demonstration, because we wanted the evidence to appear completely impartial and not tainted by the lead officer in the case. So all my huffing and puffing in Merton was for nothing.

While they played back the video, I watched the jury. They seemed engaged, rigid in their seats, not fidgeting. A good sign.)

Date: Tuesday 13th November
Time: 10:00
Location: 5 Odin Court

Today was a trip for the jury to Asgard, which I was not allowed on. Clive Hendy showed them around, and reported back that there was now a For Sale sign outside the house.

> **PJ's audio log Tuesday 13th November**
>
> I was surprised to see my tall gaunt next door neighbour take the stand as a witness against me. He's never said anything to me in the whole time I've lived there and now he's chipping in to say that I looked suspicious as I was standing outside my home waiting for the police. I think he just wanted to stick his oar in and have something to say in the witness box. What a jerk. I think Jennifer Janus took him down and showed him up. I've always thought he looked creepy and he's far more likely to be a killer than I am.
>
> When I saw my golfing buddy Chops take the stand. I was thinking Et tu Chops?
>
> But what could he possibly say that would be incriminating against me? I was pleased that in the end they just got him to rattle off all the dates he'd played golf with me. It gave Jennifer Janus the opportunity in cross-examination to say that I seemed like a top bloke and not the type who would murder his wife. Cheers Chops.
>
> He was the last of the prosecution witnesses. As the court was called to a close, my head was swimming with facts. On one level it all seemed rather convincing, but Jennifer Janus was a Rottweiler in cross-examination, planting seeds of doubt into everything.
>
> That jury trip to Asgard was deeply unpleasant. I was told that I had to go, as the accused must see all the evidence that is presented to the jury. I hadn't been back there since that horrible day, and I never want to go back there ever again. I had already made arrangements to put the house on the market. Can you imagine moving back there and then running into my next-door neighbour after he's tried to put me away for murder?
>
> Whatever the outcome of the trial. If I lost I would use the funds from selling the houses for my appeal. If I win, I would move far away.

Date: Wednesday 14th November
Time: 10:00
Location: Kingston Crown Court

Before calling the defence witnesses, Jennifer Janus played to the jury the audio of the wire that Samantha had on her. But any reference to the first wife Kelly or her death was edited out.

Then she played an edited version of the video PJ was making with Dougal MacPherson. 20 minutes in total. Again any reference to Kelly Hill and her death was cut out. They clearly thought this video was exculpatory.

Clive Hendy objected and said that the jury should see an uncut version of the video. He wanted the jury to see the numerous takes – which would make PJ seem less spontaneous and genuine. However rather than subject the jury to the whole six hours of unedited torture, he showed a cut down 40 minute version of the video, with some of the re-takes. Once again any reference to Kelly Hill, her name, her life, her death was airbrushed out for the benefit of the jury.

> **PJ's audio log – Wednesday 14th November**
> They showed the video in court today. I felt strange and uncomfortable seeing myself on the big screen talking for half an hour about my most private thoughts. Stranger still then to sit through an uncut version at the insistence of the prosecution. They clearly thought me asking for another take because the peacocks were squawking too loudly would make me appear fake.
>
> But Janus was delighted that we were able to put it into evidence. It allowed the jury to hear me proclaim my innocence in my own words without being subjected to cross-examination. She regarded it as a big win and I was heartened by that.

Date: Thursday 15th November

Time: 10:00
Location: Kingston Crown Court

The defence chose to call just six witnesses, and none were experts to rebut the evidence of our team of experts. On the order of play we had:
- Terry Snape
- Chloe Lund
- DCS Christopher Harris aka Slack Harris
- Samantha James
- Dougal MacPherson – the video producer
- Zico Pinheiro

Defence Witnesses
Terry Snape

(Before he took the stand Terry Snape was told away from the jury that he must not mention the YouTube Video, which to me really made no difference either way. I grabbed a moment with Clive Hendy to tell him that a good strategy was to get a defence witness to slip up and reveal that PJ's first wife had died under questionable circumstances. But Clive Hendy waved this suggestion away. I just hoped he knew what he was doing. I really wanted the jury to know that his first wife had died mysteriously.

On the stand to Jennifer Janus, Snape said much the same stuff as he did on the YouTube clip though without mentioning any Hippopotamus.)

Cross-examination
Clive Hendy – Before the death of Ligia, when was the last time you met with PJ James? Remember you are under oath.
Terry Snape – Well we've stayed in touch via email.
Clive Hendy – Yes – but when was the last time you actually met with PJ James?

Terry Snape – Errr. We're both very busy.

Clive Hendy – Yes but when?

Terry Snape – Not since Shipton Village.

Clive Hendy – Well that was several years ago.

Terry Snape – Yes.

Clive Hendy – So you're not exactly bessy mates then?

Jennifer Janus – Objection – the prosecution is mocking the witness's provincial accent.

Clive Hendy – I was not m'lord.

Judge – I trust you were not doing such a thing Mr. Hendy – please proceed.

Clive Hendy – Like many of PJ's associates you stopped seeing him after he lost his job at Shipton Village. So you have not been able to witness the bitterness seeping into his life.

Terry Snape – PJ's not bitter. I know him.

Clive Hendy – Normally a character witness is a person who knows that person very well. Not someone they can't be bothered to stay in touch with ...

Terry Snape – No. No. I know him well. We've worked together. Spent ages together.

Clive Hendy – No further questions.

(After Terry Snape stepped down Jennifer Janus announced that they were hoping to call Chloe Lund as a character witness, but her commitments would not allow it.

I jumped up at this, and from the gallery made over to the prosecution desk, grabbed hold of Clive Hendy and hissed into this ear – Clive Hendy listened to me and got to his feet.)

Clive Hendy – Objection your honour. By the defence saying the name of someone as a character witness and not delivering that character evidence, you must not allow that to imply that the person would in fact provide a character witness.

Judge – What do you mean?

Clive Hendy – We cannot allow the jury to think that this person is endorsing the accused, when she is not actually here to do so.

Judge – Mr. Hendy. Please calm down. Listen. Chloe Lund was called as a character witness – she is not here to provide it. So she is not a character witness. That's it. May we move on with the case? Thank you.

Clive Hendy – But it's important that the defence does not infer to the jury that Chloe Lund would have provided a character witness.

Judge – Yes. Mr. Hendy. You've made your point.

(I was furious. Just by having the name Chloe Lund mentioned as a character witness would make the jury think that PJ was friends with a popular TV personality. Yet we were not allowed to name her in the complaint made against him and why he lost his job on Shipton Village. The law really is an ass.)

DCS Christopher Harris

Jennifer Janus – You were the lead investigator into the death of Eduardo Pinheiro?

DCS Christopher Harris – Correct.

Jennifer Janus – What did you find?

DCS Christopher Harris – We found him dead in the driving seat of his car. He had put a tool box down on the accelerator pedal. There was a garden hose attached to the exhaust pipe and the other end was placed inside the car through the driving seat window. In consideration of all the evidence, I found it to be a suicide. The clincher for me was the hand written note sellotaped to the window.

Jennifer Janus – You also looked into Eduardo Pinheiro's life. What did you find?

DCS Christopher Harris – There had been a terrible tragedy in his life. His youngest son died in a car crash, in which he was driving and he was considered responsible. This contributed to the break up of his marriage. So he was the sort of person who would commit suicide.

Clive Hendy – Objection! The witness is speculating.

DCS Christopher Harris – Well I say that because he was being treated by the NHS for depression.

Cross-Examination

Clive Hendy – With regards to the note sellotaped to the window. Do you have any idea where the paper came from?

DCS Christopher Harris – No.

Clive Hendy – Did you find the pen used to write the note at the scene?

DCS Christopher Harris – No.

Clive Hendy – Any idea where the pen that wrote the note came from?

DCS Christopher Harris – No.

Clive Hendy – If the pen was not found on the scene. That strongly indicates that the note was written somewhere else.

DCS Christopher Harris – Could be.

Clive Hendy – Could be? Don't you think as lead investigator you should investigate such things?

DCS Christopher Harris – Yes we did. It was inconclusive.

Clive Hendy – You are sitting on this stand saying, I quote "The clincher" for you was the hand written note sellotaped to the window to conclude that it was a suicide, and yet you have no idea where the note was written – or any details at all about it.

(I was so hoping that Hendy would bring up the "slack" Harris nickname, which would have completely buried him, but sadly Hendy let him go after that.

Jennifer Janus next announced that Samantha James was not taking the stand. She did not offer any explanation. From where I was sitting, I could not see the upstairs public gallery, so I had no idea whether she was in court that day or not.)

Dougal MacPherson – the video producer

(In his testimony Dougal slagged us off for our harassment of him and his friend. He said we were heavy handed and insulting. He objected to me calling him the Witch-finder General, though I do not remember ever calling him

that to his face. It may have been my investigator Tom, who was the one who made the original observation.)

Cross-examination
Clive Hendy – You have a TV production company with PJ.

Dougal – Yes.

Hendy – You had a number of projects you were working on?

Dougal – Yes.

Hendy – Were you working on a TV series idea about young people studying at Oxford? Remember you are under oath.

Dougal – No.

Hendy – Did PJ ever mention to you about the idea of a TV series about young people studying at Oxford?

Dougal – No…but that doesn't mean.

Clive Hendy – No further questions…

Dougal – Hold on it doesn't mean he didn't have one. He might not have been ready to tell me about it yet.

<u>Zico Pinheiro</u>
Jennifer Janus – You have suffered an unimaginable loss. It's understandable that you would not want to believe that your father murdered your mother and then killed himself.

Zico Pinheiro – It's understandable that I should hate the man who killed my mother and father.

Judge – Please control yourself.

Zico Pinheiro – He would not even go to her funeral. He left it to me to identify the body.

Jennifer Janus – The defendant was too upset to identify the body. He was still in shock.

Zico Pinheiro – And what about me? I am her son. Why did I have to do it?

Jennifer Janus – That's the fault of the Surrey Police.

Zico Pinheiro – No that's his fault *(points to PJ in the dock)*. And Chloe Lund thinks he's a creep. She insisted he got sacked from Shipton Village. No way was she ever going to be a character witness.

Jennifer Janus – You are not allowed to say her name. Please strike…

Zico Pinheiro – Why the fuck not? Because it's the truth? And what about his first wife?

Judge – Quiet! Please remove this man form the court. He is held in contempt.

(As the athletic, strapping Zico was escorted out of the dock by the geriatric Albert the usher and his equally aged colleague, Zico glared at the man in the dock and shouted– "you will not get away with this."

Did calling Zico as a witness backfire for the defence? I know they wanted to show that Zico had influenced me in pursuing PJ, but the outburst showed his raw emotion to the jury and he was able to get two truths out that were officially suppressed by the court.)

PJ's audio-log – Thursday 15th November

I was shocked by Zico's hatred towards me. I've never been on the receiving end of such a display of loathing. It was so violent, so full of anger. A homicidal rage so fierce that for the first time ever it occurred to me that it could have been Zico that killed Ligia and Eduardo. Surely not.

Nevertheless. it really bothered me that someone should hate me so much. I wanted to talk to him, to try and convince him of my innocence. But I think that would be irretrievable. I decided that if I was going to get acquitted, I would write him a letter to try and get him to think differently of me.

With regards to the case – what did bother me was that the prosecution had wheeled out all these different experts, pathologists, entomologists, blood splatter experts, cadaver dogs, and we had put up no experts to counter that. Jennifer Janus explained that all the conclusions they put forward did not prove my guilt. It didn't matter to my case if

> they proved that Eduardo was killed in Asgard, they hadn't proved that I was the killer. It didn't matter that Eduardo was already dead when the burglar alarm was turned off at Rye, there was no proof it was I who had turned the burglar alarm off. I just prayed she knew what she was doing.
>
> She exuded total confidence and I trusted her, but my whole life was riding on this.

Date: Friday 16th November
Time: 10:00
Location: Kingston Crown Court

Chapter 14 – Closing Arguments and Verdict

Before we get to the verdict you need to read the closing arguments. Here are the transcript highlights:

Clive Hendy – The murder of a spouse is one of the most prevalent forms of homicide. It is called Uxoricide. In the UK – 33% of female murder victims are killed by a partner or ex-partner.

But most wife murderers are not as clever as PJ. I mentioned in my opening statement that PJ realized that in order to get away with murder, it helps greatly if you can shift the blame on someone else.

We heard from Fred the next door neighbour – his testimony is no proof of guilt. Maybe it's perfectly normal for a person who on finding his wife dead, shows no emotion at all, and just sits and waits for the police and medics, and then starts screaming and hollering in a show of grief as soon as the police arrive. Maybe that's perfectly normal. But to us it appears strange, to us it appears that he is putting on an act.

Judge – Who do you mean by us?

Clive Hendy – The team behind this prosecution, my law firm, the police. Everybody I have spoken to about the case.

Judge – Please proceed.

Clive Hendy – Maybe it's perfectly normal to not go to your wife's funeral, play no part in any arrangements, claiming you are too grief stricken – and then contact your friend to make a documentary about yourself and talk garrulously in a video interview. Take after re-take to get the right nuance. To claim to be so stricken that he can't help the police with any information at all, that you can barely move, but then call his wife's employer about receiving his death-in-service payment.
 Jennifer Janus – Objection.
 Judge – Over-ruled
 Clive Hendy – To find it in you to pick up the phone to find out how much money you could get in the death in service pay out. Maybe that's perfectly normal – maybe that's how you behave when you find your wife brutally murdered. But to us it appears strange.

 The defence set great store on the fact that PJ made no admission when Samantha had a wire on her. But it proves nothing. Absence of evidence is not evidence of absence. My experience in murder cases tell me that murderers are not in the habit of casually admitting to murdering someone to people, even when asked by a close relative. If you are trying to get away with murder you tend to keep schtum about it.

 We also have the drug gang theory. PJ never spoke to the police in a formal interview, because in a formal interview he would have been required to provide formal evidence. Precise evidence – and he had none. He is smearing the name of his dead wife by suggesting she was involved in drug smuggling. It is most revealing that the defence have presented no evidence at all for that angle, apart from pointing to the fact that Ligia had traces of cocaine in her blood stream. Taking a line of cocaine does not make you a drug trafficker.

 If you were a drug gang doing a vendetta killing why clear up the crime scene, pour away her glass of wine and put it in the cupboard? Drug gangs tend not to cover up their killings. They like people to think, to know that they did it, to send out the message DON'T MESS WITH US.

The case proposing Eduardo as Ligia's murderer is full of holes.

For example: if you were Eduardo and killed Ligia in the heat of the moment – why would you bother to clear up yours and her blood marks – and then drive all the way to Rye to commit suicide?

He had his own garage in Merton he could have killed himself in.

With a note he must have written before he got to Rye. **Because it cannot have been written in the garage because the pen was not found.**

Now instead the case that PJ set it up is cast iron.

In PJ's written statement, he claims to be in Oxford all of that week-end. So why was he at Winchelsea station at 5.30 am? Why is that not in his statement? According to his statement he was tucked up in bed in a hotel in Oxford. Clearly he was not.

None of the Oxford receipts he supplied cover the time frame when the murders occurred. There is a massive hole in his alibi – that coincides exactly when Ligia was killed.

Why else would there be a fibre trail from the upstairs to downstairs? If not to drag Eduardo's dead body from upstairs to his car?

The defence question how PJ could have killed Eduardo by strangulation without sustaining any injuries. We believe that Eduardo was knocked unconscious before the strangulation. Eduardo could have been facing down so that he could not reach out and prevent his attack. Or PJ could have put handcuffs on him while he was unconscious and before the strangulation. Abrasions on his wrists were found on his dead body. Speculation I know. But very possible.

Now we have provided you with a full set of leading experts, pathologists, blood splatter, entomologists.

Instead the defence have provided no experts. Only some rather tenuous character witnesses.

One last thing – how did PJ know it was his wife in the freezer?

WPC Muldrew said in her testimony that PJ was certain that it was his wife in the freezer and he was certain that she was dead.

You heard from Roy Hughes of the Surrey Crime Scene team who was the first police to look at the body. He found the body inside a sleeping bag, covered up so that it wasn't clear it was a body at all. He had to unzip the bag and found the head inside two plastic bags, so it wasn't clear it was Ligia. So how did PJ know? Did he zip open the sleeping bag and remove the bags? If he did, he would have to have put the bags back on her head and zipped the sleeping bag back up.

All these facts work together to prove that PJ James is guilty of murder on two counts – beyond a reasonable doubt.

Date: Monday 19th November
Time: 10:00
Location: Kingston Crown Court

Closing Defence Statement

Jennifer Janus – Before my client went into shutdown mode he told the first respondent WPC Muldrew this – "She was doing cocaine. She fell in with a bad crowd! It has got to be something to do with that.

I know her first husband was back on the scene. Eduardo. They'd been meeting up."

Right there we have some leads of who might have killed Ligia James.

We spoke with Zico – who has suffered the most unbearable grief. He has lost his mother and his father. It's only natural and perfectly normal that he would want to blot out the narrative that his father killed his mother, and instead point the blame to his stepfather. Zico and PJ have never been on good terms. This is very common with step sons and step fathers – and it is this resentment that has driven this unfortunate prosecution of my client.

There is no evidence of any malice afore thought. He could have planned all this on the hoof? Really? In that fifteen minutes?

According to the prosecution my client murdered two people by strangulation. Really? When someone is strangled they put up an almighty fight – and Eduardo is a large strong man. And yet my client was found to have no injuries and no cuts and bruises. I know the prosecution say he strangled them while they lay on their stomachs, but even so – Eduardo was strong enough to lift himself up. Surely PJ would have sustained some sign of a struggle.

What about the suicide note? In Eduardo's own hand writing. In Portuguese.

We heard from DCS Christopher Harris that Eduardo was a likely suicide. He had been receiving treatment for depression.

It's all there – what really happened. You don't need to go into some weird and convoluted story about using other people's phone to lure them and fake their suicide and then get a train to Oxford and get a stranger to buy your train ticket so you don't leave a digital trail.

On the prosecution's final point in summing up – finding the dead body of your wife in the freezer is the most traumatic experience imaginable. My client cannot remember the exact details, because he does not want to remember, he does not want to play it back in his head. So it's possible that PJ unzipped the sleeping bag and zipped it back up. It's possible he even just knew by instinct that she was dead there, and he did not need to open up the bag. It's the detail my client does not remember. It does NOT mean he's guilty. It means that he has been traumatized. When trying to re-collect facts on something you don't want to remember, with the best will in the world, you may get something wrong or misremember or miss out a detail.

The prosecution made a lot of noise about the final text correspondence between Ligia and Eduardo being in English – which they are trying to say proves that the text were sent by someone else. But what about this? We know Ligia had been drinking – a seemingly large quantity of wine for a woman her size, maybe she sent the text to Eduardo by mistake – and it was intended for an English-speaking man. Eduardo saw the text and replied in English. He goes over there, gets rebuffed because she was hoping for someone else to arrive, and so attacks her. It could be. In the attack the blood of both of them is shed – Eduardo's in the spare bedroom and Ligia's downstairs.

Here's another theory – Eduardo kills Ligia in a row. He cleans up the crime scene to cover up the killing but then on the way to wherever he was going, get's racked with guilt and decides to kill himself instead. It's just speculation – but just as plausible as what the prosecution have presented to you.

The prosecution states that Uxoricide is one of the most prevalent forms of homicide. But these are usually the tragic conclusion to a sequence of violent abuse. There was no evidence of any marital violence in this case. None whatsoever. Yes – there may have been the occasional row, over the vet bills. Quite understandable – have you seen how much these people try and get away with? What married couple doesn't have rows?

Yes, there may have been a distance between PJ and Ligia. But there was no violence that could eventually lead to murder. It was a typical marriage that was not at its best place when she died.

One thing that the prosecution and the defence both agree on is that a visitor came to the house at 10.30 pm. With the testimony of Willoughby the cat this may seem laughable, but let's say a visitor did arrive at the house then. If it was not PJ – it was almost certainly Ligia's killer.

It seems likely that the visitor was Eduardo. But if it wasn't him it certainly wasn't my client.

But the visitor at 10.30 actually helps the defence story more than the prosecution. The visitor is very likely to be involved in Ligia's death in some way. It could well be Eduardo, it could also be Andy Goddard the spurned lover of

Ligia, who after laying down a digital trail alibi at home came over – we cannot rule that out. It could be a drug gang coming back to make reprisals for holding back on the drugs she brought over on her trip from Brazil.

How's this for a chain of events?

Ligia buys her bottle of Chablis and as she leaves the off licence. She is picked up by a drug gang in a car. She is forced to go with them, and they take her home. They start asking questions about some missing drugs, they get threatening, they then demand to see Eduardo Pinheiro, so she sends a text that she must see him now. When Eduardo arrives he sees Ligia killed by the drug gang, he escapes in his car, hides out in Rye where he sometimes went with Ligia, and in the garage consumed by guilt for causing this chain of events, takes his own life.

It's plausible. It's just as plausible, just a provable as the case put by the prosecution.

None of those avenues were properly explored by the lead investigator – who was clearly suffering from tunnel vision and just zeroed in on my client. In short it was a witch hunt. In fact this case has been a witch hunt against PJ James from start to finish. DCS Ferdinand has a chip on his shoulder and is clearly jealous of PJ's life. He is guilty of a most serious malfeasance. And it is clear from reading the file that the son Zico influenced DCS Ferdinand into pursuing my client. Not only did Zico not want to believe his father killed his mother, he actively went about trying to influence the investigation by supplying to the Surrey Police – Eduardo's car, Eduardo's body, after the Sussex Police had concluded their investigation. Zico even contacted the woman in Brazil and introduced her to DCS Ferdinand, who then groomed her into being a witness for the prosecution.

I must stress the prosecution needs to prove my client's guilt beyond any reasonable doubt.

There is too much reasonable doubt here, and this theory put forward by the prosecution is too elaborate and far-fetched.

It just beggars belief.

To find someone guilty of murder, the case must be iron tight. No room for doubt. If you doubt a bit, you must acquit.

(In the end I thought Jennifer Janus put on a better show. Clive Hendy did all the questions and cross-examining. His partners just held the books. While Jennifer Janus only took care of the most important parts and let her supporting lawyers do the rest. To me it meant that the jury got Clive Hendy fatigue and were less interested or even sick of hearing his voice by the end of the trial.

Nevertheless I felt hopeful. We had an overwhelming amount of forensic evidence – while the defence provided nothing.)

PJ's audio-log – Monday 19th November

With Jennifer Janus finishing her closing arguments my tension inside ramped up to become unbearable. I had set a lot of faith in her, but I thought her summing up was lacking. I wanted more emotion, more facts, more of an emphatic conclusion. That closing line "if you doubt a bit, you must acquit," – a reference to the OJ Simpson trial – I think was just corny.

I did not think her closing speech was as good as that of the prosecution counsel.

But everyone else on Team PJ thought otherwise.

I still think I should have taken the stand.

Now my whole life hangs in the balance with the 12 members of the jury. How long would they take?

Date: Thursday 22nd November
Time: 10:00
Location: Kingston Crown Court

How long does it normally take for the jury to reach a verdict in a murder case? We were on a third day of jury deliberation. If they take more than three days, what is that an indication of? Not guilty? To me it was obvious. So why are the jury taking so long?

I passed Chief Constable Hinton in the corridor, his brow was knitted and his face moulded into a frown. He too was showing signs of anxiety.

I called Clive Hendy and asked what more than three days of jury deliberation was a sign of. He said, "it could be good – or it could be bad." Thanks for that incisive legal analysis.

I received several calls from Jane Barrow of the Surrey Star. I deleted each message without listening.

PJ's audio-log – Thursday 22nd November

This is surely the darkest hour. Fear consumes everything. When I was first arrested, my thoughts were - I don't care if I go to prison, what's the point of living anyway without Ligia? But now I think – why should I spend the rest of my life in prison for something I didn't do? Ligia wouldn't want this. Ligia had a tremendous sense of justice. This isn't what's right for her.

While waiting for the verdict they put me in this holding cell in Kingston on Thames, which at least gives me a change of scenery.

Why didn't we hire our own experts to deal with the prosecution's experts? Janus said that it didn't matter. But I am sitting here now thinking that she didn't do enough.

I'd rather they put me on the electric chair than give me a life sentence.

Sitting in this cell I considered suicide. But then – they would have won.

A reporter referred to me as a modern day Sam Sheppard. At first, I thought they meant the playwright. But I got Dougal to look it up and he told me about the case of the doctor in America in the 1950s. Even though he was innocent he still did time in prison and his family were devastated by what happened. This is hardly any comfort.

Audio – Sound of a door opening. Unintelligible

> *voice.*
>
> Fuck! I've just been told to get to the court. The jury have reached a verdict.
>
> Audio – Click off.

Date: Thursday 22nd November
Time: 15:00
Location: Kingston Crown Court

We filed into the court and I took my place in the press gallery. Jane Barrow scoots up next to me and with a beaming smile asks me for a comment. I do a PJ – No Comment. Last to file in is PJ in the dock. He's shifting uncomfortably. The place is packed – but silent. The only sound was the hum of the air conditioning.

The judge addressed the jury: "Have you reached a verdict?"

The jury foreperson replies, "Yes your honour."

"Is it a unanimous verdict on both counts?"

"It is your honour."

"What is your verdict on the murder of Ligia James?"

(Turn the page for verdict)

"NOT GUILTY."

"And the murder of Eduardo Pinheiro?"

"NOT GUILTY."

I heard a howl from the gallery. I just knew it was Zico. Avoiding any eye contact I made straight for the exit.

> **PJ's video interview – Thursday 22nd November**
> *(On the steps of Kingston Crown Court.)*
>
> My faith in British justice has been restored. But I feel relief only – no elation. I am still without Ligia and nothing would ever bring her back.
>
> I also think of my parents, both sadly gone. I know they would have stood by me throughout this nightmare. I liked to think that they are up there somewhere supporting me and sending me strength. Now they are celebrating with me.
>
> But I am also celebrating with some living people – my sister Samantha, Terry Snape and of course you Dougal and the other members of Team PJ.
>
> There are a lot of reasons to be angry, but I am going to leave that for another day, because today I am acquitted and walk away from this court house a free man. For the first time in seven months I will not be sleeping in a cell.
>
> I thank my lawyer Jennifer Janus for her brilliant strategy. She shouldn't take this personally – but I hope that I will never have to see her again.

I felt guilty. Where did I go wrong? Help me out reader. You were with me on every beat of my investigation. Where did I fuck up? Why did I lose this case?

As if I didn't feel bad enough already, on the steps of the courthouse, I saw a large young man in dreadlocks charging at me. It was Zico, pointing a finger and shouting – "YOU FUCKED UP!"

His angelic face contorted with bitterness and rage. This man had suffered and lost so much, and I had added to it.

I felt like saying, 'It wasn't me. Blame that Clive Hendy."

Mercifully Zico then stormed off, chaperoned by his crest-fallen grand-parents.

My heart was heavy and my feet felt like lead as I walked down the steps of the court house.

I spotted Jane Barrow throwing herself in the direction of some of the jury members.

Outside the courthouse, I was deliberating on whether to go to the pub, maybe get Matt or Albert the court usher to join me, when I saw Jennifer Janus walking towards me and extending a hand.

"What a case! No hard feelings."

I went against my base instinct, and instead accepted her hand-shake.

"Where are you off for your celebration meal? I hear that Chinese restaurant is good – Hong Kong Garden."

She didn't get the reference, and just looked at me blankly. I went on: "What a smart strategy – telling your client to say No Comment from the very first interview. I bet you'll do that every time now."

"I didn't advise him to do that. When he didn't answer any of your questions in that first interview, I was as surprised as you."

Chapter 15 – On The Tarmac Of Heathrow Airport I Sat Down And Wept

Date: Wednesday 5th December
Time: 08:30
Location: Kingston on Thames

My impulse was to phone in sick or to ask Hinty for some time off. But then I thought – whatever is in store for me, I was going to face it with my head held high. We lost the case, and the searchlight of blame was glaring straight into my eyes, but I still thought I had done nothing wrong.

I felt sick that all the evidence I had spent hours painstakingly accumulating all blew away into irrelevance and in the end did not convince the jury absolutely beyond a reasonable doubt. I was told that after the first day of deliberation, the jury were deadlocked 9 to 3 in favour of a guilty verdict. In Scotland that verdict would have come in as 'not proven'. But in England instead they had to deliberate until they got to a unanimous verdict. But whatever – PJ was walking free. We had lost.

I was right to conclude that PJ had done it and to think I had enough evidence. Someone else was to blame – not me. That stupid jury, that twisting Goth lawyer putting Zico through even more torment just to get her narcissistic client off, and I had a big bee in my bonnet about Clive Hendy – that fat public school ponce of a lawyer who should have insisted with the judge that the death of his first wife was admissible. And how is it that the wire was admissible, but then they cut out any reference to the death of his first wife?

Was I Bitter? Only slightly.

Driving to the nick, the street lamps and shop windows were adorned with the whites, reds and greens of Christmas decorations. It brought me no festive cheer.

Before getting to the station, I drop into the newsagent to get some mints and a bottle of water. I walked in with trepidation, locking my head forward so as not to see the parade of front page newspapers displayed to my right.

As I handed over my change my phone rang. I look at the display: 'Jane Barrow – Surrey Star'. No way was I talking to her.

Turning around I look to my left and a headline caught my eye.

"Innocent Man Walks Free."

I picked up a copy of a national newspaper. This one had a picture of a triumphant PJ raising his arms aloft outside the courthouse. The caption read: "Free At Last!"

The article carried this quote from one of his team – "DCS Ferdinand of the Surrey Police has a lot to answer for. He overlooked the obvious that Eduardo Pinheiro had done it – and instead embarked on a costly grudge against the successful PJ." I saw that word malfeasance used once again in a sentence about me. Like an archaeologist, my career was in ruins.

As I was reading, the newsagent behind me was yapping – 'Excuse me. Excuse me. Would you like to buy that paper?'

I told him to fuck off, threw the paper and some change at him and left.

PJ's video log – Wednesday 5th December

I considered prosecuting the Surrey Police for what was clearly a malicious prosecution, but instead I want to leave this whole horrible episode behind me.

Nevertheless I feel I should arrange a party, as a get-together to say thank you to all the people who supported me throughout my trial ordeal. But also to say good-bye. I have decided to sell up and leave the UK. Move somewhere far, far away.

A new life. I need to forget.

Date: Wednesday 5th December
Time: 10:00
Location: Kingston Police Station

As I walked up the steps to my floor I play back my voicemails, Jane's cheery voice – "Hi! I'd be really interested in getting a comment from you about how the case went." Delete. I just wanted to lose myself in my next case, and focus entirely on that.

On switching on my PC, I get an email summonsing me for a meeting with Chief Constable Hinton in his office at 11am. Was I facing demotion? Would my next case be chasing poachers in Mole Valley, or fly-tippers in Camberley? Or even worse was I going to be booted out of the force?

I had been sat at my desk doing nothing but worrying for about ten minutes, when I get the call that Zico is in reception to see me. Maybe he wants to punch me. I don't blame him.

He was sat in reception, looking placid – he stood up on seeing me, but thankfully no fists came flying in my direction. "I've come to apologize – I'm really sorry for what I said to you outside the court house. I'm not angry with you. I don't blame you for the botched investigation."

I welcomed these words, it would be even nicer if he meant them. He went on.

"I can't hate any more. I've got to stop… But I still hate PJ. But I have to let it all go. You did your best – and to me it was obvious he did it – and the case was overwhelming, but things got twisted and that jury…"

"I am really sorry Zico."

"I've also come to say good bye. I am going to live in Brazil with my grandparents."

"Where in Brazil?"

"Rio."

"What football team will you support?"

He looked at me like it was stupid question. "Flamengo!"

"Flamengo. Zico. Of course."

"My father named us both – Leandro and me – after Flamengo players. If you are ever in Rio, get in touch."

"I certainly will."

"You are a member of an elite club."

"Oh yeah – what club is that then?"

"Only the best people get thrown out of Kingston Crown Court for contempt."

"Who else is in this club?"

"I'm the founding member. Been thrown out three times now."

"I thought they were going to charge me."

"What for telling the truth? Your outburst was the highlight of the trial."

"I spoke to that Jane Barrow this morning."

"You mustn't."

"I told her all about the murder of his first wife – and Chloe Lund. She was very interested."

Time: 11:30
Location: Chief Constable Hinton's Office, Kingston Police Station

"OK Ferdy, let me put you out of your misery. You are not being fired and you're not being demoted." He might have told me this when I was summonsed for the meeting. It would have saved me two hours of anxiety.

Hinton went on: "but we are going back to concluding that Eduardo really did kill her. At least that way we keep our clear up rate. But I cannot downplay how disastrous this lost case is for us. It's costly for the Surrey Police, not just financially but reputationally as well."

I jumped in – "It was right to charge him. He's guilty. Our lawyer should have been firmer on insisting that the death of the first wife should have been admissible. How was it his lawyer was able to say in court he had no history of violence against women when his first wife was dead, almost certainly pushed off a cliff by him?"

Hinton did not go with my scapegoat hunting: "Because the inquest concluded it was an accident. That's why. Let it go Ferdy. I am on your side. But let it go. This is not a formal warning but if you mess up like this again, it's over for you in the force. Please understand."

I sat silent, trying not to say some of the thousands of things flying around in my mind about the case. Hinton went on: "You have to stop over-thinking things. When a decent straight forward collar falls in your lap – just take it."

Also in the meeting was our Head of PR. The only thing she said in the whole meeting was: "You must NOT talk to the press. Do NOT publicly criticize the court's decision."

I was at the door about to leave when Hinton said to me: "By the way – the man's sister – she still has our recording device. Can you get it back off her? Otherwise, I'll have to charge you for it."

Time: 14:30
Location: Kingston Police Station

Back at my desk, Matt had some news – PJ had put both his properties on the market. "That was quick."

"He must have got the ball rolling while he was on trial. He planned to sell up whatever the outcome – if he was found guilty he'd use the money to fund his appeal, if he was acquitted he would take the money…and ride off into the sunset."

My phone rang – that pest Jane Barrow again. But this time I picked up. "Hey Jane. Nice to hear from you. I'd love to give you a statement. Are you at your offices? I'll swing by – I have something I want you to see."

Time: 15:00
Location: Surrey Star offices, Kingston

Jane Barrow's eyes widened as I picked out for her some of the most interesting points coming out of the Kelly Hill file. The statement from Jung Ra was the most persuasive. "I am showing you this as an un-named source you

270

understand? But here are the phone numbers of the witnesses, I'd love it for you to call them and you can hear first hand how they feel about the case."

"Can I call them now?"

"Yeah, why not?"

She dialled Jung Ra and left a message.

Next she called policeman Willie Winterburn who, like previously, was only too happy to talk about his misgivings about the inquest.

Then I told her about the Chloe Lund angle – who ruined our case by refusing to testify, and then the production company placing an injunction on us from using her name in the trial.

Then the defence misled the jury by calling Chloe Lund as a character witness, and then saying that she couldn't make it because of her busy schedule.

"Chloe Lund was never going to be a character witness – her exact words to me: That Man is A Creep!"

"I will contact her to corroborate this."

"Please do."

I left Jane sitting in silence taking it all in.

Time: 17:00
Location: Kingston Police Station

I dialled Samantha's number – this time I got through.

"Hello, I bet you lot are celebrating," I said.

"He's having a party at the Hand & Spear this Friday," she said flatly.

"That invite hasn't reached me yet. Listen, we forgot to get that recording equipment off you. Remember from that highly unsuccessful bugging exercise. Can I come over and pick it up?"

"No. No. I'll drop it by."

"Can you do it tomorrow please? Kingston Police Station?"

"Actually Woking's more convenient."

"OK Woking then. Please do it tomorrow. We have other cases you know."

"I am sorry."

"Yes so am I."

"No I'm sorry because I showed Paul the wire when I came through the door. He knew he was being surveilled."

So that was the rustling sound at the start of the recording.

"Why would you do that? That defeats the purpose of the wire."

"It was hard for me. I was conflicted – he is my brother."

"But you still think he killed your friend Kelly Hill."

Samantha was silent for a long time before saying, "Oh I don't know. I just don't."

"I think you do. He claimed that Kelly insisted on holidaying at the spot, but Kelly told you otherwise."

Silence.

"Has he paid you back yet for his stay at the sanatorium?"

More silence, until: "Look I'll drop the bugging device by tomorrow and put all this behind me."

"And what about PJ? I hear he's put both his houses on the market."

"Yes, he's leaving the country to start a new life."

"Free to go for the hat-trick in a new country. Bump off wife number three."

Time: 19:00
Location: Walton on Thames

The case I lost was a good case, but there was no point on ruefully going all Harold Melvin and the Blue Notes about it. Instead my plans for the evening was to shut myself away in my study and watch some mid-week Premiership football. I watched a bit of Tottenham verses Southampton.

I saw Harry Kane's tap in goal after eight minutes but then I got possessed with a curiosity about what they were saying about my case, so I found myself logging onto the iPlayer and caught the BBC news.

Before long I saw PJ doing a TV interview outside the courthouse: "He just had tunnel vision – blocked out all the other evidence…Nothing will bring back Ligia."

I was reminded of the quote – 'Success is all about sincerity. If you can fake that, you've got it made.'

I mused it was a mistake to make that video admissible. He did come across well.

Then outside forces found me doing searches on YouTube and I found a new video from that Northern so-called comedian Terry Snape. In this clip he was sat next to PJ. Both holding up champagne flutes. Terry spoke: "Justice has prevailed – my friend is free at last, free at last. Thank god almighty he's free at last." The bastard was impersonating Martin Luther King.

"What have you got to say PJ?"

"The police have still got my award."

I knocked back a few large brandies and started hatching a plan to make my own YouTube answer back video. But thankfully on my third large drink, I instead put on some 999, jumped around a bit, and then fell asleep.

Date: Thursday 6th December
Time: 07:30
Location: Oatlands Park, Weybridge

On my early morning park jog, I get a text from Jane Barrow.

"Pick up a copy of the Surrey Star this morning."

Ten minutes more of panting, I get a second text.

"The cover story is just factual, as in – he got off – but on page 5 I've got stuff on what the jury didn't hear about."

That really put grease in my gears. I ran to the car and made straight for the newsagent. Unfortunately it was the same one I told to fuck off the day before.

"Excuse me – you're banned," he said to me as I strode towards the counter having picked up a copy of the Surrey Star. I put two pounds on the counter (more than the cover price) and exited with a "Sorry" and what I hoped was a disarming smile.

Outside I flicked straight over to page 5 and feverishly skim read the article. A quote from an un-named jury member jumped out "I would have found him guilty if I'd known about the death of his first wife." A second jury member, also un-named "we acquitted him because there was a small amount of reasonable doubt, but we were led to believe he had no history of violence against women. But why weren't we told about the first wife, why weren't we told about all this business with Chloe Lund?"

I called Jane Barrow.

"Did you actually speak to these jury members?"

"Of course I did. Those are verbatim quotes, I can't name them obviously."

"So they are not made up quotes."

"Come on – give me a break."

This was giving me hope, but hope of what, I did not know.

"There's more to this story," she said. "Will you come to the offices? There's something I want you to hear."

PJ's video log – Thursday 6th December

That Surrey Star article was just like Brexit. They didn't like the official result, so they were trying to undermine it and get a second run at it. You lost – get over it.

But it confirmed something I suspected – that I would have this hanging over me forever.

There will always be some idiots who clings onto the notion that I am guilty. Defying logic – the armchair

274

> detectives, the keyboard conspiracy theorists twisting facts around to suit their narrative.
>
> I can never truly be acquitted – this stain will be on me for the rest of my life.
>
> It is just as well I am leaving the country.

Time: 09:00
Location: Surrey Star offices, Kingston

"You know how a journalist must never reveal their sources. But I am prepared to tell you that tip about the drug gang was an anonymous call. But we recorded it, and I can play it back to you.

She pressed the button, and I heard a familiar voice: "I know PJ James, he is a TV director of some renown. His wife Ligia was from Portugal and through her ex-husband Eduardo Pinheiro had known connections to South American drug gangs. She was mixing with a bad crowd and had been using her trips to Brazil to traffic drugs. On one trip she held back some of the merchandise and the gang came looking for it. I can tell you that cocaine will be found in her blood stream." Then a click and the dialling tone as he hung up.

The voice was hushed breathless as if he was talking in the bathroom of someone's house and did not want to be heard. Though he had never spoken to me directly, I had heard his voice enough times through playing back that video footage over and over. The voice was unmistakably PJ's.

The call was made at 6.30pm Tuesday – so as soon as he had been released by the police and allowed to stay with his sister.

What number did he call from? There was no way of knowing now. The call did not appear on his mobile phone when we seized it the day after. But he could have deleted it. Or used someone else's.

Time: 17:00

Location: Druids Head Pub, Kingston

To get myself some of that festive cheer I invited Matt to join me for an after shift drink at a quaintly Christmas decorated pubs on the market square.

He had with him a selection of some of the daily newspapers. National newspapers do a lot more checking than the local ones before they print something. But they must have got the all-clear because they were now running with the story of the death of Kelly Hill and how it was made inadmissible. This and a glass of warm mulled wine made me feel a sense of vindication. Was there a chance that all is not lost?

Matt was explaining to me how double jeopardy worked in the United Kingdom's legal system. It was not cheery. "It is possible to be charged a second time for a crime you've been acquitted for, but only in very, very exceptional circumstances. The stuff about his first wife, won't count as new evidence because it was considered the first time, and the judge is more than likely going to rule it inadmissible a second time."

As if he wanted me to feel worse, he added, "If anything that stuff in the press about the death of the first wife has ruined the chances of him facing trial again, because the defence could argue that it's now impossible to get a fair and impartial trial, because any jury would have read about the death of the first wife in a way that made him look guilty."

Matt's gloomy words seem to send the pub into a grey light. The Christmas decorations lost their shine.

"You have a slight chance of getting him on the murder of his first wife, but you can only do that if substantial new evidence came to light. But that case is so old now, that's highly unlikely. The one bright side, that is a real positive, is that The Surry Star article makes you appear less dodgy. That there were good reasons for charging him."

This was some comfort, reputation is everything. But I was so upset that this one had got away.

"Matt – how can we stop this from ever happening again?"

> **PJ's video log – Thursday 6th December**
> When I am in the right frame of mind I will put together all the footage Dougal and I have shot and make that documentary. Interview some more people and tell this story. But that won't be for months, I can't get my head around it right now.
> Right now I want to get as far away as possible.
> I am getting signals from Vietnam. Yes I had chosen Vietnam as the destination for my new life. I would tour around for 12 months or so – and then settle down and start a small TV production company – maybe doing travelogue shows or local news.
> And I would change my name.
> A whole new life. A new beginning.

Date: Friday 7th December
Time: 19:00
Location: Hand & Spear, Weybridge

I strode into the main function room of the **Hand & Spear primed** for some confrontation and looked around at the confused guests.

"Can I help you?" a burly man asked with an air of menace.

"I am looking for PJ James."

"Who?"

Wrong party.

I then went downstairs and patrolled the throng just as I did months before in the same pub when looking for Dan Lupescu and his men.

I make over to the restaurant bit and, sat at a table of eight, I see Dougal pointing a compact hand sized video camera at a man with his back towards me.

I move closer in and hear that voice again. "I was getting vibes telling me Vietnam. Ever since I saw Apocalypse Now I wanted to go there. But there's so much more to the place than the Vietnam war. More than just conical hats and paddy fields. I hear it's a great place to hang out, just a really good and laid back place."

My heart was pumping as I leaned forward waving a hand in between the camera and PJ.

"I've just come back from 'nam. Chelt-nam."

His head snaps towards me.

"May I jump in on your video? You must be so happy. It's not every day you get away with murder."

The entire ensemble stood up to confront me including, I noticed Samantha at the end of the table. I was in full palpitations now.

"Get out of here," I heard somebody growl but I could not make out who said it. PJ's lips were not moving, he was just eyeing me with a look of dread.

"Or what? You'll call the police?" Now I noticed the comedian known as Fred Snape, he was a large man over six foot –two. Now I felt a number of hands holding my shoulders and arms.

"We'll complain to the police – they'll have your job," he said.

"Uh! I'm scared. People like you off the telly have so much clout. I've come to collect some money for your next door neighbours. They've been feeding your cat Willoughby all this time, and they need to be reimbursed. These people are pensioners and you are taking liberties."

"If we give you the money, will you fuck off?" bellowed Snape.

"Yes."

PJ threw some notes at me that floated onto the table, the comedian threw some more.

I scooped them up and I pushed my head towards PJ and glared.

"I want you to know I am watching you," I said pointing at my eyes and then pointing at his.

I'd made my point, now was the time to make my exit. They watched me as I walked away, they looked ready for a proper dust up if I went back. "Get out" someone shouted and I walked away to a chorus of vituperation rising in anger and volume as I turned the corner and out of their sight.

Date: Saturday 8th December
Time: 10:00
Location: West Byfleet

I pull up outside the house where it all began. The police tape was gone and so too was the Nordic runic Asgard sign, replaced by an estate agent sign. I had looked up the asking price – £1.2 million. With no mortgage to pay PJ would have a nice stash of spending money in Vietnam.

I crunched up the gravel drive way of Number 3 – before I hit the bell, the door was opened to me by Fred, looking gaunt like the butler in a haunted house. In contrast his voice was cheery – "Ey up. Good to see yer. Rose and me are late putting up the Christmas decorations."

He led me into the living room, where Rose was putting tinsel on a real nine foot pine tree.

"8th December is a bit late," I scolded. On speaking a small blurry ball of fur ran out of the room. I assumed it was Willoughby the cat.

"We normally don't bother as it's just us two, but this year we thought – why not?"

"And we've got our daughter visiting in a couple of weeks," added Fred.

"Was that Willoughby running out just then?"

"Aye," said Fred.

"I've managed to get a couple of hundred in cash to pay you back for the cat food." I pulled out an envelope.

Fred took the envelope. "Thanks. This'll come in very handy, I can stock up the Christmas Drinks cabinet."

"Talking about money" I said, "Did you see how much next door is going for? £1.2 Million. You people are sitting on a goldmine."

"It was worth a lot less than that when we bought this place. But we aren't planning on selling. We're staying put. Do you think the murder would put people off from buying it?"

"It will with some, but not with others. There's quite a few ghoulish people out there who would like the idea."

Rose came away from the tree and suddenly looked worried.

"We've got really attached to him over the last few months, we'd hate…I mean we can't… it would just…"

"What?"

Fred came in – "We couldn't give him back. He's part of the family now."

"Relax. You don't have to."

Rose clutched her heart in relief.

"Yes – your soon to be ex-neighbour is off to Vietnam. If you want to keep the cat – he's yours."

"Do you hear that Nibbins you can stay? Oh he's gone."

"We call him Nibbins now, we didn't like the name Willoughby."

I looked over to a small table and see a framed picture of Ligia – the one that was used in the Surrey Star. I commented on it.

"It's to remind him of his previous owner. Nibbins appreciates seeing her picture."

"So the cat is very happy in his new home."

"That he is."

At least some good came of all of this.

In the car I get a phone call. It was Matt the Stat to tell me that he'd been onto Vietnam Airlines and got hold of their passenger lists. PJ is booked onto flight **VN54** from Heathrow to Hanoi going out at 21.20 that night.

Time: 20:30

280

Location: Terminal 2, Heathrow Airport

He'd bought himself a business class ticket so I had used my police ID to get into the lounge. It was like walking into a 1970s nightclub, decked out in purple velvet and silver chrome. I expected to look over to the bar to see Joan Collins sipping a Martini. Instead I saw him sat alone looking out the window at the planes on the tarmac.

I sat next to him and said something I thought would be funny: "I've come to give you a copy of the Gary Glitter guide book to Vietnam." PJ turned round with a start, saw me and then grabbed his hand luggage and ran out, leaving his cocktail behind.

I was trying my best to come across all menacing, but in reality I felt impotent. Not something I'm at all used to feeling you understand. I had my handcuffs in my coat pocket but I was most unlikely to be using them. What could I possibly do? I had lost my case and he had got away with it. He was jetting off to somewhere far away and soon would have something close to £1.2 million plus whatever he gets for the cottage in Rye in his bank account.

So what was I hoping to achieve by seeing PJ off at the airport? I wanted to put some doubt, some troubling thoughts into his sense of celebration. I wanted him to know that even though he was in another continent with a new identity that I was still onto him. That if he committed a third uxoricide, I would be there to present the evidence of the two previous deaths. Surely no court, in any country, would dismiss the evidence of the first two deaths.

I felt the need to make my point one last time, so I used my police ID again to get on the other side of the boarding desk, so I could watch the parade of business class passengers on the gangway as they walked towards the plane.

I waited for about ten minutes when I heard the tannoy call for Business Class passengers to board. PJ must have been keen to get away, as he was among the first in the parade. As he walked towards me looking at me, his demeanor was different. This time he was sneering. Waving at me as he walked past, as if to say – I'm going, what are you going to do about it? And the answer was of course sweet FA.

"See Ya!" He said with a parting wave, in the same way a football crowd mock a player of the other team who's just been sent off. He got the last laugh.

As I watched him walk away and onto the plane my heart sank into despair. I began walking back when my phone rang. It was Matt.

"Samantha the sister has still got the bugging device...," he said in a panting voice.

"Yes I know."

"She recorded him talking about the death of Kelly Hill…It's enough to convict him."

"What?"

"I'll play it to you."

"No – no time, PJ is on the plane, about to leave."

"OK. Take my word for it. It's incriminating and it's solid. Get him before he leaves."

"Are you sure?"

"Yes. GO!"

Without even hanging up I ran back towards the plane. They were about to slide the door shut, as I pulled out my ID and yelled "POLICE". I got onto the plane and turned left for the first time in my life.

I was now in the first class cabin, and there he was stretched out with his eyes shut, looking like an advert for luxury business class travelling.

I pulled him up. As roughly as I could. Holding him up by his shirt I locked into his eyes and said, "PJ James – I am arresting you for the murder of Kelly Hill, you do not have to say anything, but it may harm your defence if you do not mention when questioned something you later rely on in court."

I slapped on my handcuffs and barked at the steward to call for two policemen to take him away. PJ just looked blank, in a daze, he clearly hadn't processed what had happened.

"Sorry. But your trip to Vietnam is off."

I was still catching my breath as I saw the two uniformed policemen take PJ away. As I saw them disappear into the distance, I apologized to the flight staff for delaying their flight and walked off the gangway and onto the tarmac. I dialled Matt who played back the recording.

Here's the transcript:

"You never fully answered my questions about Kelly. You need to convince me PJ."

"What about Kelly?"

"You went on holiday at the exact same spot that we went with Mum and Dad 10 years before. You knew it was an accident hot-spot, we talked about it. One of us joked about it being the ideal place to do a murder. You said Kelly chose to go on holiday there, but she told me herself before setting off that it was your idea. That you insisted on going there."

"Yes? And?"

"I think you pushed Kelly."

"And what are you going to do about it?"

Silence from Samantha.

"Eh?"

More silence for Samantha.

"No one can touch me now."

"Did you push her for the money?"

"The money came in handy. But she was also an annoying bitch. Just like you – so don't mess? OK? Fuck off Samantha – Have a nice life."

On hearing that, my knees buckled and I fell down onto the tarmac of Heathrow Airport and wept.

I wept for all the people that had been affected by this tragedy – Kelly Hill, her friends like Jung Ra and Samantha. I wept for Ligia and her friends and her family, and for Eduardo and all of his relatives. So many people – and most of all I wept for the person who was most devastated by all of this – Zico.

At least and at last Zico would get some form of justice. The case for the murder of Ligia and Eduardo was legally lost – but the case for the murder of Kelly Hill was very much alive. PJ will deny it all of course, but this time we had his sister Samantha as a witness.

As I sat there rubbing my eyes still sat on the tarmac, a Heathrow staff member came up to me, tapped on my shoulder and said "Excuse me Sir. I know you're police, but you mustn't sit around here. Would you mind going inside the Terminal?"

> **PJ's audio log – Monday 10th December**
> What I said to Samantha was just sarcasm. I was tired and emotional. I was sick of constantly having to justify myself. Having the police put seeds of doubts in the mind of my own sister, and getting her to turn on me.
>
> My words were not a confession. It was a throw away comment. Nothing more.
>
> With every fibre of my body I will fight this. Because we cannot let these people win. What they have done to me, they can do to anybody – however innocent.
>
> I am inviting you to join my campaign, which I am extended to include all innocent people victimized by the police. Go to www.freepj.com to sign up and join the fight.
>
> Together we will fight this. Together we will win.

Biography

Paolo has worked in media sales, as a journalist, a film-maker and a promoter of raves. A Careless Husband is his first crime novel, based on a real life murder case and drawing on his experiences of working at the court house of Walton-on-Thames. Paolo lives in West London with his wife, Sarah, and two cats – Gigi and Giorgio.

Printed in Great Britain
by Amazon